The Secret Word

A Twist Upon a Regency Tale
Book 11

By Jude Knight

ARE YOU SIGNED UP FOR DRAGONBLADE'S BLOG?

You'll get the latest news and information on exclusive giveaways, exclusive excerpts, coming releases, sales, free books, cover reveals and more.

Check out our complete list of authors, too!

No spam, no junk. That's a promise!

Sign Up Here

www.dragonbladepublishing.com

Dearest Reader;

Thank you for your support of a small press. At Dragonblade Publishing, we strive to bring you the highest quality Historical Romance from some of the best authors in the business. Without your support, there is no 'us', so we sincerely hope you adore these stories and find some new favorite authors along the way.

Happy Reading!

CEO, Dragonblade Publishing

Multi-generational families can be confusing. Chris, who didn't know anything about his parents' families except that they didn't want him, certainly found it so. This brief family tree shows people mentioned in the story, and may help a reader who wants to know where people fit.

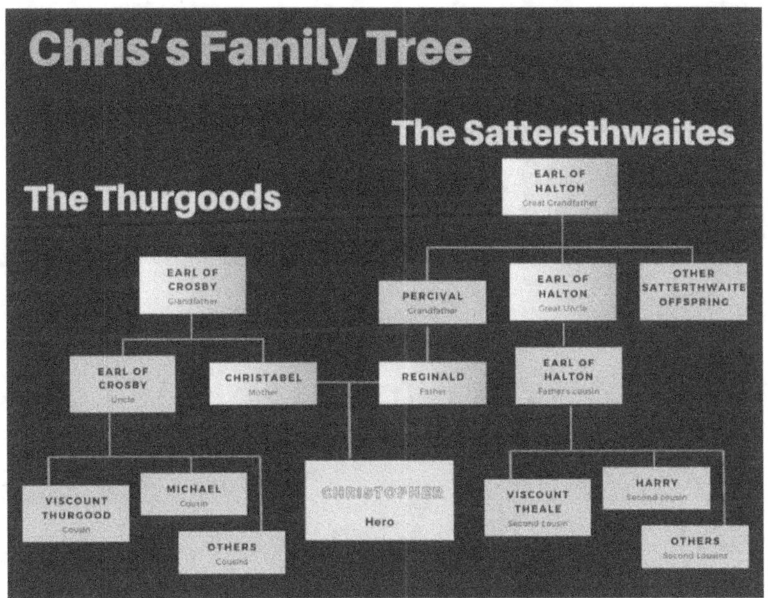

Chapter One

Devil's Kitchen, London, 1821

I F THE LADY had let go of her reticule, Christopher Satterthwaite might never have met her. A sensible person would have let Dasher Baggins take off with the scrap of lace and whatever was inside it. A sensible person would not have made a fuss in a street like this, where the law-abiding denizens knew better than to stand in the way of a villain, and where the villains would swarm like sharks at the hint of a victim.

A sensible person would not be on Bleak Street to begin with, not looking like a sweet and expensive confection in laces and silks, and certainly not screeching at the top of her voice, hanging on to her reticule for dear life, and beating the thief around his ears with her parasol.

Chris, who was mostly law-abiding, knew better than to interfere, but he couldn't help himself. He closed the distance between himself and the little tableau—outraged maiden beats off cheeky rascal—in a fast walk, designed not to attract more attention than he could help.

"Let go, Dash," he told the boy. "She's with me."

"Aw, Fingers," Dasher whined. "Don't know what she's got in there, but it must be worf somefing, way she hangs on."

"My mother's miniature, and you shan't have it," said the lady, who held her parasol ready but had at least stopped using it to beat Dash with. The poor lad should stick to mud larking. He was not a good thief.

"Get lost, Dash," Chris told him, and flipped him a farthing.

Dash let go of the reticule to catch the coin, and then demonstrated the reason for his nickname, dashing off through the crowd.

"You should have held him while I called a constable," proclaimed the lady.

"I don't know if you've noticed, Miss, but constables don't come down here," Chris replied. Up until now, he had been speaking street cant, or just far enough above it that Dash was comfortable, but now he changed accent and vocabulary to talk to the lady in a way to which she would respond. A cut above hers, in fact, for her vowels were not quite as nasal nor her consonants as crisp as Chris's grandfather's. "It is too dangerous," he elaborated. "Too many villains."

The lady huffed with displeasure, setting the ruffles on her bodice quivering. "One would think there would be fewer criminals if the constables did come down here."

"Or fewer constables," Chris argued.

She blinked at him as she absorbed the point, then huffed again. "I should not be here. I must have got turned around. Can you direct me to Meadow Court?"

"You do not want to go to Meadow Court," Chris told her. If Bleak Street did not eat her up and spit her out, Meadow Court would swallow her whole. And there'd be no spitting her out, either.

The lady's huff was more of a snort. "I decidedly do, sir," she insisted.

"Shall I tell you what will happen if you make it as far as Meadow Court?" Chris asked. It was a rhetorical question. "First, you shall be robbed of everything you have, including the clothes you stand up in. Then one of two things will happen to your naked person, depending on whether you fall into the hands of an organized gang or just a mob of the hopeless."

He fell silent and watched to see how she would react. Not as expected. Her eyes widened—they were a lovely shade of blue. Her cheeks paled. So far, quite predictable. But then she pressed her coral-pink lips together and gave a sharp nod, as if she had presented herself with a compelling argument.

"Nonetheless, sir, I have an errand in Meadow Court that will not wait."

"An organized mob will sell you to a brothel, where they will auction your virginity then put you to work servicing their clients until you drink yourself to death or die of an unspeakable disease," Chris told her.

She paled still further. Not such an innocent that she did not know what he meant, then. Or perhaps she was just responding to his earnest tone. "Nonetheless," she repeated, but her voice shook.

"A casual mob will not bother with the brothel," he continued, determined to make her change her mind. "And you will die of what they do to you." He could not bear to describe it further, did not even want to think of her intimately assaulted by one brute after another, screaming for help that never came, dying in agony of body and soul.

"Nonetheless." It was little more than a whisper, and she was so pale he thought she might faint.

"Why?" he asked. "What is so important that you are willing to die for it—die, most likely, without accomplishing it?"

She narrowed her eyes at him, considering. "I have no reason to believe you, sir," she said. "All I know about you is that you belong so well to this street, in which you say everyone is a villain, that thieves do your bidding. Ama—My friend would not have written asking me to come to Meadow Square if it was as dangerous as you say."

"I said the place had too many villains," Chris pointed out. "Not that I am one. As it happens, I am not, but you have a point. We do not know one another. Please allow me to introduce myself." He bowed. "I am Christopher Satterthwaite. And you are…?"

She curtseyed in response to his bow, "Clementine Wright."

"Miss Wright, I cannot know what your friend had in mind—you are sure it was in her hand? But have you considered she might have been threatened or tricked?"

"Why?" Miss Wright's asked. "Why would someone bother?"

Chris had recognized her name and he knew the answer to that. Wright was a common enough name, but combined with Clementine? She was the coal heiress, beyond a doubt, and her father was one of the richest mine owners in the United Kingdom.

Something about the way Miss Wright was not quite meeting his eyes hinted that she, too, knew the most likely reason criminals would attack her.

"Option three," he replied. "You must have thought of it yourself, Miss Wright. I would have mentioned it before, had we been introduced earlier. Option three is ransom, though that doesn't mean that other criminal groups will not prefer option one or option two."

Oh-oh. He had grown up in places like this, and knew better than to allow her undoubted charms to keep him from scanning the street, looking for danger. But despite that, he'd been distracted.

Had he been watching, he would have run as soon as the first of the three men arrived at the mouth of the alley that led to Meadow Court. Now that three of them were gathered, he would be hard pushed to make it out of Bleak Street. He certainly could not manage it with Miss Wright in tow.

There was really only one option. "Miss Wright, there is someone I would like you to meet. Step this way, please." He offered her his arm.

She put both of hers behind her back. "I do not think so, Mr. Satterthwaite. If that is your name. You keep telling me not to trust anyone and then insist I can trust you."

They were coming. All three of the Brown brothers, and behind them, the rest of the gang. Cautiously, for this was on the borders of Ramping Billy O'Hara's territory, and he'd not take kindly to the Brown brothers trespassing.

Chris sighed and pointed. "See those men, Miss Wright?"

She caught sight of Basher Brown's grin and let out a squeak of dismay. *Wise girl!* She moved closer to Chris.

"This way," Chris told her. He took her hand, and led her at a run up Bleak Street. To her credit, she ran like a deer, but the Brown gang was in full pursuit behind, and everyone else was turning away, pretending that they saw nothing.

There'd be no help in Bleak Street, but *if* they could get down Snitch's Alley and into Palmist Court, and *if* the back door to Fortune's Fool was open, and *if* the doorkeeper would let him bring Clementine inside, they might come out of this with their skins.

There'd be a price to pay, of course. Ramping Billy had to have his due. But at least Miss Wright would be alive.

⤙⤙⤙⤘⤚⤚

CLEM HATED IT when men told her she couldn't do something, but she had to admit that Mr. Satterthwaite had a point. She'd known as soon as she turned into Bleak Street that she shouldn't have come. Not alone, anyway. But if she had asked one of the footmen who trailed her when she left the house through the usual exits, they would have told her father, and she would have been locked up for a month.

Besides, one of the footmen might be the cause of the problem—if it was not her father. She leaned toward thinking it was her father, or why would her former maid Amanda not tell her? Had Amanda been part of a plot to kidnap her? Clem could not discount the possibility.

Or there was no such plot, and Mr. Satterthwaite's first two options were in play. She could certainly believe that the men chasing them would sell her into a brothel if there were a few pounds to be made, but she still wasn't sure she was any safer with Mr. Satterthwaite.

Certainly, he looked and talked like a gentleman, but since the beginning of the Season, Clem had learned how unreliable surface impressions could be. That he was tall and handsome, with mesmerizing grey eyes, did not mean that he could be trusted.

Especially when he tugged her sideways and led her down a malodorous alley so narrow the buildings that lined the sides nearly met overhead, so they were running into deep shadows. Anyone could reach out from the few doors, but nobody did. The men behind them were whooping with glee, as if they knew Mr. Satterthwaite had led her down a dead end. Was he in league with them?

They broke out of the shadows into a patch of sunlight. A small courtyard between buildings, no more salubrious than the alley behind them. She had worn her best walking shoes for this expedition, thank goodness, for she did not want to think about what might have seeped through less sturdy footwear.

Mr. Satterthwaite looked over his shoulder, then pulled her toward a short flight of stairs. He leapt up them and hammered on the door at the top. "It's Satterthwaite," he shouted. "Let me in!"

The men chasing them came bursting out of the alley, one after the other. Mr. Satterthwaite abandoned his knocking and shouting. "Get behind me, Miss Wright. I'll try to buy us some time." He produced a knife from somewhere.

The men stopped their slow advance across the courtyard.

"Gi'e 'er to us, Fingers," shouted one of them.

"Come here and I'll fillet you, Basher," Mr. Satterthwaite shouted back.

Then the door behind Clem opened, and Clem was pushed sideways to make way as a whole troop of large, sturdy men emerged. They were easily as big and as mean as the pursuers.

Former pursuers. Basher and his gang reacted instantly to the new players, turning and running. In moments, they had disappeared down the alley with the men from the door behind them.

A man spoke from the doorway. "Mr. O'Hara requests a moment of your time, Mr. Satterthwaite—and company."

Clem stared at him. He looked and sounded like a first-class butler, such as could be found in any house in Mayfair.

"This way, Miss…?" he said, stepping to one side and indicating the passage behind him with a subtle wave of the hand.

"Miss Clementine Wright," said Mr. Satterthwaite.

The butler acknowledged the introduction with a slight inclination of the head. "This way, Miss Wright," he said.

Clem went where she was told. She could see no other choice, but was somewhat comforted by the implied respectability of a first-class butler. Which was silly, really. For presumably a butler might be a villain, or employed by a villain, as much as any other man.

The passage ended in a small hall that had three doors and a flight of steps. The butler took the opportunity to step past Clem and take the lead up the stairs.

"After you," said Mr. Satterthwaite, but then he leaned in close. "Let me do the talking. I will get you out of here, Miss Wright."

That didn't make Clem feel better. Clearly, Mr. Satterthwaite thought they had leapt from the frying pan into the fire.

Six flights up, the butler opened a door from the plain stairwell into a sumptuous passage that would not have been out of place in one of the grandest homes in Mayfair. They walked on plush carpet, past fine side tables gleaming with polish and supporting statuettes, lamps, and other *objets d'art*. Landscapes in gilt frames lined both walls, the gaps between disclosing flocked wallpaper with a rich botanical theme.

Where on earth had Mr. Satterthwaite brought her?

Chapter Two

CHRIS HOPED HE could keep his promise to extract Miss Wright from this tangle. To be fair, Ramping Billy O'Hara was not known for abusing innocents, nor for activities any more illegal than running a series of gambling dens and bawdy houses. At least now he had turned respectable. At least for a given meaning of the word respectable.

Tiny, who was anything but respectable, stood guard outside O'Hara's office. Tiny nodded to Jameson, the butler, and knocked on the door. A single knock. They were expected. Had the visitors been unheralded but peaceful, Tiny would have given two knocks. Three knocks meant hostile but under control. Four knocks would have had O'Hara exiting by one of the room's other doors.

"Satterthwaite and guest, sir," Tiny announced them. Chris offered Miss Wright his arm and escorted her inside.

O'Hara had his head down over some papers on his desk. So, they were to stand as supplicants before him, were they?

Chris ignored the unwritten protocol that said no one spoke before Billy acknowledged them. Miss Wright, after all, was not from his world. "Miss Wright, please allow me to present Mr. William O'Hara, who has been gracious enough to give us refuge against the men who were attempting to kidnap you. Sir, Miss

Clementine Wright and I are grateful for your kindness."

Billy looked up at that, and even stood, giving Miss Wright an inclination of his head in greeting. His hazel eyes were alight with calculation. "Miss Wright. I believe I have the felicity of being acquainted with your father."

Miss Wright's eyes widened. "You are a friend of my father's, Mr. O'Hara?" The luxurious surroundings had influenced her mood. She was no longer tense, ready to jump at any movement. Little did she know it, but she was standing before the most dangerous man she had met so far today.

"I do not claim such intimacy," Billy replied, his smile not reaching his eyes. "I have been able to supply Mr. Wright with entertainment from time to time."

"Ah," said Miss Wright, enlightened. "This is a gambling den or a brothel, then."

Billy's eyes crinkled with amusement, but he kept his face straight as he asked, "And what does the great hope of the Wright family for elevation to the upper classes know about gambling dens and brothels, if I may ask?"

"*Hmmph*. Only what one might deduce about their purpose from overhearing the servants, Mr. O'Hara."

She sounded disgusted and the look Billy exchanged with Chris was pure amusement.

"I have forgotten my manners," said Billy. "Please, Miss Wright, do have a seat and tell me how you came to be in Bleak Street to be almost kidnapped by a criminal gang. You may as well be seated, too, Fingers. By the way, you'll owe me for this."

Pure O'Hara. The invitation to sit was a privilege extended only when O'Hara was inclined to be pleased with one. The offhand nature of it put Chris on notice that Billy had not yet made up his mind to be generous. The nickname was a reminder that Billy knew where Chris came from and could put him back there. And the comment about owing Billy? It was no more than Chris had expected.

Chris held Miss Wright's seat for her and then took the one

next to her. She even smelled expensive, as if she moved in an invisible cloud of flowers and spices.

She sat in comfort, her back straight but the rest of her body relaxed. She was frowning slightly, as if wondering how much to tell her host.

"I would like to help you, Miss Wright," Billy said. "Whatever you can tell me about your errand would be most appreciated."

Those who knew him had learned to be wary when Ramping Billy O'Hara was being charming, but Miss Wright relaxed still further. "It is not I who need help, Mr. O'Hara, but my maid. My ex-maid, I should say. Amanda Brown."

Billy and Chris exchanged another look, and Billy's voice was carefully devoid of emotion when he asked, "You dismissed your maid and then came to visit her?"

"Oh, I didn't dismiss her. Father did. The other servants accused her of theft, and of leaving a window unlatched for a burglar. It was just because she was the most recent hire, and all the others have worked for Father for some time. Also, I think they might have been jealous, because being my maid meant she was not under the housekeeper's authority. It was most unfair."

"I see," said Billy.

Chris saw, too. The Brown brothers had seen an opportunity to put their sister into the house of one of the richest merchants in London.

"And was there a burglar?" Billy asked.

"No, because the butler found the unlatched window. I dare say one of the footmen failed to check earlier in the evening. So, nothing was lost, and it was most unfair that Amanda was dismissed for it. Without the wages she was owed, too. I paid her out of my pin money, of course."

"You came to visit her," Billy said, returning to the point.

"She asked me to do so. She said she was with child. Someone in our household, she said, though she didn't name him. She was unwell and she did not wish to die without seeing to the babe's future. Her brother would not let her leave the house, she said. I thought… that is, I guessed, at a reason she did not want to put the father's name in writing."

"You thought the baby might be your father's," Billy commented, in the same bland tone.

Miss Wright blushed. It had occurred to her. Her overheard knowledge about what happened between men and women suggested it had something to do with the origin of babies. Logic proposed that babies no more appeared in cabbage patches than did kittens, but how they got inside maids, and whether Father was one to dally with maids, she did not know.

In any case, what she thought or did not think was beside the point. "So, you see, I had to come, and I could not bring a footman or the new maid Father foisted upon me, for they all report to my father. I do hope Amanda is unharmed. Do you think—Mr. Satterthwaite suggested that she might have been threatened and made to write the letter?"

"I think I can set your mind at rest on that account, Miss Wright. I am acquainted with Miss Brown. I saw her yesterday afternoon out shopping, and she appeared perfectly well."

"Oh." Miss Wright nibbled her upper lip, and then added, "Then I wonder why she wrote… Oh." She almost whispered her next comment. "She *was* in league with the kidnappers. Are you certain, Mr. O'Hara?"

"Perhaps you will understand if I tell you that the men who were chasing you today are the Brown gang. Miss Brown is the sister of the three brothers who run Meadow Court and a few other streets and alleys close by. I strongly suspect, in fact, that Miss Brown was in your house to do exactly the act of which she was accused."

"Oh," said Miss Wright again. Her posture had slumped, and she appeared to be trying to draw her head down into her neck, perhaps to hide her flaming cheeks. She sighed, deeply. "That is probably why I cannot find my pearl earrings, then."

One of O'Hara's eyebrows shot up, signaling his surprise at the lady's relatively calm reaction. "I imagine so," he replied.

"Sir, might I borrow a carriage to convey Miss Wright home?" Chris asked, thinking to strike while O'Hara was kindly disposed toward the lady.

That brought the full force of O'Hara's attention to focus on Chris for a few terrifying seconds, then the man laughed. "And why not? Be certain to inform Mr. Wright that I send my compliments. No. Wait. I shall write a note, and you shall deliver it, Christopher."

"I suppose you want something from him," Miss Wright commented, her tone bitter. "In which case, there is no point in asking you not to tell him how foolish I have been. And now he will lecture and complain, and hedge me about with restrictions until I go mad."

Billy laughed again. "Then I must be careful how I word my note so these dire circumstances do not befall you, Miss Wright," he said. "Excuse me for a moment, please."

He took some notepaper from a drawer and selected a pen. Miss Wright gave Chris an anguished look and then gazed fiercely at the clasped hands on her lap. Chris did his best to look relaxed, but probably did not fool Billy in the slightest.

Without looking up from the paper, Billy asked, "Where were you meant to be this afternoon, Miss Wright?"

"At Miss Clemens' Circulating Library," Miss Wright replied. "I walked there with my maid."

Billy nodded, and continued writing.

Chris was impressed with Miss Wright. No doubt her naive faith in the goodness of others would be amended in time, but her courage and her wit would see her through.

He had seen cartoons of her and read snippets in the gossip rags, and those had led him to expect a fashion doll with a fervent admiration of status and rank, and no personality. The truth was far different.

Poor Miss Wright. Whatever her personality or her wishes, the whole world knew her father was determined to buy a blue-blooded groom for her. No doubt one who was so buried in debt that he'd be willing to put a peg on his nose to help him ignore the stench of coal dust.

Miss Wright deserved better. She was so much more than just a coal man's heiress. But the husband her father wanted for her was unlikely to ever notice.

⟫⟫⟫✦⟪⟪⟪

THE BUTLER LED Clem and Mr. Satterthwaite back into the servants' stairs and through one of the doors in the little hall she had seen when she first came into the building. The short utilitarian passage opened to another that matched the one upstairs for wealth and elegance.

"I apologize for not taking you through the public ways, Miss," said the butler. "Mr. O'Hara thought it best."

Mr. Satterthwaite explained. "Some of the patrons are about, and we would not want them to recognize you."

"Goodness, no," said Clem, fervently. She didn't know which would be worse—being recognized by someone who told Father she had been here, or by someone who gossiped about her presence in Society. She might not much enjoy the Society events to which Father had managed to get her invited, but they at least offered her an opportunity to meet gentlemen.

If she did not choose a husband for herself—one of whom Father approved, then he had vowed to choose one for her. And Father's criteria would be all about rank, influence, and his own advantage, with no consideration at all given to whether the man would make her a good husband.

The passage led to a door outside, into a street where a carriage was waiting for them. "You do not have to come, Mr. Satterthwaite," Clem said as he handed her up into the carriage. "I can deliver Mr. O'Hara's letter to Father."

"I do not dare disobey Ramping Billy O'Hara," Mr. Satterthwaite said. He followed her into the carriage and took the other seat, facing her with his back to the horses. "He'll want a report."

A girl climbed into the carriage and sat next to Mr. Satterthwaite. She was modestly and neatly dressed. "Hello, Becky," Mr. Satterthwaite said. "Is Billy sending you somewhere, too?"

"I'm to be Miss Wright's chaperone," the girl explained. She grinned at Clem. "Hello, Miss Wright. Apparently, you need some female along or everyone will think Chris here has molested you in the carriage. Not to worry, love. Chris hasn't molested anyone in his life." She batted her eyes at Mr. Satterthwaite. "Not without an invitation."

"Give over, Becks," Mr. Satterthwaite ordered. "Becky and I have known each other since we were little kids, Miss Wright."

The groom had closed the door and the carriage was on its way. Clem managed a smile for Becky, but her thoughts returned to the letter. "I wonder what Mr. O'Hara had to say to my father."

"Shall I take a look?" Mr. Satterthwaite asked. Without waiting for an answer, he produced a long thin knife from his boot. "Becky will keep our secret. We're only going to read it, Becks. I shall deliver it to Mr. Wright no matter what it says, so Billy doesn't need to know."

Becky inclined her head. "If you say so, Chris."

"Shall I?" Mr. Satterthwaite asked, his knife at the ready.

Clem nodded eagerly. Perhaps she should be ashamed to be reading someone else's mail, but it was self-defense, really.

She couldn't place the man. He was dressed like a gentleman rather than a laborer. His clothing appeared to be made from good quality fabric, but both coat and pantaloons were loose for easy movement, rather than the closely-fitted garments warn by the fashionable gentlemen she knew. He wore a dark-colored cravat with the simplest of knots, and no jewelry—not even a watch fob, ring, or cravat pin. Perhaps he was a solicitor or a clerk, though she had seldom seen one so handsome and well-formed, nor with such apparent self-confidence.

While she was examining him, Mr. Satterthwaite slid his knife under the seal, working it loose until it popped free. He handed it to Becky. "Hold onto that, so we can put it back and no harm done." She looked amused but made no comment.

Then Mr. Satterthwaite gave Miss Wright the letter. "Read it. At least you will be prepared for your father's reaction."

Clem took a deep breath and unfolded the paper.

To Mr. Bertram Wright.

Dear Sir,

I had the honor this afternoon to be of some small assistance to your daughter, Miss Clementine Wright. I understand from her that she was using the facilities at Miss Clemens' Circulating Library this afternoon. She was chased by villains who intended kidnap. Mr. Satterthwaite, the gentleman who gives you this letter, saw what was happening and brought her to me at Fortune's Fool. I was pleased to be able to give her refuge, and can assure you that no one saw her beyond those immediately concerned, myself and a few trusted servants. Since arriving, she has had a maid with her for her reputation. The lady is in every respect unharmed.

I remain your humble servant.

William O'Hara.

Better than she expected. Without a single lie, he had implied that she had visited Miss Clemens' ladies' outhouse, and had been accosted there. Clem preferred not to lie outright, but she would not have the tiny amount of freedom she had managed to carve out for herself if she wasn't willing to shade the truth when necessary.

"Here," she said to Mr. Satterthwaite. "You read it. He mentions that you rescued me. He does not say that I was in Bleak Street, nor why."

"Bleak Street!" Becky exclaimed. "Not a nice place, that. It's on the boundary, you see. Not quite Billy's territory, and not quite the Browns brothers'. Boundary lands are always trouble."

She shrugged. "I wouldn't walk down there. Not alone."

"So I discovered." Clem did not bother to keep the sarcasm out of her voice. She may have been naive, but she was not a complete idiot.

Becky grinned, not in the least offended. "Cor, Chris, look at them 'ouses. *Those* 'ouses, I mean."

The carriage had turned into the street where Clem lived with her father. It was the largest house on the street, a story higher than the others and twice as wide. The carriage pulled up outside. Mr. O'Hara must have told the carriage driver where to go, for Clem had not.

While she and Becky had been talking, Mr. Satterthwaite had taken a box of lucifer matches from his pocket, lit one by scraping it on the phosphorus inside a glass tube, and melted the bottom of the seal, which was now firmly affixed to the letter again.

Clem wrinkled her nose against the smell.

Mr. Satterthwaite put the letter in his inner pocket, with a smile at Clem, and was ready to leap to the ground as soon as the groom opened the door. He turned to help first Clem, and then Becky down, even as the front door opened and the butler and Clem's maid both hurried down the steps, scolding and complaining.

"Miss, where have you been? Your father is beside himself with anger." That was the butler.

"Miss, you should be ashamed of yourself, leaving the library without me, and getting me into such trouble with the master. How could you?"

There was more, of course, but Mr. Satterthwaite cut them both off. "Silence," he demanded. "You." He glared at the butler. "Announce to Mr. Wright that Mr. Christopher Satterthwaite has escorted Miss Wright home, and requests a moment of his time." He turned his attention to the maid. "Your presence is not required. You may be about your duties."

His assumption of authority and his lordly air had the desired effect. The pair of them scurried back into the house, and Mr.

Satterthwaite offered Clem his arm. "Shall we go and beard the lion, Miss Wright?"

Becky followed them into the house and quietly took a seat in the hall as the butler returned from Father's study to say, "Mr. Wright will see you, sir."

Though Father's bellow made his true message clear. "I'll see the scoundrel, but he'll not get a penny from me."

Nothing in Mr. Satterthwaite's demeanor indicated he had heard Father's insulting words. He accompanied Clem into Father's study and bowed. "Sir, I bring you a letter from Mr. O'Hara, who explains the near disaster that befell Miss Wright." He handed the letter to Father, who snatched it with a scowl for the bearer.

"And what is your part in this, young man?" he demanded. Evidence that Mr. Satterthwaite's masquerade—if it was a masquerade—of aristocratic *hauteur* had worked. Had Father considered him to be of his own class or lower, he'd have addressed her rescuer as "boy."

Showing no sign of discomfort or irritation, Mr. Satterthwaite merely replied, "I was fortunate to be in the right place to be of some small service to your daughter, Mr. Wright."

Father broke the seal and read the letter, then turned on Clem. "You should have taken your maid with you to the outhouse, girl."

"I daresay they would have taken the maid, too," Mr. Satterthwaite told him. "They were very definitely after your daughter, and I saw at least eight of them in pursuit of Miss Wright. I doubt the maid plus the footman would have given them the least pause."

Father grunted, nonplused by the intervention and unwilling to either acknowledge Mr. Satterthwaite's point or disagree openly. "That bookseller should have guards on her back yard," he said next. "You shall not shop there again unless you have just relieved yourself, Clementine. You will excuse my mentioning it, Satterthwaite. I'm a plain man, and I call a pot I piss in a piss pot."

"As is your right, Mr. Wright," Mr. Satterthwaite said, smoothly. "But not normally, I imagine, in front of a lady such as your daughter. It is your current emotional distress over her near escape from kidnapping or worse, I make no doubt."

Another grunt from Father, and then the surprising words, "Sorry, Missie." But it was all for Mr. Satterthwaite, not Clem, for he added, "My Clementine *is* a lady, Satterthwaite, and make no mistake. Thousands I've spent on governesses and tutors and dresses, and all for one purpose. And do you know what that purpose is?"

"Your daughter's happiness in a marriage suited to her grace, her beauty, and her excellent character?" Mr. Satterthwaite asked.

The question being rhetorical, Father was taken aback to have it answered, but he rallied. "Find her attractive, do you? A Satterthwaite, you say. I used to know a Reginald Satterthwaite. Something of a ne'er-do-well. But out of the top drawer, there was no doubt of that."

"I have the honor to tell you the gentleman was my papa, sir," said Mr. Satterthwaite. Father missed the heavy ironic overtones in Mr. Satterthwaite's voice. Clem doubted he saw any honor in his statement, and also sensed he would have preferred a less dignified term than "gentleman."

"Old Reggie's son? Is that right?" The gleam in Father's eye was familiar to Clem, and her heart sank. He had a scheme, and given his plans for Clem, she could guess what it was. She would have to warn Mr. Satterthwaite to run. Not that he was objectionable to her from what she knew of him so far, but Clem would come into marriage with lead strings, every one of which would be designed to bind both her and her aristocratic husband to her father.

"Clementine," said Father, "run along. Go wash and change. Rest, even. You have a ball this evening. Satterthwaite, can I offer you a brandy? Run along, Clementine, or do I have to take a switch to you?"

Chapter Three

M ISS WRIGHT RELUCTANTLY left, while Chris called on all his self-control to keep from finding the switch and using it on Wright. Coarse, arrogant, nasty old man. No wonder he had been a friend to Chris's father, who was just such another one, though his coarseness was masked in the impeccable public behavior that was taught to gentlemen.

He could think of only one reason why Wright was being so affable, and he did not for a moment imagine it was to thank Chris for saving Miss Wright from certain kidnapping and probable rape and murder.

"Sir, just so it is clear, I am Reggie Satterthwaite's son. Between them, he and my grandfather dissipated my patrimony before I was out of short dresses. As a marriage prospect for Miss Wright, I have nothing to recommend me but my blue blood."

Wright's eyebrows shot up, and he grunted a couple of times, then he finished pouring the brandy and handed one to Chris. "I appreciate plain speaking in a man, so I'll give you the same in return. My Clem has nothing to recommend her to the likes of you except lots of money. She's plain spoken and plain of feature. She is too independent and too stubborn. Her education was as much like a lady's as money could make it, but to give you the truth without the bark on it, she somehow isn't quite a lady, for all of that."

"I do not find her plain, sir, and I appreciate her plain speaking. As to her independence, I appreciated that, too, Mr. Wright. When I met up with her, chased by kidnappers, she did not faint or dither, but picked up her skirts and ran in the direction I told her."

Another grunt from Wright. "Not what a lady would have done," he insisted. "All that money I've paid, and she still speaks her mind. Now that's all well and good for us lesser folk. But not for a lady. Not at all. Not what I paid for. Here's the point, lad. I can marry her to someone that'd dive into a midden for enough cash, and don't I know it? Easy enough. But I've not met one to suit me, somehow."

More to the point, Chris had received the impression they didn't suit Miss Wright. Still, while that might the important factor to Miss Wright, and to Chris, clearly her father was not of the same view.

"None of them will turn my girl into a lady, see. And it's a lady I need. My girl is straw. Highly polished, but still straw. I need someone who will spin her into gold. What do you say, Satterthwaite? Are you the man for the job?"

"To tutor her, sir?" Because he couldn't mean what Chris wanted him to mean.

"Tutor her, yes. To start with. And when I see her shine, lad, to marry her." His smile would have been envied by a crocodile. It said, as clearly as words, "do not buy a horse from this man."

Before Chris could prevaricate, for he didn't dare say yes and didn't want to say no, Wright added. "*If* you meet my other conditions. I'm being honest with you, Satterthwaite. I want an heir. My wife only gave me a daughter, so I need to marry her off to someone who can breed her and give my blood a future."

Chris had not liked Wright from the first, and his opinion was dipping lower with every word the man said.

"In every way, that man will be a son to me," Wright went on. "I've a fancy for him to be a blue-blood, and to have entry in places denied to me. Good for the business, that. A pleasure to me, too, to have a son people look up to. People like your grandfather, who never thought I was good enough to be friends with his son."

The crocodile grin broadened. "But I'll have the last laugh when my grandson is good enough to marry their daughters, even if I don't live to see it. The man who marries my daughter will teach her to be a lady, Satterthwaite. A lady as if she was born to it. He will also show me he can learn how to run my business. And he'll do my bidding, same as a son would. Let me be quite clear about that."

Chris couldn't help but be curious, though he wasn't considering the proposition. Was he? "And what does that lucky man get, apart from Miss Wright?" he asked.

"A sum of money on the marriage. A house in the best part of town for him and my daughter, where my grandson can rub his elbows with the upper crust. Enough money to keep up the lifestyle—the carriages, the clothes, the horses, the houses. And beyond that? His son will be my heir, young man. And if that man is smart enough, he'll make a lot of money for me and for him. Is that enough for you?"

An odd thought crossed Chris's mind. Clementine Wright would have been enough for him. But the rest was tempting. Very tempting. Except it would turn him into the puppet of this man, and even Miss Wright was not tempting enough to make him swallow that.

"You have given me much to think about, Mr. Wright," Chris said. A polite nothing.

Wright stood and put out his hand for Chris to shake. "Don't take too long," he warned. "I have other candidates. My daughter will be married to the man of my choice by the end of the Season. If you wish to be considered, be here at two o'clock tomorrow afternoon for Clementine's first lesson. Good day to you, Satterthwaite."

"Take the carriage," Chris said to Becky, when he joined her again in the front hall. "I feel like a walk."

A walk in which to think about Wright and his outrageous offer. And about Miss Wright.

He heard a sibilant sound and sought the source. It was Miss Wright, peering through the garden fence, hissing at him to attract his attention. Chris looked around quickly, but if Wright had put spies on him—or on his daughter, for that matter—they were well-hidden.

Ah well. A little risk made life interesting. Chris strolled over to the gate and lifted his hat in greeting. "Miss Wright, hello again."

"What did you and my father talk about?" Miss Wright demanded, without any preamble.

Not a ladylike way of approaching a conversation, at least according to the "lady" lessons Ramping Billy held for his female employees. Chris liked Miss Wright's directness, though. It certainly saved time and misunderstanding.

"He is determined to see you married to someone whose blood runs blue, Miss Wright. I imagine you know that. He seems to think I might be a suitable candidate."

Miss Wright grimaced. "I suppose he told you that he needs a male heir, and that a grandson will have to do, since my mother was only able to provide a daughter."

She put it as baldly as her father had, though her tone and her expression turned it into a scathing comment on her father's opinion. And no wonder. "I am sorry," Chris told her.

Her eyes widened. His apology surprised her. "For what?"

"I am sorry your father is a dunderhead," he said. "And that he is a disappointment to you." Chris had personal experience of fathers who were disappointments to their children.

She narrowed her eyes with apparent suspicion. "If you are planning to offer for me, you should be aware that my father plans to control my husband's life as he controls mine," she said. "He may promise you wealth, but marriage to me would be nothing more than life in a gilded cage." She paused, and sighed.

"You rescued me, Mr. Satterthwaite. You deserve better from my family than to become nothing more than an expensive slave at my father's beck and call."

That was the truth with no bark on it. "Yes, I'd guessed that." Chris grinned at her. The knowledge didn't put him off. People had been trying to control him all his life, and he'd been figuring out how to work his way around them since he was a child. "Or at least that he would try."

"I suppose you think being a man and nobly born will keep you safe from his control," Miss Wright scoffed.

Chris told the truth again—not his usual strategy, but he thought Miss Wright would appreciate it. "No. I think that you and I are both smarter than your father, and that we can outwit and out-manipulate him. Miss Wright, once you marry, you are no longer his to control. If you pick a husband who will be on your side, you will have the upper hand. He needs to be in favor with you, or you can refuse to let him visit his heir."

Rather than appreciation, he received a snort of derision. "Fine words, but the man who controls the purse string wins the game, Mr. Satterthwaite."

"Chris," he said. "My name is Chris. And yours is Clementine. May I use it?"

"Clem," she responded. "But no. I do not think we shall be on first-name terms, Mr. Satterthwaite."

"Do you have a better prospect, Clem?" He showed no reaction to her pronouncement and her scrunched-up brow, showing that she'd recognized that he'd ignored her denial of the use of first names. "For your father says he will see you married to the man of his choice by the end of the Season."

Clem winced. "I shall have to find one. But he will not be a man who frequents gambling dens, Mr. Satterthwaite, and is on intimate terms with a man called 'Ramping Billy'." Another brow scrunch. "What does that mean, 'Ramping Billy'?"

"It's what he used to do before he turned respectable," Chris explained. He could see she was about to protest, and corrected his remark. "Sort of respectable. To 'ramp' something is to take it from somebody else by force. When he was a boy, he used to specialize in taking parcels from shoppers. Then, when he was older and bigger, he used to seize goods from people who were in debt to one of the money lenders and could not pay. He saved all his wages and became a money lender himself. He raised enough to start a gambling den and then another and another. And now he is a wealthy man. He is a legend for it."

He pursed his lips. "The name is—an honorific, I suppose. Like 'earl' or 'duke'. In fact, when you come to think of it, most nobles have ancestors who received a title because they ramped for whomever was king at the time. Billy's title recognizes his prowess. He is part of the aristocracy of the gutter."

"You sound proud of him, but the man is clearly a villain. Is that how your ancestors managed to make it into the top drawer? Taking things from other people?" Her tone made "top drawer" into a sneer.

Chris chuckled. "Probably. The only members of my father's family I have ever met were my father, who was a do-nothing and a dirty dish, and my grandfather, who is a scoundrel through and through. They are not good advertisements for their ancestors, but perhaps it speaks well of the family that they cut my grandfather off, and then my father in his turn."

He didn't normally tell people the truth about those two reprobates, but Clem would soon discover the facts if he really did court her. Might as well be the one to tell her.

"And you?" Clem asked. "Have they cut you off?"

He'd not given them the opportunity. "I have not met them," he repeated. "As far as I know, they have never shown any interest in me, so I cannot tell what they would do if I introduced myself." He had been tempted. The current earl was the son of his grandfather's brother. The earl's son—Chris's cousin, he supposed—occasionally played at Fortune's Fool.

He returned to her previous remark. Once again, only honesty would do, for the facts were widely known. In any case, he wanted her to know the truth of him and choose him anyway. "I grew up in one of Billy's gambling dens," he offered. "I cannot say I am a close friend, or any kind of friend at all—I do not think he has any friends. But I owe him a great deal. Not just for letting me stay when I was a boy, but for seeing me educated. Now I work as his bookkeeper. That's why I know Tiny and the others, and why I hoped they would let us in."

"I see," she replied. "I suppose I can understand why you admire him, then."

They were interrupted by Clem's maid. They heard her shout before she came into view. "Miss Wright!" She came around a shrub and caught sight of them. "Oh. There you are." She glared at Chris as if he was up to no good, but addressed herself to Clem. "Your father wishes to speak to you."

"Miss," Chris said.

Both lady and maid looked at him in bewilderment. Chris addressed the maid. "'Your father wishes to speak to you, *Miss*.' Your master requires his daughter to behave like the lady she is. As the maid of a lady, you must address her correctly. I am certain Mr. Wright will see the truth of that when I point it out to him."

Clem lifted an eyebrow and directed a speculative gaze at her maid. "He makes a good point," she commented.

The maid turned her shoulder to Chris. "You are keeping the master waiting," she insisted.

"Miss," said Clem. She glanced at Chris, her eyes laughing, though she kept her face straight.

Two could play at the ignoring game. "Sleeps with the master, does she?" Chris asked. It was an educated guess, and did not entirely miss the target. The maid's face flared bright red, but with anger rather than guilt. "Do not!"

"Not for lack of trying," Clem told Chris.

"I'll tell him you are not coming, shall I," threatened the girl.

"I shall tell him you are an impertinent baggage who flirts with the footmen instead of attending to your duties," Chris retorted. "It does not speak well of his control over his household." Another shaft fired not quite at random. For Clem to escape the mouthy maid's supervision in the bookshop, the maid must have been preoccupied with something else. This one struck the bullseye. The maid flushed an even deeper red, and muttered, "Miss. If you please, Miss."

"Enough, Mr. Satterthwaite," Clem decided. "Martha, tell my father I shall be with him in a moment. Mr. Satterthwaite, good day, sir."

Chris took his dismissal. "Good day, Miss Wright." He resumed his walk home. He had a lot to think about.

➤➤➤❯❮❮❮❮

MR. SATTERTHWAITE WAS far too observant. Martha had been flirting with Papa since the day he employed her to be Clem's maid. Papa flirted back, and Martha thought herself too good for service as a result. Not that Papa would do more than flirt. Or, at least, he never had in the past. Clem had no idea what he did outside of the house, but he left his servants alone.

Meanwhile, Martha consoled herself with the footmen. However, between her hopes of becoming Papa's mistress and her imitation of Papa's own dismissive attitude, Martha was not treating Clem with the respect due to one's employer.

Clem had had enough of Martha's impertinence. She could try the kind of subtle threat that Mr. Satterthwaite used so well, but she was more comfortable with direct dealings. "Martha, I must go to my father, but afterward, you and I are overdue for a chat. Wait for me outside his study."

Father merely wanted to crow about finding her a suitor to suit his needs. He was so delighted that his language reverted to the patterns of his youth, as it tended to do when he was in the grip of a strong emotion. "Young Satterthwaite's family is top of the line, my girl. 'Is da was a wastrel. Yes, and his gaffer, too. But the gaffer was second son of an earl. The current earl is young Satterthwaite's cousin. Top shelf, I tell ye. 'As never taken an interest in the boy, but that's all the better for us, Clementine, isn't it?"

"Is it, Father?" Clem asked, her heart sinking. What made Father think Mr. Satterthwaite, from a line of wastrels—yes, and drunks and rakes, she'd be bound—was any different than his father and grandfather?

"O' course, girl. Listen. The boy's mother came from the best bloodlines in the business. An earl's daughter, and some sort o' cousin to a marquess. I'll 'ave to look into it. Charmed 'er, I 'spects, then spent all her money. We won't be 'avin' none o' that, Clementine. Ye can trust me to tie it up right and tight."

He chuckled and rubbed his hands together, unable to contain his glee. "First-class bloodlines and no family what cares what 'appens to 'im. Couldn't be better. Except... Na. The current earl's got three sons, I reckon, and I heard tell one o' them's married. Not much chance of being a countess, Clementine, but ye have to take what ye can get, and yer not much to look at, and that's a fact."

"Thank you, Father." She had heard the comment often enough for it only to rub a little raw, and after all, her own mirror confirmed the truth of it.

"Ye've done well, my girl, to be rescued by Satterthwaite. And he stood up for ye, mind. Said 'e didn't think ye plain and 'e liked that ye did not dither, or some such. Trying to turn me up sweet, like as not, but there ye are."

"How nice of him, Father." If Mr. Satterthwaite really wished to please Father, he would praise Father's business rather than his daughter, but it was nice of him to praise her for being decisive. If that was indeed what he meant.

"I've told 'im I'll pay 'im to give you lady lessons," Father said. "Keep him close, like, so I can see what 'e's made of."

"Lady lessons!" Clem exclaimed, moderating her tone immediately to say, "I have *had* lessons in how to be a lady, Father."

"I should know. I've paid enough for them," Father grumbled. "Ye speak right, and ye know all the fancy-pants manners, but ye don't talk right, Clementine, no matter how much I whip ye for it. Talking business! And worse things. Politics, they tell me. Arguin' with gennelemen, as if any man wants a woman who thinks she knows better 'n 'im. But it don't matter none. It's just to keep 'im close till I decide whether I want 'im. And if I do, my girl, it don't matter what ye and 'im think, so ye might as well make up yer mind to it. I'll see ye wed, or out in the street in yer shift, my girl."

"He might not agree, Father," she couldn't help but protest, and on another day that might have won her a bruise or two, but Father was in a good mood, for he just laughed.

"'E won't 'ave no more choice than ye, Clementine. I'll find somefin' on 'im. Trust yer old da for that. Now run along. Tell Cook I'll be out for dinner." He was already standing up and putting on the coat and hat that he kept by the outside door from the study.

He had a habit of coming and going that way to avoid the notice of his servants, for he'd spent so many years paying other people's servants to provide him with information that he used in his business dealings, that he had no trust in his own household. He paused with his hand on the door. "Run along, I tell ye."

Clementine left, but she heard the outer door close and lock again as she went. In the hall, she called for Martha, and waited, the ire she did not dare release on her father fueling her anger with the faithless. lazy maid.

"Martha," she shouted at last. "Stop cavorting with Charles and come here this instant."

Charles was one of two footmen currently sharing Martha's favors, and Clem happened to know that Frederick, her other paramour, had been sent to take the mail to the posting house.

The strategy of shouting Martha's perfidy outside of Father's study produced rapid results. Martha hurried down the stairs, tying her apron and tucking her hair back into her cap. "Miss! Are you trying to get me dismissed?"

"That is one of my options," Clem told her. "As it happens, Father has gone out, but remember this, Martha. I know things about your behavior when you are out of Father's sight that you would prefer Father did not know, and now Mr. Satterthwaite has seen them, too. And I have matters I would prefer Father didn't know. Keep my secrets and treat me with respect as your employer, and your secrets are safe with me. If not... I am the daughter of the house, and about to fulfill Father's ambitions for him. If he has to choose between us, who do you think will lose?"

And so, the day was not a complete loss. She had been tricked into putting herself into danger, had nearly discovered at first-hand what the old ladies meant when they talked about "a fate worse than death", and had been told she had no choice in whom she would marry. On the other hand, she had discovered how to get at least reluctant cooperation from her maid.

Whether Mr. Satterthwaite went on the plus or minus side of the ledger remained to be seen.

Chapter Four

CHRIS FULLY EXPECTED to be summoned by Ramping Billy as soon as he returned to his office at Fortune's Fool, and sure enough, he had not been seated above a minute before one of the herd of small boys that infested the gambling den poked his head around the corner and said, "Billy wants yuh, Fingers."

Actually, Tom was not that small anymore. Good food and good treatment had prompted a growth spurt. Like many of Billy's boys, he had no memory of his mother and only a random guess at his own age, but Tom was probably older than most of the other boys, though he'd not been here as long as some.

He was a bright lad, and no doubt Billy was taking his time to decide what best to do with him.

Billy's study was just along the corridor from Chris's, though it was four or more times the size of his own and much more elegantly appointed. "Himself wanted to see me," he told Tiny, who was lounging against the door.

Tiny straightened, knocked, opened the door, and yelled, "Fingers to see yuh, Boss."

At Billy's "Send him in," Tiny stepped out of the way so Chris could enter the room.

When Billy chose to be inscrutable, as he did now, it was impossible to tell his mood from his voice or his face. His expression was neutral, his voice bland as he greeted Chris. "Christopher."

"Sir."

"Sit. Tell me how Wright reacted."

How had Wright reacted? "He appeared gleeful, sir. The kidnapping and the danger to his daughter, he more or less dismissed. His main focus seemed to be on me. He recognized my name, or rather, he asked me if I was related to Reginald Satterthwaite."

Billy nodded. "Carry on."

"He seems to think I can be useful to him. He wants a husband for his daughter who will give him a doorway into the ton but be completely under his control. He thinks I might be that man." Chris's attempt to be as emotionless as Billy failed when he added, "He doesn't care what his daughter thinks about it. He intends to force her into a marriage to please himself."

"That offends you? It is common enough."

"Yes, it offends me. Just because it is common doesn't make it right." And there went any facade of indifference.

His boss allowed himself a small smile. "You care what happens to the girl." It was not a question.

Chris didn't argue the point. Billy was right, as usual, though why Clem affected him so, he had no idea. "He'll soon realize I am useless to his schemes. I have no links to the ton."

"You could have, though," Billy observed. "You could introduce yourself to your cousin the earl, or call on your mother's cousin the marquess. Or, better yet, your mother's brother the earl."

It was uncanny how Billy could pluck a half-formed idea from a man's head. "And say what?" Chris said. "Hello, I am the son of the late, unlamented Reggie Satterthwaite. I found him no more reliable than you did, but was fortunate enough to be caught picking the pocket of a gang boss, who took pity on me and had me raised by the professional women in his gambling den. Kiss me, cousin."

"Perhaps a little less information and a shade more formality," Billy suggested.

"They will throw me out on my arse."

"Perhaps." Billy pursed his lips and tilted his head from side to side. "Perhaps not, if we approach it correctly. It is worth doing, you know. You shouldn't settle for being my bookkeeper for the rest of your life. If you are acquainted with your family, it will open doors to almost any life you might want, especially if you have access to Miss Wright's money."

The assumptions in that statement sent Chris's head reeling, and all he could think of to say in response was, "If Wright has his way, I'll not have access to anything he doesn't dribble out to me."

"We can handle Wright." Billy's grin suggested he had several enjoyable strategies already planned. "That man is not half as clever as he thinks he is."

"I said something similar to Miss Wright."

"Yes, the girl is sharp," Billy agreed. "Fetching, too, if not quite in the common way."

And now Chris was feeling a sharp stab of jealousy at his benefactor and boss. He was disgusted with himself. Clementine Wright had had him at sixes and sevens even before her father's outrageous proposal set his mind seething with plans and dreams.

"Think about it, Christopher," Billy said. "Decide if you want Miss Wright and her money, if you want to make contact with the respectable side of your family. I will help you with both or either. Now. To business. Do you have the summary figures for last month?"

"I do, sir." Chris stood, grateful to put the confusing questions to one side to return to the straightforward financial records he kept for Billy's multiple enterprises. "I will get them for you immediately."

IT COULDN'T HURT, Chris decided, to turn up at the Wright townhouse the following day at two o'clock, which was the time Wright had appointed for Miss Wright's first lesson in being a lady. One lesson did not commit him to marrying the lady, after all.

"I was not sure if you would come," Miss Wright said, when he was shown into the drawing room where she waited, with the maid Martha in attendance. *No. I didn't imagine my reaction to her. What is it about her that turns my heart over in my chest?*

"I wasn't sure if I would come, either." Chris grinned at her, inviting her to enjoy the joke. "It would do no harm to talk, I told myself. But truly, I just wanted to see you again."

She rolled her eyes, suggesting she thought he was serving compliments with a shovel. This had the paradoxical effect of delighting him. "It is true, you know," he said. "But you have no reason to believe me. You do not know me. Not yet. In further-ance of our acquaintance, shall we go for a walk to discuss your father's requirements and how what we might go about satisfying them?"

From Clem's expression, she was trying to work out whether walking with him would be a concession too far. She had not yet understood what he was about. Chris let her know by speaking to the maid. "Martha, my plan is to walk to Leicester Square and then stroll around the gardens. Once we arrive at the gardens, you will walk behind us, out of earshot but well within sight. That will cover the proprieties while allowing Miss Wright and myself the privacy to speak our minds."

That worked. Clem's face cleared and she nodded briskly. "Yes, Mr. Satterthwaite. Martha, please fetch my bonnet, my pelisse, and my walking boots. Also, your own."

"May I suggest a shawl?" Chris asked. "There is a brisk wind."

Soon, they had covered the short distance to Leicester Square. Billy had suggested the destination and provided a key to one of the gates so they could walk in the private garden that filled the center of the square.

Apart from a sharp look when Chris pulled out the key, Clem did not react to him claiming resident's privileges. As soon as Martha had lagged far enough behind them, he answered the question she hadn't asked. "Ramping Billy gave me the key. I didn't ask where he got it."

The answer was not to her taste, Chris could tell, but he had no other, so he changed the subject. "Shall we talk about the choices each of us has before us?"

"Do I have choices before me?" Clem asked. "Father has already said that the decision is his, and that if I refuse the groom he offers me, I will be—and I quote—'out in the street in your shift, my girl.'"

Nasty old man. "Then you have three choice. Cooperate with me to convince your father I am the preferred suitor. Make common cause with another suitor. Simply sit back and let come what may."

Clem bowed her head so all he could see of her was her bonnet. A pretty confection, but he'd have preferred it back in her wardrobe so her face was visible. If he could see her face, he would know what she was thinking. She had not mastered the art of keeping her thoughts to herself, which was probably what her father meant by saying she needed to be more ladylike.

Personally, Chris preferred her openness.

"But if you are at risk of being thrown out, Clem, send for me, and I will meet you with a cloak and take you some place safe."

She turned her head up at that and searched his face. Let her. He meant every word. Some of the women who had raised him took to their way of life because they'd been thrown penniless into the street—by a lover, a father, even a husband. For their sakes, he'd come to the rescue of anyone in such need.

Perhaps she did not believe what she saw. Certainly, her harrumph sounded dismissive. "What choices do you face, Chris?" she asked.

That was a victory! She had called him by his preferred name.

He hoped his exultation did not show on his face. "Two, but each has options and both, benefits and costs. Do I accept your father's challenge or do I walk away? If I accept, can we manage your father's expectations or will we end up paying his price? I think we can avoid being his puppets, and I know Billy will help, but what will Billy's price be?" He paused for her comment, but she said nothing. That pestiferous bonnet was back in the way again.

"If I walk away, what will your father do to force my hand? Or can I convince him that I would be too much trouble, so that he dismisses me? And what of Billy? He is taking an interest in this match. If I refuse it, what will it cost me then?"

She had a tart comment about that. "My, Mr. O'Hara is taking an interest in my affairs. I wonder you let him push you around. I know you owe him, but does he own you?"

"In much the same way as your father owns you, Clem. And I dare say Billy has been as much a father to me as my own was. More, in fact, for he..." He trailed off, not sure if he was ready to share that particular piece of dirty laundry.

He expected her to demand that he finish his sentence, but instead she asked a question that got almost to the heart of his discomfort with her knowing his past. "Why do they call you Fingers? The people at Mr. O'Hara's?"

They turned a corner and walked along the next side of the square. She didn't press the question except by her silence.

Well, and why not? If she rejected him once she knew his story, so be it. If they were to decide to marry, he wanted a relationship based on honesty and trust. "When I was nine, my mother died," he said, eventually. "My father had not been home for some time. I found out later that he was dead, too, which I suppose is why his debts were called in. The debt collectors took everything and left me homeless and alone."

He was skipping the complication that was his grandfather, but the outcome was the same. He'd finished up out on the street. In more than his undershirt, but that didn't last. A gang of boys beat him up for his clothes, which still had plenty of wear, though they were not new.

Fortunately, the boys were impressed at how well he'd fought and how many of them it had taken to subdue him, so they took him back to the den they'd made in the cellar of a burnt-out building.

"I was lucky. I found a place to live with some people who taught me a skill with which I could pay my share of food and board." For nearly a year, he worked in a team, lifting purses and watches, swiftly graduating from decoy to pick pockets as his skill grew. "They taught me to be a pickpocket, Clem."

An indrawn gasp was her only comment. After a pause, he picked up the story. "Until I was caught. Ramping Billy had me, and not only that, he recognized me, because he was one of the men who had collected money from my father in the past, though not one of those who stripped my mother's rooms. He took me back to Fortune's Fool—at that time, it was his only establishment. He handed me over to the ladies who worked there."

Chris could remember exactly what Billy had said to them. *"Wash him, delouse him, dress him in something that isn't rags, and put him to work. We're keeping him."*

"He told them to watch me, because I was light-fingered. So, they called me 'Fingers', and they still do."

He shuddered at the memory of that hungry, terrifying year between the time his grandfather had abandoned him and when Billy had found him. He'd been well aware of his fate if he were caught by constables, and he'd been scared every time he lifted something.

But from the moment he entered Fortune's Fool, he never stole again. Billy had made it clear that if he was caught stealing from Billy or any of his employees or customers, he'd be out on his ear again. By that time, he'd been a street rat for long enough to know how lucky he had been the first time. Being beaten and stripped was far from the worst fate to befall a handsome boy alone in the stews of London.

"So, that is why they call me Fingers, and that is why, between your father and Billy, I'll take Billy every time. He is a villain, Clem, I'll grant you that. But he's an *honest* villain."

"Whereas my father is a dishonest upright citizen. I accept your point, Chris."

She was not yelling for her maid and stalking off in outraged disgust. That was a bonus. Instead, she seemed to have decided on an interrogation. "Do you gamble?"

"Only for pleasure and never more than I happen to have in my pockets. My father couldn't leave the tables alone, and so my mother moved from rented room to rented room, outrunning the bailiff, never quite making ends meet. I won't ever do that to those who depend on me." He paused as a realization made him amend his statement. "Not that I have anyone dependent on me yet."

She nodded. "Do you drink alcohol?"

"I do, but I am not a drunkard. From what I understand, both my father and my grandfather spent their lives intoxicated to a lesser or greater extent, which is probably why they were such poor gamblers that my grandfather had to flee overseas when my father died. You might not think much of my position with Billy, but it is a responsible job overseeing his finances, and pays well. I won't put that at risk just for the sake of a temporary escape into dreams. No opium for me, either, or ether parties, or the like."

Clem nodded, and he thought that turn-about was fair play, but before he could ask her the same question, she floored him with a question about the third vice of the disorderly—the one he had expected her maidenly sensibilities to ignore. More the fool, him. Clementine Wright was made of sterner stuff than that.

"Do you disport with women?"

It silenced him for a moment, but he had been blunt and honest so far, and had no intention of stopping now. If she had the knowledge to ask the question, she should not be offended by the answer.

"I am not a virgin, Clem. I have not been a virgin since I was fourteen, when one of O'Hara's women took me on as a charity case. I have, in recent years, lost my taste for mindless coupling, but I have had temporary lovers—women who had an interest in my company and I in theirs. Hearts were not involved, except that we were friends—and in most cases still are. I do not have a lover at the moment."

Come to think of it, he had not had a lover for months. Perhaps that was the reason Clem had bowled him over. Perhaps he should find a willing woman with whom to exorcise her.

Except he didn't want to, and in any case, he was reasonably sure it would not work.

"I see," said Clem.

Chris decided to take over the conversation. "My turn. Same questions. Do you gamble?"

"I shall simplify matters by saying that I do not gamble. I do not drink alcohol. And I am a virgin. However, I reserve the right to change all three once my father no longer monitors how often I breathe."

His smile was involuntary. What a delight she was.

Her smile was sour. "And I suppose that is the sort of comment you are expected to train me not to make."

"The fact you already know that shows you don't need any training," Chris pointed out. "All you need is the motivation to monitor what you say if the situation calls for it."

She set her jaw. "I do not see why I should."

"Yes. Exactly. And frankly, neither do I! Unless you do it as part of a strategy to placate your father until you get what you want."

Chris had taken another two steps before he realized that she had stopped. She was standing on the path, looking as stunned as if his comment had been a flour sack to the head.

And Martha was approaching. She ignored Chris and spoke to Clem. "Miss Wright, you are 'at home' this afternoon. We should get back."

"Yes," said Clem. "Yes, Martha, you are correct. I see we have completed a circuit of the square, Mr. Satterthwaite. Shall we retrace our steps to Father's townhouse?"

"Indeed, Miss Wright. And might I be so fortunate as to take you driving with me tomorrow afternoon?" In a phaeton, if he could hire one, with no room for a maid.

"Thank you," the lady replied. "I should like that."

Today's mission could be accounted a success, then. He had not scared her off, he had given her food for thought, and they had an engagement for the next day.

He had only one problem. He had never before driven a phaeton or, indeed, anything more than a donkey cart.

However, he had a plan.

Two years ago, Ramping Billy O'Hara had branched out from debt-collection, gambling dens, brothels, and residential property (which was a fancy expression for warrens of once fine buildings repurposed to accommodate dozens of families each). More recently, he'd begun buying successful businesses around the fringes of the area he ruled, and even beyond the reach of the crime bosses who ruled the worst parts of London.

Since Chris kept Billy's books, he was one of the few people aware that Billy now owned the King's Arms, which was one of the terminal inns for the Great North Road, an important link in a chain of transport for people and mail that branched out across the breadth and length of the country.

So, it was to the King's Arms Chris went, to ask if he could rent a phaeton and team for the following afternoon, and whether someone could teach him how to drive it. The groom laughed in his face and asked him to wait a minute.

Some fifteen minutes later, he was explaining his request to the stable master, and then to the innkeeper. Both were as amused as the groom.

"*Ee*, lad. Driving a high-bred team is not learned in a minute," the stable master said, when he'd stopped laughing.

"And even if it could be done, I've not the people to spare nor the horses," the innkeeper said. "You might be Billy's pet, but even he can't expect miracles."

Right. So much for plan "A". All Chris had achieved was making an idiot of himself for the pleasure of the innkeeper and his stablemaster. He gave it up as a bad job—he was due back at work, in any case.

The problem was, he did not have a plan "B". He continued to worry at the problem for the rest of the afternoon. He could hire a carriage and a driver, but that wouldn't give him the privacy with Clem that he wanted. Perhaps he could hire horses, for he could ride well enough. He had no idea, however, whether Clem did or did not.

He was finishing up for the day when one of Billy's boys came looking for him. "Mr. Satterthwaite, there's someone for you in the stable-yard," he said.

When Chris went to look, he found an elegant phaeton occupied by a smartly-dressed man he'd seen from time to time in Fortune's Fool.

"Christopher Satterthwaite?" the man called out.

"I am, yes."

"I'm John Bagshaw. O'Hara sent me to teach you how to drive a phaeton. If you learn to drive, he'll write off my gambling debts." He moved over on the seat. "Come on up."

Another favor from Billy. When the bill came due to be paid it was going to be enormous, but turning Billy down was even more dangerous. Chris mounted the steps and took the driver's seat. Laugh at him, did they? If he could master this skill—or at least make not too bad a fist of it—he'd have the last laugh.

Chapter Five

"I COULD TRY a new style, Miss," said Martha.

Clem realized that she had been frowning at the mirror, but her appearance had not been what made her frown. She had given up hoping she would grow taller and more slender, that her face would become less blocky and her bosom less robust. She had long since accepted that her fair hair would not suddenly change color to the more fashionable brunette and develop more of a curl, and that her eyes would always remain irretrievably and blandly blue.

But why not try a new style? "Yes, thank you, Martha."

If nothing else, her encounter with Chris Satterthwaite had inspired her to take a firmer line with her maid, and the past two days had been much more pleasant. And there she was, thinking about him again. The sad truth was that her life was a dull round of fashionable events at which nobody spoke to her, and afternoons during which nobody visited her.

She had concluded somewhat sadly she had been ready to believe Amanda Brown's lies, not because she was kind, but because she was bored. Being nearly kidnapped, rescued by Chris, and introduced to Mr. O'Hara had been the most excitement she'd had in a long time.

And yesterday afternoon had been lovely. Chris had spoken

to her, and not to her breasts. She supposed he was after her money, but he was at least putting in some effort to court her, instead of assuming that the person to woo was her father. He took her questions seriously and answered them.

Such a contrast to the ball she had been to the night before last, where, as usual, she had stood with her chaperone, and spent the evening being ignored while the woman chatted with her friends. And to last night's musicale and the subsequent event, a rout, at both of which the same scenario replayed, except she was approached by one of the more persistent fortune hunters who her father had already rejected. He seemed to think she was the one who had refused him and that the way to persuade her to change her mind was a series of fulsome and insincere compliments.

"There, Miss," said Martha.

Clem focused on the mirror, and was stunned. "You are a magician, Martha." She turned her head from side to side, and Martha picked up a hand mirror to show her the back. Instead of pinning everything tightly back, she had pinned a wave into the sides, teased a few strands to drift over her ears, and caught the remainder up into a soft roll.

"I don't look nearly so square jawed," she noticed. "Martha, I love it."

"It's pretty, Miss. And if I might be so bold…"

"Please, if you have any more ideas, I would like to hear them."

"Can I take some of the flounces off your dresses, Miss? They are too fussy for you. Make you look wider and shorter, if you don't mind me saying so. The colors aren't the best they could be, but we can't do nothing about that unless you want to start again. But we could take the frills and fuss off."

The frills and flounces had not been Clem's idea. "My sponsor, Mrs. Bellowes, insisted that my gowns were highly fashionable and appropriate for a girl making her Season, but I agree, Martha. They are too fussy for me. As to the colors, I don't think Father would let me start again, but I would be very grateful if you do what you can. What do you think of the carriage dress I have out for today?"

Martha narrowed her eyes. "I can have that flounce off in a few minutes, Miss, and if you wear it with the pale blue redingote and your cream scarf, it will do very well."

It did very well indeed. Clem could not claim that she was pretty, but she looked smart, for once. The difference was astonishing. "Martha, if I can talk Father into new dresses, you must come with me to help me choose," she said.

Goodness. Who would have thought two days ago that Martha would become an ally!

A knock on the door proved to be Charles, to announce Mr. Satterthwaite had arrived and was in the drawing room. With a lift of her heart that was not entirely due to her new hair style and the improved gown, Clem went down to meet him.

His eyes widened when he saw her. "Is that a new way of wearing your hair?" he asked. "I like it."

"I do, too," Clem said. "Martha is good with hair."

Chris grinned at Martha, who had followed Clem, carrying her coat and hat. "Good day, Martha. Well done with the hair. Are you ready, Miss Wright? My mentor tells me that one must not keep the horses waiting."

"Your mentor?"

"You shall meet him in a minute, and I will explain," Chris promised, taking the coat from Martha and holding it for Clem to put on. Martha fitted the bonnet to Clem's head and tied her ribbon, and Clem pulled on her gloves. "I am ready, Mr. Satterthwaite," she said. "Thank you, Martha."

A smart phaeton was drawn up at the bottom of the steps. The man at the reins doffed his hat to Clem. "Miss Wright," said Chris, "allow me to make known to you the Honorable John Bagshaw. Mr. Bagshaw has been kind enough to take me on as a pupil to learn how to drive a fashionable vehicle such as this."

He leaned close, as if to impart a secret, but he did not lower his voice as he said, "He tells me I am not ready to drive through the streets, Miss Wright, but he will drive us to Green Park while I ride behind in the tiger's seat. There, he will trust me at the reins until it is time to come back through the streets again."

"The horses are very well trained and know their business, Miss Wright," said Mr. Bagshaw. "You will be perfectly safe."

"You are meant to tell her I have been diligent at my lessons and show great promise," protested Chris, but he was laughing, and Mr. Bagshaw laughed with him.

Clem allowed herself to be assisted up into the passenger seat. "*Has* he been diligent at his lessons, Mr. Bagshaw?" she asked. Chris leapt up behind and Mr. Bagshaw coaxed the horses out into the traffic.

"Yes, I have to admit that he has," said Mr. Bagshaw. "Both of them."

Clem twisted in her seat to look at Chris. "Two lessons, Mr. Satterthwaite? How many times have you driven a carriage or other vehicle?"

"Not counting donkey carts," insisted Mr. Bagshaw.

"Twice," Chris admitted. "Yesterday evening and this morning."

Clem realized her mouth was opened and took it back under her control to say, "I see. And how many times have you driven donkey carts, may I ask?"

"Perhaps a dozen? There are some similarities, Clem."

"Yes," Mr. Bagshaw agreed. "Horses and donkeys both have four legs and a tail. And a donkey cart and a phaeton both have four wheels."

"You are not helping, John," Chris retorted, and Mr. Bagshaw laughed again.

At least it is not a high-perch phaeton. Yes, and the horses were calm in traffic and not inclined to be restive.

"That reminds me," said Chris. "Do you ride, Miss Wright? I suggested a phaeton because I thought it would be easier to talk, but if you ride, I could hire horses tomorrow instead."

"Better to use the phaeton, dear boy," said Mr. Bagshaw. "You could use the practice."

"I have never learned to ride," Clem admitted. "Father could not see the point."

"The point," said Mr. Bagshaw, "is to see and be seen. In the country, I grant you, we ride because it is a pleasure, and also often the fastest way from place to place. In London, we ride to be seen and admired. Who has the finest seat? Who the best top hat? Who the most expensive horse? Your father, if you will forgive me for saying so, Miss Wright, does not know how the game is played."

"No," Clem agreed. "He does not."

"And here we are at Green Park," said Chris, with satisfaction. "Go and find a bench to sit on, John. We don't need you."

"Cheeky!" Mr. Bagshaw retorted, laughing. "Your tutor should cane you, boy." He negotiated the gateway and drew the horses up out of the way of any other carriages.

Chris laughed back. "I'd like to see you try." He leapt down from the back and came round to Mr. Bagshaw's side of the phaeton, then the two men changed places. "Don't become so distracted by the lovely lady that you forget to mind your horses," Mr. Bagshaw reminded him.

Lovely lady, indeed. Clem restrained herself from snorting.

The horses started off again without any trouble. Clem said nothing, not wanting to distract Chris from driving, but he had no such qualms. "You are, you know," he said. "I saw your expression when John called you lovely, but you are wrong to think he dissembles. You are not in the common way of what people call 'pretty', I'll grant you. But your eyes are fine, your complexion is excellent, your hair is becomingly dressed for the first time since I met you, and I particularly like your determined chin."

On the whole, Clem had no time for compliments, which usually sounded as if the speaker had copied them out of a book, and was bound and determined to repeat them whether or not they were appropriate to the recipient.

This one was different, for the features he mentioned were the very ones with which she sometimes consoled herself. Her eyes were a boring blue, yes, but they were bright and well-shaped, with long full lashes. As for her skin, it was clear and pale.

The comment about the hair was true, too, and honest. And he liked her determined chin!

"Thank you." It was all she could think of to say, but then her most obvious flaws crowded into her consciousness, demanding to be recognized. "I am short and portly." Bother! She hadn't meant to blurt out the words.

"You are diminutive and shapely, though I must say one usually has difficulty seeing your shape past all the frilly stuff."

"Flounces and ruffles," she informed him, her mind repeating the words *diminutive* and *shapely*. "My chaperone says they are fashionable. Martha says they make me look wider and shorter. She took the flounce off this gown."

"Martha is being helpful?" Chris asked.

"We had a little chat. I promised to keep her secrets from my father if she kept mine from him. We are getting along well now. I should have put my foot down with her weeks ago." She smiled at him, though he wouldn't see it, for he had his eyes on the horses. "I owe you my thanks for bringing to my attention how to deal with her."

"I'm glad I could be of service."

"Again. I have not forgotten you saved me from the Brown brothers."

Chris shot her one of his cheerful grins. "Again, then. And whenever you need me, really. Have you thought any more about what we discussed yesterday? Do you have any further questions for me?"

Clem had thought about little else. "Why me?" she asked. "Why do you want to marry me? Is it just…"

He had put up a hand to stop her, and she would rather that he kept both his hands firmly on the reins. "It is not just your dowry. And I am not delighted at the prospect of the ongoing battle with your father to keep my soul intact and to protect you. But I think it will be worth it."

"Protect me?" What on earth did he mean by that? Who did he think she needed to be protected from?

"Clem," he said, and somehow the fact that he sounded exasperated made him all the more convincing. "Clem, if we marry, if you become my wife, it will be my duty and my honor to put you at the center of my life. I haven't seen that many successful marriages, and heaven knows my own parents' marriage was a primer in what not to do, but I have seen enough to know that a man and a woman who want to be happy together must each put the other first. It will be my job, my privilege, and my honor to protect and defend you from any threats. That includes your father. I will not allow him to bully or manipulate you, and I fully expect explosions over the matter."

The warm feeling spreading through her had to be ignored. "I shall not be your property, whatever the law says," she warned him.

"I should hope not, except in so far as I shall be yours. In fact, it could be said I was more your property than you are mine, since you are, in effect, paying for me. Or at least for my bloodlines."

That was certainly a different way of looking at it, but it led neatly to the next question. "Why do you want to marry for money?"

Again, he didn't hesitate. "Money is nice to have. I could afford to marry if the lady to favor me with her hand in marriage had less money than I have myself. I am well paid for the work I do, and I have been able to save. But grateful though I am to Billy, I'd like to leave his employ, Clem. If I married a poor woman, I could not afford to do that. Still, I would not be contemplating this course if I had not met you. In all truth, I like you, Clem. I think we could be good for one another."

He was convincing, she'd give him that. But then, by his own account, he'd been raised by one rogue after another. Of course, he was convincing. On the other hand, none of the other suitors for her hand had bothered to court her at all. They had all applied their efforts to wooing her father, and if they spoke to her at all it was to talk about themselves.

Since none of them had won over her father, she did not have to consider them—though who else was Father considering?

"If you left your position with Mr. O'Hara, what would you do, Chris? Do you contemplate a life of leisure?" She did her best to keep her feelings about such a life out of her voice. Gambling, the endless social round, womanizing, foolish pursuits involving horses, overindulgence in alcohol and overspending on clothing. Those were the entertainments of the gentlemen she knew.

"I can hear your sneer, you know," Chris said. "You despise the kinds of gentlemen who have made Billy rich, and so do I. No, I cannot see myself as a gentleman of leisure, though I doubt successful gentlemen have as much leisure as we think, since they have investments to manage and estates to run.

"But those are not for me. I have an idea—a dream, if you will. But we are already within sight of the gate. Can we leave discussion of that for tomorrow? I'd like to talk about your lady lessons. I have an idea about what sort of worm your father has in his brain box. May I tell you?"

A worm in his brain box. Clem, who had begun to bristle at the mere thought that Chris could teach her how to be a lady, giggled.

"Do tell," she said, wondering if she really wanted to know.

"Your father, I am thinking, is not acquainted with many ladies of the ton, and so his opinion of ladylike behavior is formed from impressions he gained from others. He has paid for you to be raised as a lady—by which he means he has paid for a governess, I assume?"

"A series of them, and music teachers, dance tutors, painting instructors. I have mastered all the lessons I had a scrap of talent at, but please do not ask me to sing."

One of Clem's music teachers had suggested voice training,

but the voice teacher resigned after two lessons, telling her father she was musical enough, as evidenced by her piano playing, but she had the voice of a crow, and should on no account be permitted to sing in public.

"So, you were as well-prepared for your come out as any other damsel, but I'm guessing that your father cannot attend events with you, and that he doesn't know any suitable lady, so he hired one. Am I right so far?"

"Yes, Mrs. Bellowes. She was recommended by another mine owner, whose daughter she sponsored. The daughter married a baron."

"And did the daughter meet the baron through Mrs. Bellowes? I am guessing not. I believe she has few contacts in the circles your father wants you to enter, and has been unable to attract invitations to the premier events or to introduce you to suitable gentlemen. I surmise she has told your father that her failure to find you a husband is your fault."

Clem jaw had dropped open again. How had she not realized that? "You are right. Now that you've pointed it out, it's obvious to me. The lords and ladies the newspapers write about are never at the events I attend, and I have never been to any of the events that appear in the newspapers. *She* is the one who says I am not ladylike!"

"That is my guess," Chris said. "Also, those suitors your father has negotiated with—I am assuming there are some?" At her nod, he continued. "I imagine they were critical of you as a negotiating tactic. The swine. 'Plain' and 'no lady'." He snorted. "You! They were either lying or blind."

He sounded aggrieved, and Clem warmed to him still further. If this was all a strategy on his part, she would never forgive him.

"We are nearly back to Bagshaw, Clem. Please note that I have not overturned you! Will you come out with me tomorrow?"

"I will, Chris."

He had been keeping his eyes fixed religiously on the horses, but at that, he turned to beam another smile at her. As he did, a dog rushed out of a small stand of shrubs and ran across almost under the horses' hooves. Naturally, they startled.

In a blink, Chris had his attention back on them again, his hands firm on the reins, his voice, assuring the beasts in a calm soothing tone.

In a moment, he had them back under control. They shook their heads and snorted but trotted the last twenty yards to where Mr. Bagshaw waited as if nothing had happened.

"Well done, Satterthwaite," he called. "Miss Wright, I told you, you would be safe."

Would Chris keep Clem safe? She was increasingly convinced she could rely on him physically, but could she trust him with her heart?

Chapter Six

BILLY APPROVED OF Chris's driving lessons, and told him to take whatever time he needed. "You can ride well enough," he commented. "But you'd better practice, Christopher. Get Barney Griggs to take you up to Wimbledon Common, and put you through your paces on Thunder."

That was a facer. Thunder was Billy's own thoroughbred. Chris hated to think what he was going to have to pay when the bill came due. "That's very kind of you, Billy," he said, wondering if Billy might respond to the hint. No point in asking straight out. Billy would only be offended, or at least would feign being offended. It was hard to tell with Billy.

"You're going to have to start going to ton events," Billy said next. "If you are serious about the girl, that is. Her father wants her to be in fashion, and that will have to be up to you, for the old dragon he has sponsoring her is not up to the job."

"I am not invited to ton events," Chris pointed out.

"You will need to change that."

How do you suppose I can perform that miracle?" Chris asked, not quite daring to let his mental scoff show in his tone."

"I am sure you'll think of something," Billy replied. "I have faith in you, Christopher. You'll need a better wardrobe, though. Actually, even to take Miss Wright riding or driving in Hyde

Park, you'll need to look more like one of them and less like a solicitor or a clerk. I suggest a visit to Pettinger's. Here is their card."

Billy handed over the piece of pasteboard. "If that will be all, Christopher, we both have work to do."

Which, since it had been Billy who summoned him, was either irritating or funny. Chris opted to chuckle and make himself scarce.

He worked until seven that evening, catching up on the bookkeeping he'd neglected earlier in the day. Then he strolled home to the rooms he rented in one of Billy's buildings. He hadn't intended to stroll past Pettinger's, and it wasn't on his direct route. But apparently his legs were taking instructions directly from Billy, because there it was on his left as he walked. The lights were still on, but someone was closing the shutters over the expensive bay window, where a single tailor's dummy displayed a gentleman's evening coat, with a top hat tipped at an angle over the neck.

"Good evening," Chris said, and the man replied in kind.

"You do not happen to be Pettinger, do you?" Chris asked. Surely not. The man was no more than Chris's age—mid-twenties. And Billy had been using the tailor for his own elegant clothing for at least the last decade.

"Not *the* Pettinger," the other man acknowledged. "I'm Stephen Pettinger, one of his sons. Were you looking for my father? He has finished work for the day. In fact, he has gone out to dinner with a local widow, and my brothers and I have high hopes!" He waggled his eyebrows and grinned.

Chris grinned back to acknowledge the man's revelation before saying, "I just happened to be passing. I did want to make an appointment, though. My employer tells me I need a whole new wardrobe. I am going courting, you see, and the lady is used to gentlemen of fashion."

"You're Mr. Satterthwaite," said Mr. Stephen Pettinger. "Mr. O'Hara told my father you would be visiting. Look, if you'd like to come inside, Mandy—she's my brother David's wife—has made far more stew than we can eat. You can join me and my other brother, Thomas, for dinner. We can have a chat while we eat."

Chris finally left the Pettinger household at ten that evening, having been measured and even fitted—the Pettingers kept a number of half-made items in various sizes that could be fitted to a customer and supplied in a day or two.

He had ordered buff pantaloons for daytime wear, others with a different cut for riding, and several pairs of breeches for evening wear. He had coats to go with all three, all in black. "Black is fashionable," Mr. Thomas Pettinger had conceded, when Chris had expressed a preference for that color. "But we would not wish people to assume you are in mourning, Mr. Satterthwaite," and in the end, they persuaded him to order coats in dark shades of navy, gray, a bright, bottle green, and even a very dark red.

Hats, too. The Pettingers did not themselves make hats, but they displayed those made by another merchant, and measured for them. He chose a black silk flat-topped hat in the collegian style for evening, and a tilbury in cream beaver for day time. His own bicorne was pronounced tolerable for more casual occasions.

He had also tentatively chosen fabrics for an array of waist-coats, which would be, he had been told, his point of difference. "You will express your character and personality in your waistcoats, Mr. Satterthwaite," Mr. Stephen Pettinger instructed. "Fabrics, cut, number of buttons, stitching. Those, and the way you tie your cravat. The leisured classes make a study of such things, and if you wish to appear as one of them, you must, at the very least, hire people who know how to choose for you."

"You will need to see them in daylight," said Mr. David Pettinger. "Return tomorrow morning so we can fill the order as quickly as possible."

"You will also need cravats, stockings and shirts," Mr. Thomas advised. "Those you have are all very well for a tradesman...

but you have expectations, Mr. O'Hara says."

That set Chris back on his heels. He had been swept away by the enthusiasm of the brothers Pettinger, but what was all this going to cost? He asked, finally.

"Oh, that is not a problem. Mr. O'Hara said to send the bill to him," Mr. Stephen said.

Not likely. "I would prefer not to be beholden to Mr. O'Hara to that extent," Chris said. "How much?"

"Will a round figure do, or do you want a detailed accounting?" asked Mr. David, beginning to scribble amounts on a notepad.

"A round figure. A detailed accounting can wait for the final invoice," Chris told him.

Mr. David bent over the pad and his pencil flew, while Mr. Thomas wrote the names of recommended purveyors of cravats, stockings, and shirts.

"And shoes," Mr. Stephen added. "Your boots are acceptable, Mr. Satterthwaite, or will be with a better polishing agent. But you will need dancing shoes and walking shoes." He frowned. "You have riding boots, of course?"

More money. "No, Mr. Pettinger, I do not have boots specifically for riding. Do I need them?"

The three brothers exchanged glances, and Mr. Stephen acted as their spokesperson. "If your family was in good standing with Society and you were known to be wealthy, Mr. Satterthwaite, any deficiencies in your personal presentation would be regarded as eccentricities, and would be tolerated. But it is my understanding that neither of those fortunate conditions apply?"

Sadly true. His family—his immediate family—had no standing at all in Society, and he was far from wealthy. "You are correct," he admitted.

"That being the case, you need to give the impression by your clothing, your demeanor, and your speech that you are well-born and have independent means. That is, if it is important for you to be accepted in ton circles?"

It was, of course. It became more important every time he met with Clementine Wright. Only because it mattered to her father, but that was everything, for he had little doubt that Clem would marry the man her father chose for her. More and more, Chris wanted that man to be him.

That was why, when Mr. David told him the lump sum, which would halve his bank deposits, he gulped and agreed. Better to deplete his bank account than to owe Billy yet another favor.

At least the Pettingers were far cheaper than their Bond Street counterparts. Chris thanked them all for his dinner and their professional services, and went home to bed.

The following morning, when he went to confirm his waistcoat fabric selection, they had ready for him everything he needed to turn him out as a gentleman of fashion for his afternoon drive. Even a waistcoat in stripes of cream, green, and maroon.

"This," said Mr. David, "is the mercer we usually work with. He has a selection of cravats and stockings for you, Mr. Satterthwaite, and can also supply shirts of a finer quality than those you currently wear."

Chris was almost afraid to ask how much this would add to his bill, but the sum was reasonable. "We do not pay Bond Street rentals, Mr. Satterthwaite," Mr. Pettinger senior explained, "nor do we have to charge our solvent customers to cover the expense of those who think we should be delighted to dress them for free. Our clients are businesspeople like ourselves, and know the value of the work that we do. We have very few unpaid bills."

On the strength of that, Chris ordered a dozen shirts and—at Mr. David's insistence—twenty cravats.

Encouraged by the mercer, the three Pettinger brothers and Mr. Pettinger senior, Chris dressed for his driving lesson and his afternoon engagement in all his new finery. Mr. Thomas was good enough to arrange his cravat, while explaining each step as he folded it, put it on, tied it, and arranged it. How fashionable gentlemen ever had time to get anything done was beyond him.

The Pettingers clucked over his inability to produce a cravat pin, and Mr. David insisted on providing one—a little gold bird with chips of garnet for eyes. "Not an expensive item, Mr. Satterthwaite, but charming. And the garnet reflects the subtle red stripes in the waistcoat."

"Very nice, Mr. Satterthwaite," said Mr. Pettinger senior.

The reflection in the Pettingers' mirror agreed with him. It showed a Christopher Satterthwaite who was recognizable but not the same. More assured. More elegant. More aristocratic.

"Thank you, gentlemen," Chris said. "I am amazed."

"We are not amazed, Mr. Satterthwaite," said Mr. Stephen. "You were already a gentleman. We merely provided the clothing that made it obvious."

Chris was not so certain. The son and grandson of villains raised in a gambling den? A gentleman? If he was accepted as one because of his clothing, did that make it true?

Perhaps it didn't matter. After all, while working for Billy, he'd met any number of men who were highly regarded in Society but whose behavior out of the public eye was hardly gentlemanly.

Another—more important—thought occurred as he donned his new hat and made his way out into the street, because for what other reason was he amassing this new wardrobe and expenses: What would Clem think of his new look?

⤚⟫⟪⟞

CLEM WAS LOOKING out the parlor window and saw Chris arrive. And Mr. Bagshaw, of course, but it was Chris who was driving and Chris who, as always, caught her eye. He drew the horses up in front of the house and sat a moment longer, saying something to Mr. Bagshaw as he handed over the reins.

There was something different about Chris today. He looked

more put-together, somehow. Wealthier. More aristocratic. Perhaps it was the hat. He had been wearing a softer lower hat each time she'd seen him before, but today he wore the same kind of hat as Mr. Bagshaw—one of those brimmed hats with high straight sides and a flat top.

He was standing in the front hall holding it in his gloved hands when she emerged from the parlor. "Good afternoon, Mr. Satterthwaite."

Formal names in front of the servants, and in a way, that pleased her. Calling him "Chris"—having him call her "Clem"—felt like a delicious secret that only the two of them shared.

He appeared to be amused by it, for his eyes danced as he said, "Good afternoon, Miss Wright."

Mr. Bagshaw repeated the greeting when Chris escorted her outside. "Good afternoon, Miss Wright. I enjoyed our dance yesterday evening."

"Good day, Mr. Bagshaw. I enjoyed it, too." Even if she did wish that her partner had been Chris.

Chris was glowering at his friend. "You didn't tell me that you danced with Miss Wright."

Mr. Bagshaw grinned. "No need to be jealous, Satterthwaite. I was there. She was there. We danced."

Was Chris jealous? Clem should not be so pleased about the possibility, but she could not deny the thrill it gave her to see him put out on this matter.

"If you attend a ball I am attending, I will dance with you, too," she informed him.

"There you go, Satterthwaite," Mr. Bagshaw said cheerfully. "What affairs do you attend tonight, Miss Wright? If I have an invitation to it, I'll undertake to get Satterthwaite along."

"I've nothing this evening, Mr. Bagshaw, but I shall be at the Hartford ball tomorrow evening." She slid her eyes sideways to see how Chris was responding to Mr. Bagshaw's machinations.

"I hardly think Lady Hartford would care for an uninvited guest," Chris protested.

Mr. Bagshaw laughed. "Then you are wrong," he said. "The hostesses are always pleased to have extra men, particularly those willing to dance with the wallflowers. And it is not as if *Mrs.* Hartford can expect a crush. She is not one of the premier hostesses who only invite the cream of the cream. And from what you said about your tailors, you can be dressed to the part by tomorrow night."

More evidence that Chris was right about Mrs. Bellowes, and her inability to procure the invitations that would put Clem in the same room as the kind of gentleman her father wanted her to meet.

Her grimace was misinterpreted. Mr. Bagshaw flushed and said, "I beg your pardon, Miss Wright. I'm sure it must be the thing if you have been invited. If you help Miss Wright up, Satterthwaite, you can take the driver's seat, and I shall ride in escort."

For the first time, Clem noticed the horse tied on behind the phaeton. Goodness. Chris was so distracting that she'd not noticed it.

Today, he drove them to Hyde Park, maneuvering the team through the traffic competently, if not expertly. Mr. Bagshaw rode alongside the phaeton, keeping his eye on the team, but nothing happened that required his intervention.

"It is too early for the fashionable hour," he said, as they approached the gates to the park. "Which is all to the good, because it will not be as crowded. Now easy through the gates, Satterthwaite, and then I shall leave you to it. Do the circuit, my friends, and I shall meet you back here in an hour."

"New clothes?" Clem asked as Mr. Bagshaw rode away. "I *thought* the hat was new."

"Everything," Chris replied, somewhat mournfully. "From the skin out, if I can be so indelicate. Billy said I had to look the part. At least the tailor to whom he sent me hasn't charged me more than I can afford. I do not want to be any more beholden to Billy than I already am."

He shrugged. "I live simply and I don't gamble. I have savings. Dressing to impress your father and the ton is not going to beggar me. The thing is—I told you I had a dream, Clem. May I tell you?"

"Of course." Clem had been wondering what it could be since yesterday afternoon. Not a gambling den or anything on the wrong side of legal. He wanted to get away from Mr. O'Hara, but that didn't mean it would be either wise or safe to set up in opposition to him.

"I want to open an orphan asylum," Chris confessed. "No, not that exactly. More of a school, but one at which boys like me—poor boys with no relatives—have a chance to be educated so they can make something of themselves. I teach a few classes for the errand boys who work for Billy, so I know I could do the teaching. But I have no idea about the rest of it. Which is why it is a dream, you know, and not a plan. For example, it would be very expensive. Most orphanages make the orphans work to raise funds, but I do not want them to be cheap labor. I want them learning things that are useful for a decent life once they are adults."

Clem thought about that. She understood where his impulse had come from. Becoming an orphan had landed him in the streets, after all. "You could have a few rich orphans, and even rich, neglected children who are not orphans. People who could afford your fees."

"That," said Chris, "is a very good idea. Would you..." Chris's forehead creased into a frown, and then he started again. "Would you want to help with something like that? Would you mind some of your money being spent on something like that? Setting it up, I mean. I see your point about having some paying pupils."

"You could also save on servants by having the boys do some of the housework," Clem suggested. "I spent a year at a school that was supposed to give me good contacts with the ton, though none of the girls there were actually from the ton. We had to do three hours of chores a week, which meant we learned to work together, to manage our time, to follow instructions—and how to boil a kettle and scrub a floor. I am not," she pointed out, "suggesting you use them as 'cheap labor', but as a way to learn what it's like to do domestic work. It would be advantageous for some, as they'd learn the right way to do what they'll need to do as adults, and for others—those who might never need to do domestic chores to making a living—it would create an understanding and an appreciation for those who do the hard work to make their living easier. In theory, at least."

She chuckled. "Some of the girls at school had large allowances and paid others to do their chores, and that worked well for me, for Father never gave me an allowance. He won't like your plan, Chris."

"I am aware that I'll have to change it a bit," Chris acknowledged. He was silent for a moment. The carriage drive they were on intersected with another, and he gave all his concentration to the horses while he turned them to the left.

That accomplished without incident, he picked up the conversation. "I can work for your father and manage the orphanage, or at least provide useful oversight. And perhaps teach for an hour or two several times a week. After all, your father currently manages his mines from here in London, where he is out every night and most afternoons."

"Yes, and sleeping in during the mornings," Clem agreed. "But he still will not approve of you having an enterprise he has no hand in, and especially one with a charitable purpose. Father does not believe in charity. He says that he raised himself from the pits, and if others do not do likewise, it is their fault and none of his affair."

Chris drew the horses to a halt and turned in his seat to regard her with a steady gaze from his blue-gray eyes. "I do not intend your father to rule our lives, Clem. I will give him his due, but I won't give him my soul, or allow him to take more from us than you and I agree."

"Do not underestimate my father, Chris. He did 'raise himself from the pits', as he puts it. He didn't care then who he had to betray or step on to gain an advantage, and he cares even less now."

"I know, my dear," Chris said. "But I ask you not to underestimate us. You and I together, with your knowledge of your father and mine of villains in general, and with our courage, our intelligence, and—"

He paused and then finished the sentence. "Our love, Clem. I believe in us. We will be fighting for our future, remember. He will only be fighting for spite and his need to bully and control." He collected the reins into one hand and used the other to pick up hers and lift it to his lips for a kiss. "I believe in us."

And in that minute, there in Hyde Park, with the sun shining on them and Chris turning his attention back to the horses and giving them the direction to continue, Clem believed, too. *Our love, he said. Does he love me, then?* That raised another question, one she had not thought to expect. *Do I love him?*

✦ ✦ ✦

Chapter Seven

Mrs. Bellowes was not impressed by the alterations Martha had made to Clem's gowns. She normally met Clem at the evening's ball or musicale or whatever else was on, but on the evening of the Hartford Ball, she turned up at the Wright townhouse, inspected Clem's gown and hairstyle, and demanded that Clem change immediately.

"Thank you for your advice," said Clem. "I shall continue as I am, however. I believe fewer flounces and a looser hair style are more flattering to my person."

The snort from Mrs. Bellowes spoke volumes. "That is a lost cause, girl, given how plump you are, and how plain."

Clem stood firm, and Mrs. Bellowes demanded to speak with Father, who was, for once, at home.

"You hired me to puff your daughter off, Mr. Wright," the harridan scolded. "How am I to do it when she defies me like this? Just look at her!"

Clem faced her father's glower with a firm exterior, doing her best to follow Chris's example. *Firm but polite, and ruthlessly honest.* That was the ticket. "The flounces and frills do not suit me, Father. I look like a cream puff. Furthermore, the over-fussy decoration Mrs. Bellowes ordered for me is not in fashion, so next to the other ladies, I look ridiculous in those gowns."

Martha had also performed other miracles. For example, she had removed some of the width from this gown, as well as adding a matching ribbon that had the effect of lowering the high waist. Clem continued, "The changes Martha has made on my gowns are an improvement, though I have been unable to do anything about the insipid colors."

Father was examining her, his face impassive. When Mrs. Bellowes started to speak, he held up a hand to silence her. After a long minute, he said, "Ye don't look so plump in that. Shapely, but that's to the good. Men like shapely, whatever the fashion. As for the hair—it stays. You'll do, Clementine."

As near a compliment as she'd ever had from her father. "Thank you, sir." She curtseyed.

"That is not acceptable, Mr. Wright," Mrs. Bellowes snapped. "You pay me to teach Miss Wright how to compete with her betters, and—"

Clem interrupted. "I am Clementine Wright, daughter of Bertram Wright, who pulled himself up by his bootstraps from pit boy to one of the richest men in England. He need acknowledge no man as his better just because they can trace their ancestors back to some thug who bullied the poor and pandered to the king. I am grateful, Mrs. Bellowes, for your sponsorship. But I draw the line at any insult to my father."

It was a master stroke. Father puffed out his chest and Mrs. Bellowes deflated. How Chris would smile when she told him.

"Your transport is ready, Miss Wright." Charles the footman entered the room.

Clem swept her father another curtsey, and led the way out to the carriage. Perhaps, at that, she could talk Father into paying for a few more gowns.

It wasn't over, of course. Mrs. Bellowes grumbled for the fifteen minutes it took to reach the Hartfords' townhouse. True to Mr. Bagshaw's prediction, it was on the extreme edge of the fashionable area, which gave Clem the confidence to put an end to Mrs. Bellowes' scolding and complaints.

"If you are unhappy as my chaperone and sponsor, Mrs. Bellowes, we can put an end to the arrangement. I can tell my father that you are neither as knowledgeable nor as well connected as you claimed, and we shall part ways." She smiled.

She had noted that Chris used his smile like a lethal weapon, charming people into going along with him before they noticed they had been cozened. "Thank you for your efforts on my behalf," she added.

Chris had also demonstrated that politeness disarmed, and it worked on this occasion, for Mrs. Bellowes subsided with a muttered, "There'll be no need for that," and was silent for the rest of the journey.

Chris was already at the Hartfords', waiting by the ballroom door so she could see him over other guests as the receiving line made its way to the waiting host and hostess. Just the sight of him made Clem happier and more confident, and his smile drew forth an answering one from her just as she and Mrs. Bellowes were greeted by Mrs. Hartford, who took the smile as being for her, and smiled back. "Miss Wright, is it not? How lovely of you to join us, Miss Wright. Girls, this is Miss Wright. Miss Wright, my daughters, Prudence and Charity. Mr. Hartford, Miss Wright."

The gentleman of the house peered at her over the top of his glasses. "Nice to see you, Miss *Er...*"

"Good evening, Mr. Hartford," said Clem, with a curtsey.

His eyes were distant, but his smile was kind. "I hope you have a lovely evening, my dear. Mrs. Hartford, we shall have to make certain that Miss... *Er...* has plenty of partners."

"Thank you, sir," Clem said, before she and Mrs. Bellowes had to move on to make way for the next guests to take their place with the Hartfords.

"You look lovely this evening, Miss Wright," said Mr. Bagshaw, who was with Chris.

Which was as may be, but Clem did not have the breath to answer him. A nod and a smile was all she could manage now she had an uninterrupted view of Chris Satterthwaite in all his new evening splendor. He was breathtaking. It was the only word. From his dancing pumps to the top of his head, there wasn't a detail that didn't shout 'quality'. And fit, lean, handsome, gorgeous quality at that.

"Which of these is your young man?" Mrs. Bellowes demanded.

Clem ignored the rude question, but realized she had been remiss. "Mrs. Bellowes, may I make known to you Mr. Satterthwaite and Mr. Bagshaw." She indicated each gentleman in turn. "Gentlemen, Mrs. Bellowes has been kind enough to sponsor me this season."

Father had clearly given Mrs. Bellowes Chris's name, for she examined him closely. "You *look* like a gentleman," she commented, "but it is not only fine feathers that make fine birds."

"How kind you are," said Chris, as if she had paid him an extravagant compliment.

Mrs. Bellowes was not armored against Chris's brand of ruthless courtesy, so she huffed out a breath and then spoke to Clem. "You shall be fine with your friends, Miss Wright. I see someone I wish to speak with. I shall find you later." She marched away.

Chris and Mr. Bagshaw watched her go. "Not the thing, to go off like that," Mr. Bagshaw announced. "She has only just met us."

"Does she usually abandon you like this?" Chris asked.

"Usually not this early, but she seldom stays near me for more than half an hour. She doesn't have a friend, by the way. Or, at least, she doesn't usually. Unless the bottle of gin in her reticule counts as a friend. By the time I am ready to leave, she is usually very much on the go."

Chris and Mr. Bagshaw exchanged glances.

"We'll not desert you," Chris said.

"I should think not," agreed Mr. Bagshaw.

"Thank you," Clem said, "but I do not mind. She only complains and criticizes. This way, I can watch the dancing and imagine what it must be like."

"Yes, but you should not be left on your own," Mr. Bagshaw insisted. "Especially not looking like that."

So much for their flattery! "It has been the same all Season," she protested. "Nothing has happened to me."

"It will now," said Mr. Bagshaw, casting a dark look around the ball room.

Chris bent forward to bring his face closer, so she could hear his quiet voice over the buzz of conversation. "What Bagshaw is carefully not saying, Clem, is that you were safe as long as you looked like a plump, frilly frump. But now that your clothing fits you and suits you better, things will change."

He smiled then, a genuine smile. "You always look lovely to me, Clem. But the gown is charming, and I really like what Martha has done with your hair. Bagshaw says I may have no more than two dances unless we are betrothed. Shall I propose right now and ask for three?"

Clem shook her head. "You may have two, Chris, the first dance and the supper dance." She was very tempted to simply say 'yes', though. She was beginning to believe that marriage to Chris was a very good idea. She was stopped only by the thought of her father's probable reaction if they made such a public display before he had given his formal approval to the marriage.

"I should also like to request two dances," said Mr. Bagshaw.

In the end, Clem danced eleven dances—two each with Chris and Bagshaw, three with men introduced to her by Mrs. Hartford, and four with men who asked for an introduction from one of the other men.

Perhaps her friends were correct and she looked almost pretty, or perhaps all it took to attract partners was for her to dance with other nice-looking and perfectly presentable men. Either way, it was astounding.

Mrs. Bellowes returned not long before the final set. "We can go now," she said, without preamble. "The ball is nearly over. If someone was going to ask you to dance, they would have done so by now."

"I have a partner for the last set," Clem told her. "In fact, Mrs. Bellowes, I have had nine partners this evening."

The look on her sponsor's face could only be described as flabbergasted.

She turned away from the pleasing sight to address Chris. "I suppose, Mr. Satterthwaite, that Mrs. Bellowes and I will need to be 'at home' tomorrow afternoon. Could our drive be a little earlier or a little later?"

"Later," Chris proposed. "If you are willing, we can do the fashionable hour at Hyde Park."

Clem felt a delicious shudder—not of fear or excitement at the idea of Chris's driving, but entirely because she was thrilled by his constant and public attention. She was grateful now that none of her previous suitors had pleased Father, for she would not have missed getting to know this man for the world.

➤➤➤◄◄◄

On the following day, Mr. Wright emerged from his study when Chris arrived to take Clem driving.

"Ye've done it, young Satterthwaite," he crowed. "Six men—six lords' sons, or close. And all in my drawing room, flattering my Clementine. The house looks like a flower shop, too. Demmit if it don't."

"I'm glad you are pleased, sir," Chris said. He wasn't. Well, he was for Clem's sake, because she deserved to know what she was worth. But he had sat for the requisite thirty minutes in her drawing room earlier in the day with the group of men, and had determined that at least three of the six were looking for a rich wife. And they were, as Wright said, lords' sons, or close. One of them might suit the selfish old man better than a lord's estranged great grandchild, like Chris.

Wright echoed his thoughts, saying, "Maybe I could do better than you, Satterthwaite. I reckon I could, now my Clementine has come into her own."

"I don't doubt it," Chris admitted. "She charmed them, Wright, the way she has charmed me."

Wright grinned. "You've put in some effort to charm her, too, haven't you, lad? Not just lessons, was it? Dancing with her and the like?"

"It was what you asked of me, sir," Chris replied. He wasn't about to confess to Wright that he was head over heels in love with the man's daughter. He didn't know what Wright would do with such leverage, but it would be something.

"It was. It was. And you've succeeded, lad. I'll keep my word, don't you worry. It's good business. Besides, they all have nosy, pushy families."

Whereas Chris had Billy. Loath though he was to become further indebted to Ramping Billy O'Hara, Chris would call on him if he had to, and he'd back Billy over Wright on any day.

"Next, I need to see what you know about the coal mining business," Wright said. "Not tomorrow, but the next day, present yourself at my office at nine in the morning. Here. Follow me and I'll give you my address."

He ducked back into his study, and bent over his desk for a minute, scribbling on a square of paper, which he blotted and handed to Chris. "Now run along, Satterthwaite. Take my daughter to be seen by the smart folks in Hyde Park. I'll see you at nine the morning after tomorrow."

Chris left him in his study, rubbing his hands and muttering, "My Clementine with six lords' sons!"

Chapter Eight

"BILLY," CHRIS SAID, when he had reported on Wright's response to Clem's sudden popularity, "I do not know anything about the coal mining business, and I have slightly more than a day to find out."

"I'll see what I can do," said Billy. "Christopher, for the next little while, you are going to be spending most of your time wooing either Miss Wright or her father. I have found someone else for your position as my bookkeeper. You can continue in your current accommodation until the Wright situation is resolved."

Chris felt as if he'd suddenly run into a wall when expecting a door. Yes, it was true he had been wondering how he was going carry out his responsibilities to Billy. It was, after all, a full-time job.

And so was winning Clem as his wife. He had not only to acquire the gentlemanly skills that had not yet come his way, but also learn how to be a coal mining industrialist. Plus, he needed to spend time with Clem and satisfy her father that he was worth teaching.

Failing was not an option. Somewhere between taking her hand as they ran from the Brown's gang and delivering her back to her father, he had tumbled head over heels in love, and each day only deepened his feelings.

But if he did not have his paycheck from O'Hara's bookkeeping, how was he to live? His savings were rapidly disappearing.

"What if it is not resolved in my favor?" he asked. "I am almost certain that Clem feels as I do, but I cannot know which way Wright will decide." *And I shall need money to run away with her if he decides against me*, he thought, but did not say.

"Wright needs someone he can control," Billy said. "He knows that most of the other men who might offer for Miss Wright have influential families who care about them, and who will help them keep Wright at bay if he becomes troublesome."

Billy looked into the middle distance, as if at some memory that pleased him. "He thinks you are alone, Christopher, and that is of benefit to him. He has been trying to work out how I feel about you, since he has more sense than to knowingly set himself in opposition to me. I, too, am a self-made man."

He allowed what Chris considered to be his most shark-like grin to spread across his face. "I have made it known that you are nothing to me, and that I am displeased with your failure to put your duty to me first, and am thinking of dismissing you."

Chris saw the point of the strategy, but had to know. "Are you displeased, sir?"

"Of course not, Christopher. I have reasons of my own for promoting this match. Have no fear. If everything fails, I will find you some sort of a job. But it will not fail. Just continue charming Miss Wright and her father, and we shall see you married within a few weeks."

"What are those reasons, Billy? What is the benefit to you?"

But Billy merely smiled, and told him to be about his business. "You'll need to be up early in the morning to prepare to hand over the accounts to someone else, and then to meet with whomever I find to give you a quick lesson on coal mining. And I dare say you are romancing Miss Wright this evening. A visit to the opera, is it?"

Bagshaw had managed to produce an invitation to view the

opera from a box owned by a duke whose son Bagshaw had known at school. Clem had declared herself thrilled. "I have never been to the theater," she had told Chris, "and I have always wondered what it is like."

Bagshaw and Mrs. Bellowes would be there, of course, as would Lord Thornstead, the duke's son, and his lady wife, so it was not as if Chris would have Clem to himself. On the other hand, he was not going to have to settle for two dances and spending the rest of the evening watching Clem dance with other men. So it would be an entire evening sitting next to Clem. Chris was looking forward to it.

⟫⟫⟫✕⟪⟪⟪

CLEM WAS ENJOYING her first visit to the opera, though she thought she might enjoy it even more if not for the audience. Aristocrats were rude, she decided. Not to one another, of course, but to everyone else, and especially to the players, who were largely ignored in favor of conversation, visiting between boxes, and preening in front of their peers.

She shut them out as best she could, and concentrated on the performance with such success that, when the curtain came down, she emerged as if in a daze.

"How are you enjoying yourself?" Chris asked.

"Wonderfully. But I thought he would win the fair Arianna," she said. The poor heroine had been carried off by her father, to be married to a very villainous character. Clem could not help but sympathize with her whole heart.

"He will," Lord Thornstead told her, kindly. "But there are two more acts, my dear. This is the intermission, to allow the players to change and the audience to refresh themselves."

Clem could not help herself. She gave a wriggle of delight. "Oh, I am so pleased. Have you seen the performance before, my lord?"

"Not with this group of singers, Miss Wright, but yes. I have seen it several times. It is something of a favorite with my dear wife."

Lady Thornstead joined in the conversation. "I think this Arianna is very good," she declared. "And Count Balsario! Did it not make your skin crawl when he laughed over his wicked plan to make her his own?"

"Oh, it did!" Clem agreed, and enjoyed a delightful discussion about the entire first act, while the gentlemen vacated the box to fetch drinks for the ladies. Mrs. Bellowes made a comment about seeking out the lady's retiring chamber, and also went, leaving Clem and Lady Thornstead to their conversation.

None of others had returned when the box received a visitor, a lady who was edging elegantly into old age, still upright and vigorous, and richly dressed in the latest fashion.

"Lady Thornstead?" she said. "May I come in?"

"Lady Fernvale. Yes, please do. Here, come and sit next to me. Have you met Miss Wright? No? Let me make her known to you. Miss Wright, this is Lady Fernvale."

Lady Fernvale smiled somewhat absently at Clem, and commented, "Are you making your debut, my dear? I must be becoming more absent-minded than I thought, for I do not believe I have seen you."

"Indeed I am, my lady," Clem replied. Chris was correct again. The Season was as ruled by hierarchy as everything else the ton did, and Clem had only had access to the lower levels of events.

"She and her escort are friends of John Bagshaw, Lady Fernvale," said her hostess. "And very amiable people, I have found them. Miss Wright quite agrees with me that tonight's Count Balsario is the scariest either of us has ever seen."

Clem did not point out that her life total of Counts Balsario was the one present tonight. It would be rude, and was beside the point, besides.

"He is deliciously evil, is he not?" Lady Fernvale agreed.

"Your escort, Miss Wright. What is his name, my dear?"

There was something curiously intent about her as she asked the question, and for a moment Clem toyed with refusing to answer. But of course, their host and hostess knew the name, and Lady Fernvale would find it out soon enough. "Christopher Satterthwaite, my lady," she replied.

"I knew it!" Lady Fernvale leaned forward in her chair. "The son of Reginald and Christabel Satterthwaite." It was a statement, but the lady's raised eyebrow made it a question.

"I do not know his mother's name, my lady, but his father's name was Reginald."

"My mother's name was Christabel," said Chris, who had entered the box unobserved, just ahead of Bagshaw and Lord Thornstead.

"Christopher Satterthwaite," said Lady Fernvale, standing up so she could study Chris as intently as she had been looking at Clem. "My dear Christopher, and I may call you that, my dear, for I knew you when you were a babe in clouts. I do not suppose you recognize me?"

She sounded so hopeful that Clem hoped Chris could answer in the affirmative. He didn't, quite, but he took another look at the lady and looked thoughtful. "I think... I am sorry, my lady. You seem familiar, but I cannot imagine where I might have met you. Did you know my parents?"

The lady looked around at the rest of the company, smiling even as tears welled in her eyes. "You must think I have lost my mind. Please forgive me. Mr. Satterthwaite is the son of a very dear friend—my closest friend of my girlhood. Chrissie Thurgood died far too young, and I have not seen Mr. Satterthwaite since her death, even though I am his godmother. Indeed, until this evening, I believed you to be dead, Christopher. Or, I should say, at first, I thought you had gone overseas with your grandfather after your father died. But you did not, did you? For he returned six months ago, and you were not with him."

Her emotions overflowed, and she took both of Chris's

hands, clung to them, and looked up at Chris though her tears. "But here you are, alive, my dear, and looking magnificent. Did you go with your grandfather after all? Wherever it was he went?"

Chris was shaking his head. He looked dazed, as if he had received a blow to the head.

He needed a rescue, so Clem gave him one. "Lady Fernvale, may Mr. Satterthwaite call on you tomorrow? This has been a shock to him, as it has been to you, I am certain."

"Yes," said Lady Fernvale eagerly. "Will you call on me, Christopher?"

Chris felt inside his coat and pulled out a stub of pencil and a small notebook. "Tomorrow afternoon, my lady? Shortly after two?"

"That will be wonderful," said Lady Fernvale. "Oh, Christopher. I do not know whether I am on my head or my heels. I am so happy! Excuse me, Lady Thornstead, for intruding. Good evening, Miss Wright, Lord Thornstead, Mr. Bagshaw. Tomorrow, Christopher. I shall be looking forward to it!"

The bell rang to indicate that the second act was about to start, and they all took their seats again. Clem could not sink back into the story again, though, as she had before, for she could not help wondering whether, if Chris found his way back into his rightful world, he would still want to take on the bother of Clem's domineering father for the sake of marrying Clem and her dowry.

❯❯❯❯❮❮❮❮

GRANDFATHER WAS BACK. Chris had hoped that Lady Fernvale— 'Aunt Fern', as he had apparently called her when he was a child—was mistaken, but Grandfather had actually called on Lady Fernvale, hoping she would be able to give him news of Chris.

"He thought his brother might not have wished to have kept

you, dear Christopher, but that he would have sent you to the Thurgoods, your mother's people. Of course, Mr. Satterthwaite—Mr. Percival Satterthwaite—knew he could not call on them. Not after how he and his son—your father—deceived them so as to trick Christabel into marrying Reginald."

Chris remembered his father speaking of romancing his mother off her feet, but not deceiving her. That didn't sound good. It fit his father's *modus operandi*, though, and his grandfather's. Clem, who had agreed to come with him, squeezed his hand. He looked down surprised to see their fingers twined. He had not even been aware they were holding hands. Even so, it bolstered him and gave him courage he didn't know he needed. "Instead, my great uncle put me out into the street," he said.

"Oh, dearest boy," said Aunt Fern, her eyes filling again with tears, though she had sworn three times in the past half hour that she 'was not a watering pot.' "Darling, your cousin's wife told me that your grandfather tried to leave you with them, but that they refused. They thought you should be your grandfather's responsibility since he was the person that you knew. A grieving boy, you know."

Chris, who had always done his best not to think about that day, had a sudden memory. "My grandfather and the man who looked like him argued, but in the end, grandfather took me to the other side of the square, where our carriage waited. Then he gave me my bag and told me to return, and to knock on the door. He said he would wait until I was safely inside. But he didn't, Aunt Fern. The person who opened the door told me to go away, and when I looked for Grandfather, he was gone."

His face was wet. It had been wet then, too, he remembered. *No. Not remembered.* What was happening to him now as he recalled that moment was stronger than that. He was that boy again, running frantically in the direction the carriage had been heading, calling out for his grandfather, longing for his mother, who had been in her grave for two years, or even his often absent but always cheerful father, whose funeral had been only the day before.

After he'd given up the chase, he'd thought of returning to his great uncle's, but the angry voices between the brothers, the cold rejection from the butler—he could not face it. He had wandered and cried, cried and wandered, until he fell in with a gang of street rats, who robbed him of his bag and all his possession, then—with careless kindness unfathomable then and even now—gave him some rags to wear and took him home with them.

Their voices echoed in his mind, their cant almost unintelligible to his ten-year-old ears. In English, it went like this.

"Here! What are you crying for?"

"Because my grandfather has left London without me."

"Go home to your ma, then."

"My mother is dead."

"That's tough, shrimp. Losing your ma. Go home to your pa, then."

"My father is dead."

"Bad luck. Unless he was a drunk. If he got drunk and beat you all the time, good luck." The hard cynicism of these miniature street toughs struck him even at that moment. However often his father had disappointed Chris, he had never beaten him.

But Chris didn't see any reason to feel sorry for them when they had his money and he had nothing. "Now I am all alone, and you have taken all my money and my clothes, so I shall either starve or freeze."

One of the boys, bigger, with a wisdom greater than his apparent years and yet somehow and inexplicably kinder than the rest, had considered him, shrugged, and turned to the others. "He'd better come home with us then, gang. Right?" he'd asked in a way that was more of a command, and the other boys had agreed.

And that was Chris's introduction to a life of crime.

"However did you survive, Christopher?" his aunt asked, recalling him to the present day. "Did some kind people take you in?" She and Clem both had tears in their eyes.

"Yes, they did, Aunt." Let her imagine a kindly shopkeeper and a life of honest labor. She didn't need to know the worst of it. Which, at that, could have been much worse.

Aunt Fern was able to tell Chris about his family, both the Satterthwaites and the Thurgoods, and he and Clem stayed much longer than was appropriate for an afternoon call.

When he tried to apologize as they were leaving, Aunt Fern hugged him and said, "Those rules do not apply to family, Christopher, and you are the son of the sister of my heart. I am so happy to have found you. I cannot wait to tell all your cousins."

That would never do. "Aunt Fern, I have a favor to ask you," Chris said. "I have a particular reason for not wanting to see the rest of my family yet. In fact, I'd rather not have them know I am here in London until I am able to work out a few things."

"Chris," said Clem. "Tell her why. We can trust her."

"You tell her," Chris said.

Aunt Fern was looking bewildered, and well she might.

"Lady Fernvale, Chris and I love one another and we want to marry," Clem said. "My father wants me to marry someone with aristocratic bloodlines, and he favors Chris because Chris, as far as my father knows, has no family, so Father thinks he will be able to control him by holding on to my dowry unless Chris and I do what he wants."

"We have a plan to manage him," Chris explained. "I will work for him as he wants, but in return, I want a small country estate—one where Clem and I can live and raise a family. That is our dream, mine and Clem's."

"But Christopher..." Aunt Fern's eyes were wide and troubled. Here it came. Chris had expected her to oppose her godson's marriage to a coal miner's daughter, but so far, she had been everything amiable to Chris's beloved.

What she said, though, was something very different. "You *have* a country estate, dear. Your Thurgood grandmother left it to you in her will." She frowned. "It is not particularly small, though." She frowned. "In truth, I am not certain we can keep your existence a secret. Or the fact that I have acknowledged you. After last night, I expect word will have gone around the ton after last night, dear. Bagshaw is a dear boy, but a rattle, and Lady Thornstead is worse."

She brightened. "Would it work, do you think, if we cast you off for marrying down, Christopher? Begging your pardon, Miss Wright. But I dare say it is what your father will expect us to think. We can keep the estate secret, of course. Nobody needs to know about that."

"By 'we', you mean my Satterthwaite and Thurgood relatives, as well as yourself, Aunt Fern," Chris said, slowly.

Clem tipped her head on one side, her mind clearly working behind lively eyes. "It will work if nobody finds out that you are so pleased to have Chris safe and alive, that you don't care who he marries."

Aunt Fern gifted her with a bright smile. "Oh, it is not quite as bad as that, dear. If you were poor, and your father still dug coal out of the ground with his own hands, it would never do." She chuckled. "But the rules about like marrying like have never been as solid as some people wish to think, and it seems to me you have been raised as a lady, Miss Wright, even if you were not born one."

"I would love Clem if she were as poor as a church mouse," Chris declared.

Aunt Fern patted him on the arm. "Of course, you would, dear. And very sweet, too. But how much nicer that she is rich. Now, my loves, I think we should sit down and make a plan, since I suppose we cannot safely meet again until after your wedding." She beamed. "You shall contrive to send me the date, time, and location, and I shall be there with a veil on. I do love weddings. Come back into the parlor, my loves, and I shall send for pen and paper."

Chapter Nine

CHRIS HAD ALWAYS had the ability to quickly comprehend new information and to remember it accurately. It was what made him so useful in Billy's enterprises, and it was what saved him now.

He had spent three hours with the coal mining expert Billy had found—an investor who believed he needed to understand the ins and outs of any industry to which he gave his money.

That information was helping Chris this morning, as Wright snapped questions at him, and the three men with Wright trotted out facts and figures, each from their own area of expertise.

Apparently, this meeting with key employees was a weekly event, and the chief way in which Wright kept up with his empire. Today, however, Chris was the entire focus of the meeting.

The clerk in charge of the books was easiest. He used the same double entry bookkeeping system that Chris had been taught. It had been invented in Venice at the dawn of their merchant empire, and had spread across the Western world because, in the hands of someone who understood it, it saved time and supported good decision-making.

The mining engineer was much harder to match, and Chris would have been lost in a welter of terms that might as well have been foreign for all the meaning they'd had for him before yesterday's tutoring session. Gins, baulks, rolley ways, Davy lamps, and so much more. Picking his way through the thicket of industry-specific words, Chris was able to make intelligent remarks and ask pertinent questions. Or, at least, he hoped they were intelligent and pertinent.

The third man was the manager—the man who made it possible for Wright to ignore his empire, confident that it was running smoothly in his absence. "Josh Flint watches all the people who work for me," Wright had said, during the introductions, "And I watch Josh Flint."

Flint spoke less often than the other two, but his questions were the hardest, for he was interested in Chris as a manager of people, and Chris had never managed servants or employees—for himself, or for other people.

Except that perhaps he had, for something Clem had said yesterday afternoon came to his rescue. They had been riding home after the visit to Aunt Fern, and he had been wondering whether his relatives would co-operate with a masqueraded estrangement.

"You will talk them round," she had said. "You have a gift for understanding what people need and talking them into believing you can give it to them."

He repeated some of that to Flint. "I am not in charge in my current position," he said. "I cannot give orders to those who are not under my authority, and no one is under my authority. But I can persuade, and I do. It is a matter of understanding what motivates a person—what will make them want to oblige me. Perhaps I show people how they will benefit from doing what I ask or giving me the information I need. Or perhaps they are motivated by praise, or by interest in what they are doing." He shrugged. "It works for me."

"Arrant nonsense," grumbled Wright. "I give orders and they are obeyed."

"Because you are the man with the power, sir," Chris pointed out. "They know it is in their interests to do as you tell them."

"That is true," the manager said. "They obey because otherwise they fear they will not have a job."

Wright nodded. "And quite right, too."

The manager nodded. "I have Mr. Wright's full authority in my daily activities, Mr. Satterthwaite, but I have often found it more effective to explain why a particular action should be taken. Cheerful co-operation can be more pleasant and more productive than grudging compliance."

Wright made a grunting sound, but whether it indicated agreement, disagreement, or merely distaste at the line of conversation, Chris could not have said.

What would Clem say?

Chris usually had no trouble focusing on the task at hand, but today his mind kept drifting to Clem, or if not her, his relatives. He had an estate! Or, at least, he *probably* had an estate. If the trustee refused to accept that he was who he said he was, how would he prove it?

Billy knew who he was, of course. Billy remembered him tagging along behind his father from time to time. But would they accept Billy's word? Would Billy even give it? And what would he want in return? Chris's debt to Billy was growing to alarming proportions, all the worse for being undefined.

Grandfather would be able to identify him, too, if the old scoundrel cared to do so. But Chris had no idea where his grandfather was, and in any case, Chris was even less inclined to owe a favor to his grandfather than to Billy. Even before he was abandoned, the child Chris had known Grandfather was not a man to rely on.

And once again, he was letting himself get distracted. Fortunately, the one part of his mind that was still attending to Wright could replay what had just happened. Wright had asked his three employees to rate Chris's chances of being useful in the business.

"The best yet, sir," the bookkeeper had said.

The manager had agreed. "Not that the others would have

done at all. Mr. Satterthwaite is at least not afraid of hard work."

"He has a lot to learn," the engineer was saying when Chris forced his attention back to the conversation, "but I am cautiously pleased, sir."

His pursed lips said Wright was not entirely pleased with their responses. "If I let him marry my Clementine, will he do?"

Do for what, precisely? Was Wright planning to retire?

The bookkeeper expressed it in blunt terms. "You mean, if—heaven forbid—something happens to you before your grandson is old enough to take over, will Mr. Satterthwaite keep your enterprises thriving?"

"Aye," Wright replied, though the twist to his mouth suggested that he was not pleased to contemplate his own demise.

"You appear hale and hearty, sir," Chris commented, wondering if the man had had some bad news from the doctor.

"I am as yet, but I'm a realist, Satterthwaite. As you need to be. I was thirty-five when Clementine was born. Perhaps I should have wed again after her mother died, and if I had, perhaps I'd have a boy growing up who could take over in a few years."

He looked into the middle distance, perhaps contemplating that desirable possibility. "Clementine's Ma was my second wife, you know. My first died and so did both her children. I didn't have the heart to try a third time."

Chris felt a surge of pity Wright, a quite unexpected sentiment towards a man who had, up until now, had provoked only irritation or even anger.

Wright waved a hand, as if to dismiss his unusual retrospection. "I didn't, and now I'm fifty-three. Hale and hearty, aye. That's true. But who's to say that I'll make another ten years?"

"Let us hope," Chris said. "Quite apart from the business, Miss Wright would be distressed to lose you." *Probably. In some ways.*

"*Humph,*" said Wright. "I was a coal miner, lad. For fifteen years, from the time I was a boy of eight, I went down the mines every day. Coal miners don't make old bones. Even if you and my girl marry tomorrow, and my grandson comes along in nine months, it'll be seventeen years until he can start learning the business and twenty-six years, I reckon, before he'd be able to run it without someone to check up on him, like. You, if you're the one to marry Clementine. My boy's father."

Sympathetic moment over, and straight back to irritation. The child, if child there was, would be Chris's boy. His and Clem's. "I see," Chris said. "It sounds like a sensible plan."

"It is the only plan," Wright said. "I built this business, Satterthwaite. Hour by hour, day by day, year by year. My determination. My sweat. My blood." He thumped his fist on the table. "My blood, Satterthwaite. My blood will carry on when I am gone. It is the only plan."

Perhaps he regretted his emotional outburst, for he stood up, then, and announced that Chris could go. "We have other business to discuss. Run along and take my daughter somewhere the ton can see her."

Irritation. Definitely irritation. The man was fundamentally unlikeable.

"So I HAVE no idea whether I passed his tests today or not," Chris reported to Clem. She and Chris were once again driving around Hyde Park, this time without Mr. Bagshaw.

Clem was hopeful. "He told you to take me out. Only two other men even made it as far as talking to his inner circle of employees. Quite what happened I do not know, but they did not call on me again, or approach me if we were at the same entertainment." It was a good sign that Father had sent Chris to her, but even so, Clem was not certain Chris would, in the end, be allowed to marry her. Father was, as he called it, "playing his cards close to his chest." He enjoyed keeping people uncertain.

She had news for Chris. "I have an invitation to Lady Fernvale's ball tomorrow evening, Chris, and one for you, too." It would be the most prestigious event she had ever attended. If Chris agreed that they should go.

"Should we attend?" he asked her. "Will people wonder why we have been invited?"

"I think we can assume at least some of them have figured it out," Clem told him. "After all, Lady Fernvale walked into the box where we were sitting, and in full view of the audience, held your hands and talked to you with great affection and animation. If I know anything about the way Society works, one of the older generation will remember that your mother and Lady Fernvale were close, and that your mother chose Lady Fernvale as your godmother."

"Perhaps we should stage that argument with Aunt Fern at her ball."

Clem shook her head. "I don't think word will have reached Father yet, and even when it does, he won't see Lady Fernvale as a threat. She is a woman and a widow. He will assume that she is powerless. It will be the Satterthwaite and Thurgood men that he will want to guard himself against."

"I will need to talk to the Thurgoods about this estate," Chris commented. "It makes your father's approval less important, Clem. If it has been cared for, and if it is big enough, we might have sufficient income even without your dowry."

It warmed Clem's heart that Chris wanted her even without the money that would come from her father, but she saw no reason why they shouldn't have both.

"It is wonderful that you will have something of your own, so you do not feel beholden to me. But if our roles were reversed, and I had nothing while you were rich, I wouldn't like it at all, Chris. If we can, we should keep Father happy. Just think how many orphans we will be able to educate with my money and your estate!"

"I wonder how far away from London the estate is, and how big it is," Chris mused. "I'll need to be in London at least some of the time, and up in Yorkshire, too, if I'm to learn your father's business and then run it."

"Why would you want to do that?" Clem asked. "I thought that we would, once we had my dowry, cut ties with Father."

"Do you want to cut ties with your father?" Chris sounded surprised. "He made a good point today. He said his grandson would inherit everything, probably before the boy was old enough to manage it. He would need a trustee who could teach him his duties and guide him until he was ready. I should be that trustee, do you not think? As the boy's father?"

"You make a good point," Clem had to agree. Which was annoying, for she had been looking forward to telling her father she was no longer his to command.

"Mind you, Clem," Chris said. "We are not going to let him push us around or bully us, and if he does not like it, then we will cut those ties. Even if he disinherits his grandson. I don't think he will, because he has no one else. But I'd rather that than allow him to give you one moment of distress."

When Chris said it so firmly, Clem believed him, at least at that moment. And even if Father proved to be too much even for the pair of them working together, Clem loved how protective Chris was. It really was very sweet.

Chapter Ten

C HRIS WAITED ANXIOUSLY in the private room at Miss Clemens' Book Emporium and Tea Rooms. He was about to meet cousins from both sides of the family, and he was far from certain about the reception he was about to get.

Clem squeezed his hands and he smiled at her. He wasn't at all certain he would be facing this if not for her. She gave him strength.

She had done so at Aunt Fern's ball. Both his mother's brother, the Earl of Crosby, and his father's cousin, the Earl of Halton, were there. Later, he found that the public repudiation had been organized by Aunt Fern. But whether they meant it or not was the question.

Both reacted with the same disdain when Chris was presented to them.

Lord Halton said, "Reginald Satterthwaite's son? I have no wish to meet anyone associated with that scoundrel."

And Lord Crosby looked Chris up and down and declared, "No, thank you, Lady Fernvale. With all due respect, I see no reason to acknowledge this person."

Chris wanted the floor to open up and swallow him, and then Clem had slipped her hand into his, and all was right with his world. He had not had their approbation before, and had not felt the need for it. He did not need it now.

Nonetheless, as the minutes ticked by, he acknowledged to himself his deep yearning for a family. He would have Clem, of course. Somehow. With or without Wright's blessing. But, for as long as he could remember, he had longed for brothers and sisters or—failing them—cousins. Perhaps, if this meeting went well, his children with Clem might grow up knowing their cousins.

The first to arrive was Lord Crosby's son, a tall man with that gaunt, stretched look of a youth who was still growing—one who ate like a horse and put on no weight. "Are you the son of Reggie Satterthwaite, who ruined my father's sister Christabel and ran off with her to Gretna Green?" he asked. "I am Michael Thurgood, Lord Crosby's son and your mother's nephew."

He held out a hand to be shaken, so Chris figured his somewhat hostile first question could safely be ignored. "Clem," he said, figuring a female—and a non-family member at that—might help to keep the conversation civil, "May I present my cousin Michael Thurgood? Thurgood, Miss Wright has done me the honor of accepting my suit. I have yet to convince her father."

"Miss Wright." Michael Thurgood's nod was perfectly polite, but his attention remained on Chris. "Is it true, what Lady Fernvale said? That your grandfather abandoned you in the streets after your father died?" he demanded. "Father says he would have taken you in if you had come to him."

Chris was about to protest that his nine-year old self had had no idea where the Earl of Halton lived, and no expectation of being welcomed, in any case. But they were interrupted by another arrival. A second man, this one around Chris's age, so perhaps five or six years older than Thurgood.

Chris would have known him for a Satterthwaite, even if he had not been expecting him. He look more like Reggie, Chris's father, than Chris did, though his hair and complexion were fairer and his chin was firm and determined where Reginald Satterthwaite's had been weak. He wore the flashy uniform of a horse guard. "If you're Satterthwaite, so am I," he growled. "Hello,

Thurgood."

Thurgood nodded. "Satterthwaite." He gained a bit of respect from Chris when he then turned to Clem. "Miss Wright, may I make known to you Captain Satterthwaite of His Majesty's 27th Regiment of Horse, and Satterthwaite, this is our cousin Christopher Satterthwaite and his betrothed, Miss Clementine Wright."

As with Thurgood, Satterthwaite greeted Clem politely, but then turned his attention back to Chris.

"Is it true you did not go overseas with your grandfather? My father wants to know why you didn't come to us. We would not have turned you away."

"You did," Chris said, dryly. "Or at least, your grandfather had me and my grandfather thrown out of the house, and when my grandfather sent me back on my own, the butler would not let me in."

"You were nine or ten," the guard's officer said.

"I was nine."

"You went back out into the road, and then what?"

"I ran back to where my grandfather had been, but he was gone. I called out for him. I asked other people if they had seen him. Then I ran down the street he'd left by. But I never found him."

"I saw you," Satterthwaite said. "I was watching from the schoolroom. You turned at the corner. Do you remember? You shook your fist at the house."

"I did," Chris said. He had forgotten that detail until this moment. "I was angry with my grandfather and with yours."

"It *is* you," Satterthwaite said. "Chris, isn't it? Chris, I'm Harry. I'm pleased to meet you at long last. I told my father what I had seen that afternoon, and he went after you, but he never found you. We hoped you might have caught up with your grandfather." Harry shrugged. "Better that than the streets."

"I didn't," Chris said. "I haven't seen my grandfather from that day to this, though Lady Fernvale says he is back in England, or was six months ago, when she saw him."

"He came to my father, six months ago," offered Thurgood. "Father saw him, if only to ask about you, but he said what you did—that he hadn't seen you since he left you with Lord Halton. Which we knew he hadn't, for Harry's father, had come all those years ago, asking mine if he knew where you were. If he's going to be Harry to you, I'd better be Michael. Once all the secrecy is over, you'll have too many cousins to be Thurgooding and Satterthwaiting everyone."

"What is the secrecy for, by the way?" Harry asked. "Lady Fernvale said something about Miss Wright's father? Will it not help you for him to know you are supported by your family? Everyone knows he has been looking to breed his daughter to a blueblood."

He choked on the last word and cast a guilty glance at Miss Wright. "I beg your pardon, Miss Wright. Should not have said that."

"It is true, nonetheless," Clem told him, "but not in the way you might think. He wants a blueblood, as you call your class, as a grandson, which means a blue-blooded husband for me. That much is true. Chris, you worked it out. You explain."

"His hopes are pinned on his grandson," Chris agreed. It bore repeating. "He wants no interference in how the boy is raised. Indeed, he wants the grandson's father to be utterly under his thumb, without allies who might support any rebellion, or, indeed, any attempt to influence the grandson's upbringing."

Michael was nodding. "That explains why he has been turning down some of those who are hanging out for a fortune. I take it you mean to marry Miss Wright, then let Wright know you have an estate of your own and family who will acknowledge you?"

Harry looked as if he was bursting to say something, but it appeared Clem's presence was inhibiting him. Clem must have thought so, too, for she said, "Spit it out, Harry. I will try not to take offense."

Harry was the sort of fair-skinned man on which every blush was painfully obvious. He reddened, but still said, "No offense intended, Miss Wright, but Chris, you don't need to marry for money anymore."

"And is that not fortunate?" Chris said. "Clem will be able to walk down the aisle knowing I married her for her own lovely self, and not for the dubious rewards that her father might or might not distribute my way."

Michael's eyebrows shot up again. "This is a love match then? Well. Our family would certain not wish to stand in the way of true love. Not again, anyway. My father thinks that, if he and his father had stood by his sister, we would have been able to save her life, or at the very least save you."

"Yes," Harry agreed. "I don't have the authority to speak for my father, Chris. He and his cousin did not get on, and that is putting it mildly, I gather. He'll need to know more before he decides to take you into the bosom of the family. But he won't queer your pitch." He paused. "What do you need us to do?"

Chris exchanged glances with Clem. This had all been much easier than they expected. "Thank you," he said.

Michael handed Chris his glass in a mute request for a refill. As Chris refreshed all the glasses, his cousin asked, "Who rescued you when you were turned away by Harry's grandfather, if I might ask? Lady Fernvale said some kind person took you in."

Again, Chris and Clem exchanged glances. They had been tolerant so far. But how would they react to his personal history as a street rat, a pickpocket, and then an errand boy for Ramping Billy? Ah well. It was the truth, after all.

"A gang of pickpockets," he said. "They robbed me and then took pity on me. They gave me some rags to wear and taught me their trade."

Harry was staring at him with his mouth open. "You were a pickpocket? Good God!"

Michael, meanwhile, was chuckling. "I cannot wait to tell my father. You must have been a good one, for here you are."

"Not good enough," Chris said. "Ramping Billy O'Hara caught me picking his pocket, and decided to keep me. You've heard of Ramping Billy?"

Harry nodded and Michael whistled. "He was your kind person?"

"When I told Aunt Fern that, I meant the pickpockets, but yes. Billy has been surprisingly kind to me. He gave me a job upstairs in the brothel above his first gambling den—emptying chamber pots, sweeping the floor, and collecting dirty linens, mostly. And then different tasks as I grew older. He made sure I was educated. And when I showed some talent with mathematics, he hired me as his bookkeeper."

"I've never seen you at O'Hara's places," Michael commented.

"I work out of sight and I don't gamble or frequent the ladies," Chris told him. "I mostly work out of Fortune's Fool."

Michael whistled again, and this time Harry shook his head. "Ramping Billy. My father is not going to like that."

"I didn't like being put out on the street," Chris retorted, irritated on Billy's behalf.

Harry gave him a wry smile. "I'll make sure to point that out to him, cousin."

"Did you really work in a brothel?" Michael asked, then seemed to remember that Clem was there, for he shot her a glance and muttered, "Never mind." Clearly, he wanted salacious details. He was doomed to be disappointed, for Chris wouldn't share the few he had available.

"This place runs a depository for letters," Chris said, changing the subject. "If you need to reach me, or if I need to let you know something, write to me here. I'll be collecting letters addressed to C. Waite."

"Oh fun," Michael said. "I've always wanted my own secret correspondent, like in the Gothic novels. I'll be M. Good, shall I?"

"What can I be?" Harry asked. "H. Satters might not be different enough, if someone asks the right questions. C. Waite writing to H. Satters would give it away immediately. Let's say S. Henry."

"Very good," Chris approved.

The cousins parted in charity with one another, and Clem reflected Chris's feelings when she said, "That went quite well, I thought."

Better than Chris had expected, and certainly better than his next encounter with family.

The sign that something was wrong came from one of Billy's boys. He was waiting by the door under the supervision of Billy's lieutenant, Tiny, and approached Chris nervously. "Mister, I'm sorry, mister. I di'n't know I shouldn't, only 'e said 'e were yer gaffer, so I let 'im in."

Chris looked at Tiny over the boy's head. "My grandfather?"

"Seemingly. The boss said might as well see him now as later."

Chris crouched to look the boy in the face. Like most of them, he had old eyes in a young scrawny body. He flinched, as if expecting a blow, then peeked at Tiny and straightened, setting his chin and squaring his shoulders, as if determined to take whatever happened. Jim, this one was called, though whether it was the name he had as a baby or one he'd adopted since was anyone's guess.

Jim was a recent addition to Billy's crew. Chris might have been the first boy Billy took from the streets, but he was far from the last. Billy's people fed them, civilized them, educated them in useful skills and in basic writing and arithmetic, and when they were finally of some use, they disappeared. But others always took their place.

People had dozens of theories about what happened to the trained boys, some more lurid than others, none even close to the truth. Chris, as Billy's bookkeeper, knew they all went to legitimate positions. Households and businesses throughout England hired on Billy's former boys.

If Chris managed to set up his school, he planned to ask Billy to send the most promising to him, for he himself was the only boy he knew about who had been educated beyond the basics. Chris thought that was a waste, for there were other intelligent lads who would go far with the right education.

"Is my grandfather in my office, Jim?" Chris asked.

Jim nodded. "I'm sorry, mister," he repeated.

"You weren't to know, Jim," Chris told him. "If it happens again, though, tell the person who calls that they must wait. That study is where I write things down about Mr. O'Hara's business. You wouldn't want Mr. O'Hara's enemies finding out things they are not meant to know, would you?"

Jim shook his head so fast that his cheeks wobbled. "No, sir, mister," he said fervently.

Chris nodded and went to face his grandfather. He wasn't truly worried about the records he kept for Billy. Everything was locked away whenever he left the room. Tiny knew that, and so did Billy, or Grandfather's time in the room would have been short indeed. But let Jim worry a little. It would help the lesson to stick.

It was lucky that Chris had no expectation that Grandfather might have changed. The way the man bullied his way into a room he should not have entered without Chris's invitation showed he was the same man who cheerfully abandoned Chris to his own devices in one of the world's wickedest cities.

"Grandfather," Chris said, as he opened the door. The man hadn't changed. Perhaps he was a little greyer, a little older. But he turned from the window as the door opened, caught sight of Chris, and went straight to the point without a smile or even a glint of recognition in his eyes.

"Wright. He's worse than a commoner. He's a coal miner. You cannot marry his daughter."

"I intend to marry his daughter," Chris told him.

"I forbid it," Grandfather declared. "You are a Satterthwaite of Blethering. Marry an heiress who doesn't belong in the gutter. And what are you doing here? Working for a debt collector? It won't do, Christopher. You must resign."

"You cannot tell me what I can and cannot do, Grandfather. You gave up that right when you abandoned me in the street."

"Don't talk nonsense," Grandfather said. "I left you safely at my brother's house."

Chris had been over this painful ancient history often enough in recent days to speak calmly. "You left me in the street outside your brother's house, from which we had already been turned away once. I was turned away again, and had nowhere to go. I could have died in the streets that first winter. I very nearly did."

"Fool boy. You should have tried your mother's people."

"I did not know my mother's people," Chris pointed out. "I was a child."

"That is hardly my fault," said Grandfather, and then he waved a dismissive hand. "I did not come here to discuss ancient history, Christopher. Your father was a disappointment to me, falling in love with your mother and running off with her when all he was meant to do was be paid off by her father."

That was good to know. Chris felt slightly better about his father, knowing he had loved his mother when he ruined her.

Grandfather had not finished his rant. "I expect better from you, boy. I have plans for you, and they do not include being married to a coal miner's daughter. But if we play our cards correctly, she could be worth something, for all of that."

Chris opened the door which he had closed behind him when he entered. "I want no part of your plans, Grandfather. Please leave."

"Shut the door, boy, and I'll tell you about the bride I have chosen for you. I think you shall be pleased."

"I'll have no part of any of your plans, Grandfather," Chris insisted.

"Her father is Morton Vaughan," Grandfather said, ignoring him. "Born a gentleman, mark you, Christopher, though he does work in trade. Tea, and as rich as Croesus. The girl is pretty, too. I'd have married her myself, but he won't have me for her. Says she deserves a handsome young husband."

"I am marrying Clementine Wright, Grandfather," Chris said, wishing the man was twenty years younger, for he would be happy to hurl him down the stairs and out the door into the stable yard.

"You've no choice, Christopher. I've signed the marriage agreements. You are marrying the Vaughan filly."

Obnoxious turnip! Chris struggled to maintain the appearance of calm while his temper seethed and bubbled. "Your signature is not valid. I am an adult, and have not agreed, and will not agree."

"You will do as you are told, Christopher," his grandfather growled.

"I will not," said Chris, firmly.

His grandfather complained, harangued, and eventually left, muttering about serpents' teeth and thankless children.

Chapter Eleven

"Yer young fella's gaffer came by to threaten me today. Me! At my work! Happen I'll lurn him that Bertram Wright ain't to be pushed round by a useless blot of an upper crust snot rag. Says that scoundrel of a grandson is already betrothed!" Father was furious. His careful speech, much like that of the class he aspired for his grandson to join, had been slowly and thoroughly learned. Slipping back into the words and accent of his youth showed how angry he was.

Another sign of his wrath was the way he was pacing, to and fro. across the parlor rug.

Fortunately, Clem had already heard from Chris the probable topic that had so upset her father. "Our Mr. Satterthwaite was angry with his grandfather when we met this afternoon, Father. Apparently, the man turned up in Chr—Mr. Satterthwaite's office this morning, demanding that Mr. Satterthwaite stop courting me as the older Mr. Satterthwaite had already signed a marriage agreement for Chris. Of course, Mr. Satterthwaite told him where he could put his plans."

That stopped Father's furious pacing. "He did? Yes, I suppose he did. Though the man *is* his grandfather."

"The man abandoned our Mr. Satterthwaite sixteen years ago, when he was a child. To turn up now and dare suggest Chris owes him anything? Chris told him in no uncertain terms that whom he marries or does not marry is not the business of Mr. Satterthwaite senior, and he wants nothing to do with the man."

"Is that right?" Father had taken up station in front of the fireplace, rocking back and forth, his hands in his pockets, and with a smile on his face. His temper was gone as if it had never been.

"When are you seeing 'Chris'? Tonight, is it?"

Father had not missed her slip of the tongue, then. It was too late to unsay it. She could do nothing more than hope he wouldn't find a way to turn it to her disadvantage. Hers and Chris's.

Honestly, why did the pair of them have to be cursed with such conniving, selfish, vicious old men?

"Yes, Father. He is escorting me to the Sutton ball."

"Sutton, as in the Earl of Sutton? That's the Duke of Winshire's heir."

At her nod, he whistled. "Sutton, eh? You are flying high, Clementine, my girl. When Satterthwaite arrives, tell him I want to talk to you both before you go out."

Clem could do nothing but agree, and wait with as much patience as she could muster for Chris to arrive.

Hours later—it seemed much longer—evening rolled around and with it came Chris, looking incredibly desirable in his black evening coat and silver-grey breeches and stockings, this time teamed with another waistcoat—this one in a dark blue silk brocade.

He must have chosen it to co-ordinate with her gown, which he had asked about during their afternoon drive. It was silver-grey and embroidered in dark blue, and was one of two new gowns she had had made. Father had reluctantly agreed to pay for a single new ball gown, but Clem had taken a leaf from Chris's book and gone off Bond Street. The modiste was so reasonably-priced compared to the Bond Street shop that Clem was able to purchase two.

"Father had a visit from your grandfather," Clem told Chris.

"The vile old villain," said Chris. "I should have expected it. What did he want?"

"Do you know? Father never said. I just assumed it was that you couldn't marry me. I told him about Mr. Satterthwaite's visit to you, and how you dealt with it. He cheered up, then. He wants to talk to us before he goes out, Chris, but he didn't say what about."

"We are about to find out, then," Chris said, "for here he comes."

"Ah, Satterthwaite," said Father. "Come into the parlor. I have a bone to pick with you."

"I am sorry my grandfather angered you today, sir," Chris said, as he escorted Clem to a chair in the parlor and took station slightly behind her and to her right. "I want you to know that I don't agree with him. I knew nothing about his plans on my behalf, and I'll have no part of his schemes."

"I'm pleased to hear that, my boy," Father said. "You know what he came about, then?"

Clem, who knew her father well, could tell this was a trick question. It wasn't what she had thought, then. It was too late to warn Chris. She held her breath as Chris answered.

"I assume to tell you he would not allow me to marry your daughter, sir. That is what he told me when he called on me today. That he had plans for me, and they did not include marrying the daughter of a coal miner. That he had signed a marriage agreement on my behalf, without my knowledge or consent! Well. I'm a man grown, and no thanks to him. I'm not a dog to be whistled at when he wants me. He ignored me for sixteen years, and I'd be happy to spend another sixteen ignoring him."

Chris was breathing heavily when he had finished, and when she turned to look over her shoulder at him, his color was high. She turned in her chair then to see that his eyes were flashing and his hands had formed fists.

Father, on the other hand, was grinning. "Good for you, lad, but you are wrong, you know. He didn't want to stop you from marrying my Clementine. You were determined on it, he said, and he had a mind to let you have your way." He picked up the brandy decanter. "A drink, lad?"

"Just a small one," Chris said, "and you, Miss Wright?"

Clem hid a smile at that, and said *yes*, which won her a sharp look from her father, but he poured Chris a small drink and Clem not much more than a thimbleful.

"He had changed his mind then, sir?" Chris asked. "He was in favor of the match?"

"Ah, well," said Father, well into his second favorite role, as *raconteur*. His favorite was business dealer. "Wait, and you shall see. Your grandfather said he knew—the whole world knew—I had in mind to marry my girl to a proper gentleman. 'Alas, Wright. That is not my grandson. Perhaps once—but he ran away, and ended up in a gambling den. And worse, Wright. Not the sort of man who will ever be accepted in polite Society. Such a pity. He was a boy of real promise.' He took out his handkerchief and wiped his eye."

"Chris—Mr. Satterthwaite—did not run away," Clem protested. "He was abandoned."

Father's eyes twinkled. "You will like what is coming next," he promised. "The old man said, 'I fear the rogue will break your daughter's heart, gambling and cavorting with paid women. It is what he has been raised to, Wright. And all you will get out of it is sorrow, for he'll not be your entry into the ton.' As if I wanted to enter the ton." Father sniffed his scorn.

Chris was looking mystified and Clem felt the same. What had Chris's grandfather been up to?

"I said to him, 'What do you suggest, Satterthwaite? I do not like to think of my daughter with a broken heart.' And that is when your grandfather hinted you might be prepared to change your mind about marrying my daughter. For a small fee, you understand. Payable to himself."

"So that was it!" Chris said. "The swine! The fiend. I hope you sent him off with a flea in his ear, Mr. Wright."

Father laughed. "I am glad now, that he came. I think you will be, too, young people. I had not made up my mind, but I don't like being dictated to, and I like even less to be conned out of brass I worked hard for. Young Chris—since my daughter calls you Chris, I might as well do likewise. Young Chris, do you want to marry my daughter and get her with child?"

"I do, sir," Chris said, his words laden with sincerity.

"Clementine, do you want to be Chris's wife and to bear my grandson?"

Clem ignored Father's focus on the prospective male heir for the key point. "I do, sir."

"Well, and why not?" Father said. "My advisers were impressed. They say you have a good mind. You have a lot to learn, mind, but you are not afraid of honest work. My daughter likes you and her mother would have wanted her to be happy with my choice. It will show Satterthwaite that I cannot be pushed around. Yes, I'll do it. I'll let you marry her. We shall need a marriage agreement, mind, all signed up right and tight!"

"Yes, of course, sir," said Chris, looking a little as if he had been whacked over the head. Clem felt the same way—almost dizzy with surprise, excitement, and yes—joy.

"That's settled, then," said Father. "Run along now, and enjoy your evening."

⤕⤕⤕✴⤔⤔⤔

THE MARRIAGE AGREEMENT was gargantuan, with long sentences riddled with triple and even quadruple negatives, and full of *heretofores* and *notwithstandings*. Some sentences droned on for pages before a full stop.

Chris had not expected to find it difficult to understand. He was well accustomed to combing his way through thickets of legal phrases and preparing summaries in everyday language for Billy. This document left his head reeling.

Wright had thought of every possible contingency and had ordered his legal experts to hedge them about with conditions and consequences. The enormous dowry he'd dangled before suitors was, for the most part, not a cash sum, but was made up of properties, shares in businesses and other income-producing investments.

It was divided into portions. Most of it was to be held in trust, and paid out in increments based on certain events and milestones. A small payment after the wedding. A set of small payments associated with business achievements—to be approved by Wright.

The announcement of a pregnancy would trigger another payment, and the birth of the first son, another. And so it went. Wright intended to control their marriage, their family, and their entire lives by means of a breadcrumb trail of income-earning assets.

"I will need a copy so I can study this in detail," Chris told Mr. Harcourt—the senior of the three lawyers who had appeared in Wright's office to present Chris with the document.

Wright made a harrumphing noise. Chris was learning to interpret them, and this one, he thought, meant, "I'm not going to tell the lad I approve, but he's doing the right thing."

The lawyer nodded to the most junior of the three, who took a folder from his brief case. "Mr. Wright had us prepare you a copy, sir," he said.

"Do you have a copy for Miss Wright?" Chris asked.

The lawyer's eyes widened, though he caught his jaw before it could drop. His gaze shot to Wright as he repeated Chris's words. "A copy for Miss Wright?"

Wright had begun to scowl, so Chris hastened to speak before he could refuse outright.

"Miss Wright has inherited her intelligence and her ready grasp of realities from her father. She is young, of course, but she has been well educated. Furthermore, the matter of her marriage agreement is certainly of great significance to her, and the details it contains will affect her life as much, if not more, than it will mine."

Harcourt's brow creased with worry as Wright wiped all expression from his face.

Chris tried the argument that was most likely to sway his prospective father-in-law. "Do not fall into the trap of thinking that a lady's role is merely to produce children and be decorative. Many of Society's ladies are actively involved in running great estates, charities, and businesses. The Countess of Jersey, for example. She is the daughter of an earl and married to an earl. She inherited her grandfather's wealth and is active in running Child's Bank, since she inherited his position as senior partner. She has so far given her husband four sons."

"She can read your copy," Wright conceded. "Don't need to have another made."

The lawyer's frown lightened at that, and he nodded. "Indeed, sir. That would be highly acceptable."

"We shall meet tomorrow for the signatures," said Wright.

"It is a big document," Chris objected. "Give me three days, please."

"Two," Wright countered, so quickly it was obvious he'd intended the first timeframe as a negotiating position. "Two, and I am firm on that. In two days, we shall sign the agreement."

Thank goodness Chris had been part of dozens of contract negotiations for Billy—admittedly as the most junior member of the team, holding the bag and passing the ink. But still, he'd learned enough to bluff. "Two to read and absorb the document and to discuss any issues we might have with it, one to come up with counter proposals to cover those points."

"You won't need counter proposals," Wright blustered. "This is the agreement. Take it or leave it."

Outwardly calm, but with his heart racing, Chris inclined his head. "We shall present our difficulties, our proposed solutions, and our arguments, and see what you have to say, Mr. Wright. It is surely not necessary to stop the marriage when you have not even heard what small changes we might wish to make, and why."

Wright held Chris's gaze for what must have been a full minute before making that thoughtful noise again. *"Harrumph."* He turned his glare on the lead legal advisor. "Set up a meeting for three days from now. Good day, Satterthwaite, gentlemen."

And that was it. Chris said a slightly more polite goodbye to the legal team, and the meeting was over.

CLEM AND CHRIS were still discussing the marriage agreement, which was a monster, when Clem's father dropped another verbal cannon ball to break the peace.

They were having dinner. All afternoon, Clem and Chris had been reading the marriage agreement clause by clause, and discussing what each clause meant and whether it contained fishhooks that would later catch them out. Clem invited Chris to stay for dinner so they could carry on over the meal and afterward, but when Father unexpectedly joined them at the table, they kept the conversation general.

Until Father broke into a discussion of a balloon ascension that Clem wanted to attend to say, "I have booked St. George's church for the fourth Monday of next month."

Chris put down his cutlery and turned all his attention to Father.

"For the wedding?" Clem asked, just to be certain, but what else could it be?

"Of course, for the wedding," said Father. "I wanted an earlier date, but they insisted they are fully booked."

"We could use another church," Chris suggested. "St. Martins, for example."

"I would prefer St. Martins," Clem agreed. It was her nearest church. She had been attending services there every Sunday since she was a small child.

Father, who had continued eating while Chris and Clem reacted to his statement, looked up from his plate and glared at his daughter.

"St. George's is the place where the quality marry," he said. "My daughter is having her wedding at St. George's."

"Many people—" Chris began, but Father interrupted.

"I hope you don't plan to argue with every decision I make about the wedding, Satterthwaite. I have been planning this for a long time. I know just what I need to do to make it perfect, and I will not have you and Clementine opposing me."

Clem subsided. When Father spoke like that, there was no point in arguing with him. Chris, though, cast her a quick worried glance, and made an attempt.

"It is Clem's wedding, Mr. Wright. I want it to be perfect for her."

"So do I, lad," Father said. "So do I. And I have it planned, I tell you. You, young man, will not interfere."

Chris opened his mouth again, but Clem saw her father's jaw tighten and spoke up. "Chris, I am sure I will be happy with Father's plans. What do you need me to arrange, Father? The gown? My attendants and their gowns? Bridal flowers? The wedding feast?" She was sure there were other matters such an event required. Perhaps Lady Ferndale would be willing to advise her.

Father's glare had a discomforted edge that indicated he'd not thought of at least some of the items on her list.

"Yes, sir," Chris agreed, taking her cue. "Let me know my tasks, sir. The wedding ring, the best man, and all the arrangements for the wedding trip, I assume, but I'm willing to assist with anything you assign to me."

"*Harrumph,*" said Father.

Chapter Twelve

CLEM WAS AT the next meeting with Father and the lawyers. She had met Harcourt, the senior man, before. On every occasion, he had spoken to her as if she was no more than ten years old and a halfwit. He glanced at Father in alarm when she walked in on Chris's arm, pretending she had every right to be there.

Father did not object to her presence, but nor did he greet her. "That countess you mentioned," he said to Chris. "Very important lady. No one wants to offend her, because she runs an assembly hall." He shook his head. "I don't understand the quality, and that's a fact, but the thing is, she's a banker. And a countess. Just like you said."

Chris nodded, which was agreement enough for Father, for he was talking again. "Child, her gran'fer was. Robert Child. Left her the lot because he didn't like his daughter marrying her Pa. And his widow ran the bank till the gel was old enough to take over." He shook his head. "Smart women," he said, and shook his head again.

"Like Clem," Chris said, and Father barked a short laugh.

"Very well, lad. You've made your point. I get two for one, do I? Clementine? You're going to help this lad of your'n, when he works for me?"

"Yes, Father," Clem said, clutching Chris's hand. Father appeared pleased, but he could not be trusted. Chris could. Chris would stop Father from hitting her.

"Lad, this earl, Jersey, that married Child's granddaughter—he has just changed his name. Child-Villiers, he is now. Think of that. Goldsmiths, the family was, and before that, they tell me, cloth merchants. Child was the name of nobodies, and now, through the daughter, it will be the name of earls. Think of that!"

"Wright-Satterthwaite has a ring to it," Chris said, and Father beamed.

"Just so. Just so, lad."

"Perhaps, like the Earl of Jersey, after the birth of sons," Chris suggested. "Jersey took the name after his fourth son was born."

Father narrowed his eyes as he thought about this.

"We can put it in the agreement," Chris suggested. "What do you think, Clem? After the birth of the second child, son, or daughter?"

That touched on one of the clauses they wanted to renegotiate. "Let us discuss that when we reach that point in the document," she suggested.

Father was still beaming, but the smile turned to a scowl when Chris read out their first point.

"You want cash for marrying my daughter?" he growled.

"Money to ensure I can keep your daughter in the style to which she is accustomed," Chris said.

Clem was relieved to see Father assume his business face—the one he wore when he was negotiating a deal. They had not been at all certain he would bend even a little. On certain things, she and Chris would not budge. If Father would not move, that would mean a dash for the border, and lean times as they lived on Chris's savings while they found out whether the estate from the Thurgoods could support them.

Father baulked wherever they had expected him to object—the larger cash settlement on the day of the wedding, their wish to have their own house rather than living under Father's roof, the limits Chris intended to place on his availability to Father's enterprises—three days a week but for as long each day as Father wishes.

For those items and others, they had marshalled their arguments, and Clem was very relieved that Father was prepared to listen. For example, Chris pointed out that a townhouse in a more fashionable district was one of the lures he had placed before Chris at the outset, and that the reason for it—to put his grandson's mother in contact with the ton—remained valid.

Father pushed back—in the case of a townhouse, he agreed to pay the rent on one and review it after a year. In the course of the long afternoon, they managed to hammer out most of an agreement. On two topics, Father was obdurate. His entire fortune would go to his eldest grandson, and any other children of their marriage would get nothing from their grandfather.

He would not consider settling for a granddaughter—if Chris and Clem did not produce a son, the fortune would go to Clem's unknown cousin, the son of Father's only sister.

"ON THE WHOLE," Chris said to Clem as they left at the end of the meeting, "that went better than I expected."

The lawyer was going away to write up the revised agreement—they would each have a copy by the end of the day tomorrow.

"I've been wondering if we should employ a lawyer of our own," Clem said. "I know you have a lot of experience reading lawyer-speak, but are we certain nothing is hidden in the contract that we have missed?"

Chris didn't know any lawyers, except those who worked for Billy. "I could ask Billy if I could use one of his legal men," Chris said. "Though I hate owing him even more than I do already. I have no idea what price he'll exact!"

"I would rather not pay the cost of not doing it," Clem retorted. "We need the document to be read by a lawyer who is on our side."

She made an excellent point. Would Billy's lawyers be on Chris and Clem's side, though? Yes, he supposed, provided they had no conflicts with Billy. "You are right," he told Clem. "I will ask Billy."

Her smile was, as ever, a benediction. Chris had come to realize that Clem expected men to ignore her, and though she now trusted Chris enough to argue with him, her delight when he listened showed that her trust had very shallow roots.

Billy sent for him the following day shortly after his copy of the agreement had been delivered, and before he could request a few minutes. As usual, he did not bother with social niceties. "Christopher, how did you get on at your meeting with your father-in-law to be?"

"Quite well, I think," Chris told him. He plopped the heavy sheaf of papers, still tied in red ribbon, onto Billy's desk. "This is version two of the marriage agreement. I've been over it with Wright's lawyers twice, the second time yesterday, to propose the changes that Miss Wright and I want. Those should be in this version, which has only just arrived."

"Summarize it for me," Billy said, as he always did when his employees presented him with something in writing. Billy could read—Chris had seen him do it. But Chris suspected he found it hard.

"If you have the time," Chris said. "I was planning to ask if one of your lawyers could go over it with me, but I'd value your opinion." Also true. Billy had a keen mind and a devious one. If Wright had buried traps in the agreement, Billy was the most likely one to see them.

"Tiny!" Billy shouted, and the bodyguard-aide opened the office door far enough to poke his head inside. "Clear my timetable for the next three hours, and let Anderson know I need him."

Tiny nodded and withdrew.

"Carry on," Billy said. "Anderson can catch up when he arrives."

Chris untied the ribbon and picked the first page off the top of the stack. "Names, addresses, and so on. The agreement is between Wright and me."

"His full legal name is Bertram Wright," Billy noted.

Bertram Wright, collier proprietor and merchant, of 17A Fullway Court, London and 5 Munstead Way, Sheffield, Yorkshire," Chris read. He looked up to see if Billy had any comment, and, failing a response, continued to the next page.

"The first part states Wright's motive for approving the marriage. It's a lot of words, but in essence..." He stopped at the knock on the door, which then opened, and Tiny said, "Anderson."

"Come in," said Billy. "Anderson, you're to read this agreement and make sure that Satterthwaite knows all the implications before he signs. Carry on, Christopher. 'In essence,' you said...? In essence what?"

They spent the whole afternoon on it, with Richard Anderson occasionally correcting Chris's impression of the meaning of the words. Anderson found two loopholes and a trap hidden in the thicket of terms, and Billy found one that Anderson had not noticed.

"Thank you, Richard," Chris said when Billy pronounced them finished for the day. "And thank you, Billy." He wanted to say more, but "I owe you more than I can ever repay" seemed like a dangerous thing to say to Ramping Billy O'Hara who was famous, at least in the world he ruled over, for never forgetting a debt and never doing a favor without expecting one in return.

The amusement in Billy's eyes hinted he could read Chris's thoughts, but all he said was, "We can't let the coal man take advantage of you, Christopher. Can you let Anderson have the document overnight? Anderson, can your clerks make a copy by ten tomorrow morning?"

"Yes, sir," Anderson assured him. "I'll guard it with my life, Chris. Along with my notes for changes."

After that, Chris was well-prepared for the next meeting with Wright and his people, where Chris politely pointed out the legal man's "mistakes." Wright was disgruntled, but could hardly complain, and the following day, both Chris and Wright signed the thrice-amended agreement.

Now Chris had only to wait for the wedding, and Clem would be his. *No. Not that.* He and Clem would be one another's.

FATHER WAS STILL determined to go ahead with the wedding, to Clem's relief, but had complained bitterly about young Satterthwaite being too suspicious by half. However, he cheered up when he was notified one morning that one of the many weddings ahead of them in St. George's calendar had been cancelled.

All of a sudden, the wedding was on with fewer than nine days to go. Father saw no problem with the short notice. He had booked the church, and invited his business cronies.

He also instructed Mrs. Bellowes to buy the wedding dress and organize a wedding feast for fifty people. Chris, Clem discovered, had been permitted to purchase the common license that meant they did not need to wait for banns to be called, but he had had no say in any other detail of the wedding, and Father saw no need for any further planning.

Clem was not surprised when she expressed her desire to choose her own dress, and Father told her to button her lip. He then went out for the evening.

Mrs. Bellowes was no better pleased than Clem. The budget Father had given her was totally inadequate to hiring a half-way competent modiste to make a gown in time for the wedding, let alone putting together a breakfast that would meet Father's expectations. Added to that, she had been told her services would no longer be needed after the wedding was over, and yet she was being kept too busy to seek another position.

Lady Fernvale, who had asked Clem to call her "Aunt Fern" in anticipation of the wedding, met Clem and Mrs. Bellowes in the Burlington Arcade one day just as the frustrations hit the boiling point. When Aunt Fern asked how they were, Mrs. Bellowes erupted, downloading all her frustrations, and then bursting into tears.

"Come," said Aunt Fern. "My carriage is just along here. Clementine, dear, bring your chaperone. We shall go to Fourniers, eat as many of their delightful little cakes as we can, and discuss what is to be done."

Fourniers, Clem discovered, meant a tea shop where Aunt Fern's footman had soon secured a private room. By the time the three of them were safely ensconced in comfortable chairs within the room, Mrs. Bellowes was making apologies for her emotional behavior but was unable to stop sobbing.

"Mrs. Bellowes is worried and overtired," Clem explained. "Father set her tasks to organize for the wedding, and has not given her a sufficient budget. Even if we had enough money, I do not know how we could manage a breakfast that Father would consider sufficient in the time we have to prepare. Our cook is certainly not capable, and we do not have sufficient servants for the numbers expected. As for the gown, Father does not realize that modistes are booked up months in advance, and the money is not enough, even if we could find someone with time to make it. Not even the off-Bond Street dressmaker I've used in the past has been able to accept the commission. It's quite a conundrum, and Mrs. Bellowes is most concerned that Father will blame her if all is not to his liking."

Aunt Fern frowned thoughtfully. "What sort of gown do you want, dearest? Not, I think, the flounces and frills that make you look shapeless." She seemed to avoid looking at Mrs. Bellowes' as she said this, though—thanks to Aunt Fern's words—Clem's chaperone stopped sobbing and instead looked peeved.

Clem, who had been dreading wearing whatever Mrs. Bellowes chose for, agreed enthusiastically. "No, and not pastels that wash out my coloring, either."

"Your father said…" Mrs. Bellowes began.

Aunt Fern raised an imperious brow, which temporarily silenced Mrs. Bellowes. If Clem didn't soothe the silly women's ruffled feathers, she'd have her chaperone complaining and scolding all the way home.

"Aunt Fern makes a good point, Mrs. Bellowes. While your taste is most suitable for a tall, slender debutante on the younger side, it has become apparent that it does not suit my form. So, if we obey what Father says, he is going to be angry about the results, and you shall not get your bonus." Which gave Mrs. Bellowes thoughts a different direction, Clem hoped, but did not solve their problem. "But Aunt Fern, how can we find a modiste at this late stage, and with very little money?"

Aunt Fern waved a dismissive hand. "The money is not a difficulty. I assume my godson will receive your dowry after the wedding? Ask him for the money. Tell the modiste that your father has no understanding of the cost of women's gowns, and that your husband will pay, but only after the wedding."

Clem stared at her. As easy as that! Chris had already proposed that she completely replace her wardrobe once they were married. This would simply be the first gown in that wardrobe. Sharing that promise of future—and plentiful—orders would make finding a willing modiste that much easier.

"That will solve Mrs. Bellowes' problem, too," said Aunt Fern, "since she can use the gown money for the wedding feast."

Of course! Mrs. Bellowes cheered up, but Clem still did not *have* a modiste, willing or otherwise. Aunt Fern had a plan for that, too. "I know a young woman who has just set up on her own. She is brilliant, Clem, but has not yet been noticed by the ton, which means she is a lot cheaper than you might expect, and she probably has time to make your gown. You could be her opportunity to be seen by those who matter. I shall introduce you."

It all sounded wonderful, but Clem saw a flaw. "Father will object if he finds out," she said.

"Your father *will* find out, and he will *not* object," Aunt Fern predicted. "I shall call on him myself and point out how these changes will cost him nothing and will allow him to give you a wedding to impress his competitors and any members of the ton who attend. As I intend to do."

She was as good as her word. What she said to Clem's father Clem never discovered, but he emerged from the study to see her to the door, then told Clem, "Lady Fernvale is a real lady. You could do worse than to study her, Clementine, and model yourself on her. A bit of a bossy boots, but she has good reasons for what she does. Yes. A real lady. Not like that Bellowes female. I was mistaken in her, and it's not often that Bertram Wright gets taken in. I have to give her a bonus and a good reference, Lady Fernvale says. Can't have her hinting that I'm not to be trusted, or worse. But she'll be gone after the wedding. If you doubt that, just watch me."

"I don't doubt it, Father," Clem told him. Gracious! Aunt Fern had done it! Furthermore, tomorrow morning, she was taking Clem to visit the new modiste. And Chris had said that, if she liked the woman's work, she might as well make a start on ordering her new wardrobe!

Clem, who had already been looking forward to being married, was now looking forward to her wedding.

Chapter Thirteen

CHRIS'S ONLY TASKS, Wright had said, were to visit the Bishop of London to acquire a common license, and to turn up on the day.

Wright was wrong. Chris also had to find a place for him and Clem to live, and make it a fit home for him and his new bride.

First, he wanted Clem to know what he had in mind. She was tied up with dress fittings and consultations with Aunt Fern and Mrs. Bellowes about food and decorations for the wedding feast, but he managed to steal her away for a carriage ride in Hyde Park.

"I'm hunting for a house, and I want your opinion," he said, as soon as they were in the park and he had a little attention to spare from the horses, other traffic, and careless pedestrians. "I think we should act as if the Thurgood estate will not happen," he said.

Both the Thurgood and Satterthwaite relatives were waiting to meet Chris and Clem until after the wedding, so Chris still did not know if the estate was his, and if so, how big it was and how much income it produced.

"I agree, Chris, but surely we can afford to rent a place in the country for your school from the money Father will sign over to you after the wedding?"

Chris was not counting that as certain, either. "I must admit, I have been more than half expecting your father to take offense and call the whole thing off. In which case, you and I will need to quickly use this license I have, before he stops us. I think I should sign up for a townhouse, as we agreed, but in a less expensive part of town. Then, if your father backs out, we can use some of my savings to pay the rent."

"Is that wise?" Clem asked. "If we do go ahead without Father's approval, you won't have a position with him, and you have left Mr. O'Hara's employ."

Was she saying she wouldn't marry him if her Father decided against him? Was she worried about her security? Chris hastened to assure her. "I should be able to find a job quite quickly." Even if Wright and Billy both went out and bad-mouthed him to prospective employers, he was reasonably certain he could find something. "At worst, I can return to work for Billy. I can support you, darling. You need not worry about that."

Clem made an impatient gesture. "I do not want you to obligated to Mr. O'Hara," she protested. "I just want to be sensible. If Father campaigns against you, we might have to leave London, and then the townhouse would be an unnecessary expense. Why not rent it for a quarter, and leave the rest of the money Father gives you in the bank?" Sensible, and still ready to marry him, since she said, "We might have to leave London."

She would marry him, then, whatever her father did. "A good idea," Chris said. "Paying yearly might be cheaper, but in three months, we should know about the Thurgood inheritance and we'll have received the first payment from your father." And possibly even the second, depending on how quickly Clem conceived her first child.

They discussed the location. She was happy to leave it to him, apart from agreeing she did not want or need to live in one of London's more exclusive areas, and that a house within easy walking distance of Wright was a bad idea.

"A neighborhood of merchants, bankers and lower gentry

might suit us best," Chris suggested. "We are what the newspapers call 'the middle sort', are we not? Whatever your father's aspirations. And I can tell your father that we are renting for a quarter, while we look around for a better address."

"Yes, that sort of neighborhood will be good. Somewhere for people who live year-round in London, except for a brief holiday visiting family or the like. A neighborhood for people who are comfortably circumstanced, Chris."

"I will take it partially-furnished, if I can," he said, "and once we are married, we can go shopping together for anything else we need."

Armed with her approval, he set off to make the rounds of the estate agents and solicitors, looking for anything that might be on the market. It was harder than he expected. He saw houses that were priced beyond their means, others that were little more than a few rooms with no facility for cooking and no room for servants, and some that would have worked if they were not right on the edges—and perhaps inside the borders—of some very rundown areas.

Finally, after a frustrating few days, he admitted his failure to Billy. Once again, Billy came to the rescue.

"I have been to look at a townhouse that might work for us," he told Clem. "It is not large, but not too small, either. It has four floors and a basement, with a dining room and reception room on the ground floor, two parlors on the first floor, and two bedrooms on each of the other floors. Kitchen and accommodation for the servants in the basement. It is in Primrose Square, just off Curzon Street, so not far from your father's offices."

"It seems perfect," Clem said. "But you sound as if you have doubts. Is there something wrong with it? Is it too expensive?"

"The house is perfect," he admitted. "The owner will rent it to us for one quarter, with a rent of eight pounds paid in advance. If we decide to stay on, it will be a yearly rental of twenty pounds paid at five pounds a quarter."

"That seems reasonable." Clem waited for Chris to say more.

Chris admitted his reservation. "It belongs to Billy O'Hara."

"Oh." Clem showed she understood Chris's reservations when she said, "He has done a great deal for you, Chris. Are you worried about what he might expect in return?"

"He has been very kind to me, Clem. And he is not a philanthropist."

"He is not a monster, either," Clem replied. "He is a hard man, darling, I know that. But he looks after his people, does he not? Feeds them well? Educates them? Does not allow anyone to hurt them? That is what you told me. It is a house, and he rents houses. Does it need to be more than that?"

All of that was true, but… "I owe him a favor. That's what he said, when he let us into Fortune's Fool to save you from the Brown brothers. He has told me a couple of times since then that the favor has been getting bigger."

"This won't be a favor, though," Clem insisted. "The house is empty, I take it."

At Chris's nod, she said, "Take me to see it, Chris. As far as Mr. O'Hara goes, we shall pay our rent and look after the house. We shall be good tenants. No one is doing anyone a favor."

Chris was by no means convinced, but only three days remained until the wedding, and he had seen nothing else that would do.

After he had taken her through the house, no choice remained. She loved it.

"I'll sign the lease," he agreed. "It has a bed, which I think must have been made in the room, for it would need to be chopped into pieces to go through the door. The same with the dining room table. Can we manage until after we are married?"

"We shall need beds for the servants, and cupboards for their belongings. In fact, we shall need servants! A cook, a scullery maid, a housemaid and a footman to start with, I think. Will you take me to an employment office tomorrow, Chris? I shall manage that side of it, if you can buy the furniture for their rooms. Also, a kitchen table. We shall manage with that much, I think, though we might be going out to shop the day after our wedding!"

Not the day after. Chris had borrowed a little hunting lodge from his cousin Harry Satterthwaite. It was only an hour from the outskirts of London heading south, and the kind of hunting it was used for, Chris gathered, might also go under the heading "adult games"—but Harry assured him it was an ideal spot for a new husband and wife to spend their first few days. The servants were discreet, and did not live in. The cook was excellent. The countryside was beautiful.

"We shall be going away for a few days after our wedding," Chris told his bride. "Would you prefer to spend our first night in our new home?"

"Perfect," said Clem. "Then we can decide on anything urgent and have it done while we are away."

Chris had to admit that he hoped she would have other things on her mind than housekeeping and home decoration on the morning after their wedding. They would see.

Chapter Fourteen

*I*T IS THE *morning of my wedding.* Clem stayed still under the blankets for a few moments longer, as her mind tried to grasp that enormous thought. Though she had pretended to Chris and to everyone else that she expected her wedding to go ahead, she had been certain Father would ruin it all, and announce he wanted her to marry someone else. Or that Chris would grow tired of dealing with Father and jilt her. Or that some other disaster would come between her and everything she wanted.

Yes. Things could still go wrong. But hope, only a tender flickering flame a few short weeks ago, was a raging fire, and would not be extinguished. Even the most alarming scenarios had no power to distress her, precisely because they were so alarming she could not believe in them.

A knock on the door heralded Martha, the maid, with a mug of hot chocolate and a beaming smile. They had had a serious talk, Clem and her maid. Martha would be moving with her to Primrose Square, having promised she would obey the person who paid her wages—Clem herself—and would not be bribed, threatened, or cajoled by anyone else.

"Oh, Miss Wright," said Martha. "Tonight, I will be addressing you as Mrs. Satterthwaite! I have the men coming in a few minutes with your bath water, Miss. We shall have to hurry. Lady

Fernvale is going to be here with the dressmaker in just forty-five minutes. I am so excited about seeing you in your gown, Miss Wright! It is going to be so beautiful."

Clem sipped her chocolate in her sitting room while the footmen marched into and out of her bedchamber with buckets of water until the hip bath was full. Once they were all gone, Martha helped Clem to disrobe and sink into the hot, scented water.

Bliss!

The wedding was at nine o'clock, since that was the only time available. Weddings had to be performed in the morning, before noon, and St George's had seven other weddings today.

That still gave Clem two and a bit more hours to prepare, but with Chris's godmother and the modiste due to arrive shortly, she could not linger in the bath. Besides, much as she tried to relax, her nerves were leaping. She was to be married today! It was really happening!

She had not quite finished washing when a knock on the door to her suite heralded the expected guests. Martha went through to let them into the sitting room while Clem began rinsing herself off.

"It is Lady Fernvale, the dressmaker and her assistant, and your toast, Miss Wright," Martha reported. "I have ordered tea for my lady, and told them you will be out shortly."

Dried and dressed in her chemise and a robe, Clem sat in her sitting room nibbling toast while the dressmaker, whose seamstresses must have worked day and night, showed her the gown.

She had been fitted into pieces of the gown, and on her last fitting, they had tried it on inside out, to ensure that the fit was perfect. She had not, therefore, seen the full thing. It was stunning.

Mindful of her soon-to-be husband's pocket, at least until they found out whether Father would keep his promises, she had chosen a color and style that could be worn for church services and special day-time occasions for the remainder of the Season. Indeed, the gown was of a classic cut and design that she could possibly wear for best for years to come.

Designed to suit her curves and her coloring, it was made from blue silk the color of her eyes—Chris had described them as the blue of the sky near the horizon on a bright summer day, and had declared that shade to be his new favorite color. The fabric was woven with a self-stripe in the same color, which shimmered into and out of view as the gown moved. The waist was high and the skirt cut so that the fabric clung to her waist and then curved out in a bell to skim her hips and swirl around her ankles, where a narrow ruffle in the same blue silk trimmed the hem without making Clem look shorter.

Her bodice and sleeves were the same silk, closely embroidered with flowers and embellished with crystal beads that sparkled in the light—impossible, Clem would have thought, in the time available, but the dressmaker had had a few yards of the fabric already-embroidered.

The scalloped neckline, low over the tops of her breasts, was made decent by a decorous scooped under-neckline in ivory silk, and trimmed with the same ivory lace that had been used on the cuffs of the short, puffed sleeves.

"It is a lovely gown, Clementine," Aunt Fern said, "and it will suit you beautifully."

Clem spoke directly to the dressmaker. "Thank you," she said. "It is even better than I believed possible."

"I believe it will fit, Miss Wright," said the dressmaker, "but we can make any last-minute adjustments in a trice."

Martha assisted with Clem's stays and petticoat, then the dressmaker and her seamstress lifted the gown over her head and settled it gently into place before fastening the back of the gown with five beautiful Dorset buttons made from rings and silk thread that matched the gown—the top one in cream and the other four in sky blue.

When they were done, she turned to examine her reflection

in the mirror, while the dressmaker and the seamstress fluttered around her, settling a seam, testing the fit of the waist, checking the length of the hem.

"That seems satisfactory," said the dressmaker with a decisive nod.

"It is wonderful," Clem corrected, "and it fits beautifully."

It had to come off, of course, so that Martha could dress Clem's hair, but first Clem gave a small bonus to the dressmaker and her assistant, and Martha showed them out. Their part in the day was done.

"You are going to be a beautiful bride, my dear," Aunt Fern assured Clem. Clem would be satisfied with attractive to Chris, but in this gown, she could almost believe Aunt Fern.

Martha took longer than usual to style Clem's hair. "You need something special for today," she said. She plaited and wove it, threading ribbon among the locks—sky blue and cream, with more of the crystal beads sparkling here and there. Clem could only catch glimpses, and she was not prepared for the full effect.

"Why, I look pretty," she discovered when her maid eventually allowed her to face the mirror.

"You *are* pretty, miss," Martha insisted.

"You are beautiful," said Aunt Fern, and Mrs. Bellowes arriving at that moment joined the chorus.

"You look lovely, Miss Wright."

Clem doubted Father would agree with them, but she rather thought Chris might.

Stockings and garters next, slippers that matched the gown, and ivory gloves.

The day was sunny, and too warm for her ivory pelisse. Clem sat to allow Martha to settle the blue and ivory confection of a bonnet onto her head. She then stood to view the finished effect in the mirror. *You do look pretty*, she thought. The gown would do very well.

"Father will be waiting," she said. "Let us go down."

Father stood when she entered the parlor, his eyes examining her from head to toe. "If your mother could see you now, Clementine," he said, and sighed. "You look a right treat, you do. Pretty as a picture. Well, Lady Fernvale, shall we be off to the church to see this girl married?" He chuckled. "St. George's, just as I planned!"

Clem followed them in something of a daze. She could not remember her father ever complimenting her appearance before. Or anything else about her, really. *Pretty as a picture.* Well!

⟫⟪

CHRIS HAD ASKED Harry Satterthwaite and Michael Thurgood to stand up with him. He hadn't expected Billy to attend, but there the man was, sitting on the groom's side of the church a few pews back from the front. Tiny was there, too, and at least a dozen of the other men—floor managers from each of the gambling dens, the man who operated the loan business, and managers of Billy's other shops.

The women, too, for Billy had women managing each of his brothels, as well as a laundry, a pawnbroker, two barefoot schools, and some of Billy's residential properties.

Chris had worked with them all, and was pleased to have them at his wedding, all dressed in their best clothes and looking as respectable as the other people in the pews on that side.

The others were strangers, but the resemblance of some of them to either Harry or Michael identified them. They were his Satterthwaite and Thurgood relatives, who had come to see him married. Chris was touched.

Would they take exception to the company in which they found themselves? If they did, no matter. He'd lived his life without them up until now, and it had been because of them that he did so. He could continue. Would Wright take exception to their presence? He would not arrive until Clem did. It was to be hoped that, by the time he realized that Chris's family had come out to support their relative, it would be too late to stop the wedding.

Those on the bride's side were mostly strangers, except for a few he'd met when in company with Wright. Business magnates and merchant nabobs, and the women with them presumably their wives and daughters.

Here came his godmother, and behind her Clem's maid, Martha, and the companion, Mrs. Bellowes. Aunt Fern strolled down the aisle to join those on the groom's side while Mrs. Bellowes settled on the bride's side. Martha took a seat at the back, with several other people Chris recognized from Wright's household.

And if Aunt Fern, Mrs. Bellowes, and Martha were here, then Clem must be close! Chris stood up straighter, his eyes on the door by which she would enter. His cravat suddenly felt tight. He didn't realize he was running his finger around his neck, trying to give himself room, until Michael Thurgood leaned over and told him, "You're messing up your cravat. Stop touching it."

And then suddenly the wait was over and Clem was walking toward him. Somewhere, music was playing. Presumably, Wright was escorting her. Chris saw only Clem. How lovely she was! What fools those men were who had called her plain.

His heart seemed to fill his chest, pressing his lungs so that his breath came short and caught in a suddenly dry throat. He loved Clementine Wright, and in a few minutes, she would be his wife, promised to him for a lifetime. Wright and the minister exchanged a few words, and Wright extended Clem's right hand to the minister who gave it to Chris.

Chris smiled into Clem's eyes, and she smiled back. That smile and her touch anchored him through the rest of the ceremony, when his joy made him feel so light that he thought he might float away. If Wright reacted to the presence of so many people on the groom's side of the church, Chris didn't see it.

He said his responses when prompted, trying to infuse his love, his certainty into his voice. He thrilled to hear the love in her voice and to see the happiness in her eyes when she spoke.

At last, it was time to encircle her finger with the ring he had designed and had made for her. For a moment, it caught on her knuckle, but he pushed firmly and it slid into place.

The minister prayed, asking for God's blessing on the marriage. He then took their right hands and indicated they should join hands.

"Those whom God hath joined together, let no man put asunder."

He then spoke to the congregation. But before he could finish explaining that the bride and groom had proclaimed their consent, made their vows and given and received a ring, there was a commotion—someone shouting from the back of the church. Grandfather, the swine.

"Stop the wedding. Stop this travesty. The boy is promised elsewhere!"

Harry touched Chris's arm. "I'll handle it. Carry on, Minister."

Clem started to turn, but Chris refused to give Grandfather even a look. "It is our wedding, Clem," he said. "Ignore him." And to the minister, he said, "My grandfather disapproves of my choice of bride, sir, as you can hear. But I am of age, and I have the permission of Clem's father and the blessings of my cousin and my uncle, both earls, who are respectively the heads of the Satterthwaite and the Thurgood families. Carry on with the wedding, please."

Reassured, the minister raised his voice to be heard over several voices shouting. "I pronounce that they are man and wife together, in the name of the Father, and of the Son, and of the Holy Ghost. Amen."

Next came a blessing, and during it, the altercation at the back of the church faded away. Grandfather was, presumably, being dragged off. And a good thing, too.

The minister carried on. A psalm, some further prayers, a short homily about the duties of marriage. Chris held Clem's hand. His heart was soaring, and only the occasional word made it through his triumphant joy. "Love your wife," the minister said. "Honor her." And Chris did and would. As long as they both should live. And may it be long indeed.

MR. SATTERTHWAITE SENIOR'S interruption of the wedding had had a beneficial effect, Clem discovered after they had made their way down the aisle to stand in the foyer of the church receiving the congratulations of those who had witnessed the wedding.

Father had joined the Earl of Halton in ejecting the noisy intruder, and the two of them had adopted the camaraderie of a successful sortie party. And so, since Father had already accepted Lady Fernvale, and now Lord Halton, he did not make a fuss about Lord Crosby.

Though he did tug on Chris's arm and say, "Did you invite all this lot? When did you get to know them?"

"I'm as surprised as you are," Chris told him. "The last time I saw the two earls was the evening they cut me in front of everybody."

Wright harrumphed and then invited all present back to his townhouse.

Clem cast a worried glance at Aunt Fern, who had worked with Mrs. Bellowes to organize the wedding feast. But that fine lady merely smiled and nodded.

"I imagine she has invited them all already, and planned for them," Chris murmured to her, with that uncanny ability he had to read her mind.

"Your carriage is ready, Mr. and Mrs. Satterthwaite," said Michael Thurgood, and the minister was growing anxious as the guests began to arrive for the next wedding, so Clem let Chris escort her away.

Perhaps at the wedding breakfast she would find out what

happened to Mr. Satterthwaite senior! He was gone, and there was no sign he had ever been there.

They rode to Father's townhouse in an open carriage, escorted by the younger men of the congregation on horseback, who introduced themselves to Chris and Clem, and to one another, as they rode.

There were half a dozen Satterthwaites, several Thurgoods, some other cousins with different surnames, and a smattering of wealthy merchants' sons, all of them relaxed and cheerful in one another's company.

Did men find it easier to ignore the bounds of class? Or was it the wedding that had them so egalitarian?

When they arrived at Father's townhouse, Clem met the senior members of the various families, and their wives and daughters. She was a little disappointed that Ramping Billy and his people did not arrive at the wedding breakfast, but perhaps they were correct to stay away.

She watched in awe as Aunt Fern encouraged the two groups to blend, recommending a young aristocrat to a blushing merchant's daughter as a dance partner, encouraging two grandmothers who would normally never have encountered one another to compare stories of their cherished grandchildren, and setting off a rousing debate on the corn laws among the older gentlemen.

But the debt collector-come-gambling den and brothel owner and his minions might have been beyond even Aunt Fern's powers to spread social harmony.

The breakfast had been laid out buffet-style on long tables, solving the problem of seating more than sixty people, which would have challenged even the generous space made by opening the doors between the dining room and the adjoining parlor.

Aunt Fern had organized little groups of seating in those rooms, the large drawing room, and the spacious hall that connected the two, each group with tables on which people could place their food and drink.

In addition, she had augmented Father's footmen from her own staff, and they circulated through the rooms, some with trays of food, and others with drinks.

"Did you know that lot were coming?" Father demanded, gesturing towards Chris's relatives with his chin. Chris had left Clem's side because his uncle had asked for a moment of his time.

Father was trying to glare, but his chest had the proud puff of a pigeon. He had never hosted such a company under his roof, and he was thrilled.

"No, Father," Clem was able to tell him. "Aunt Fern might have known, but I didn't, and neither did Chris. He is pleased, though, especially after the fuss his grandfather made at the wedding. Having his family acknowledge our wedding has made him very happy."

She glanced at Father's chief rival, who was the nearest person he had as a friend. "I do not believe I have ever seen Mr. Morton so flummoxed. He has long said you were foolish to try to marry me into the aristocracy, and he certainly never expected to meet two earls under your roof."

Father chuckled. *He actually chuckled!* "That he didn't, Clementine. That he didn't. Well, it is done now, and the boy is signed up to a contract. And after all, how much trouble can they cause? This could all work out for the best." He wandered off toward Mr. Morton, undoubtedly going to see if a little salt could be applied to the man's wounded pride. "Yes," he was muttering as he went, "this is excellent."

Chris had been talking to his uncle while Clem was occupied with her father, but he joined her to say, "There really is an estate, my love. My cousin Lord Crosby wants to meet with us to tell us all about it. I told him we shall be away for one week, and that we'll come to see him as soon as we are back in London." He examined her with a slight frown. "Have you had anything to eat or drink, darling?"

"I have been too busy talking," Clem admitted.

Chris took a drink from one passing footman and beckoned

to another who carried a tray of food. "Here," he said. "I don't know how long we are supposed to stay, or what you had for breakfast, but these will help."

"These" were little savories—small pastry parcels with tasty fillings. They were the only food Clem had had since a slice of toast early that morning, and she washed it down with a mouthful of wine, before one of Father's business rivals and his wife came to present their good wishes.

I hope we will be able to leave soon. As the thought crossed her mind, it suddenly occurred to her that she was actually married. To Chris. And presumably tonight he would want to go to bed with her. To do what married couples do. And wicked couples who were not married to one another, if that was the same thing. Logic suggested it must be.

Clem only knew what she had overheard of the conversations of servants, full of words she only half-understood and copious giggling, and short on detail.

She should have asked Aunt Fern. She should have asked Martha, even! She had been too embarrassed and now it was too late.

Another footman passed with a tray, and Clem finished her drink and took another.

✦ ✦ ✦

Chapter Fifteen

CHRIS'S BRIEF CONVERSATIONS with Lord Crosby, his uncle, and the Earl of Halton, his father's cousin, confirmed what Michael and Harry had told him. They would have accepted him at any time, though both remained adamantly set against his grandfather. Something with which Chris was in agreement.

There'd be time enough to think about what the family reunion meant for him—for him and Clem, as a couple.

Not today, though. Clem was his wife, and their life together had begun. Meeting the relatives who should never have been strangers was not his focus. Today, the family reunion was just background, a minor theme in the soaring orchestral crescendo that was his wedding to Clem.

Most of the people at his wedding feast were strangers, and they all wanted to meet him and Clem, so it was at least two hours before Aunt Fern took pity on them and told them Chris's carriage was being brought around to the front door.

"Let's go home," he said to Clem.

They didn't get out without a self-congratulatory speech from Wright, to which Chris replied with a speech praising his bride and thanking his groomsmen. Harry proposed a toast to the bride and groom, but at last Chris was able to escort his wife to the front steps, and assist her into their waiting carriage.

The younger people, who had accompanied them downstairs, cheered when he kissed her hand and then climbed in behind her.

And then, they were away.

It was only a short drive to the house they had rented. Chris was mindful that what was to come was new to Clem. Thanks to the efforts of Aunt Fern, their embraces so far had been nearly chaste—certainly far more chaste than Chris would have preferred.

Even so, he could control the urge to leap on her as soon as the carriage door was shut. He would have to, for he would not want to frighten her, nor did he want her to be embarrassed in front of her new servants when they arrived at their new house looking as if he had tumbled her in the carriage.

Instead, he took the seat beside her, took her gloved hand in his, and lost himself in thinking about the bedding to come. Not for the first time, he wondered what she had been told.

She was curious, he knew that. And she listened to the servants, so she knew a little. Had anyone thought to explain the details? Was she frightened? She didn't appear nervous, though. Was she glaring at him?

"Is something wrong, my love?"

Clem blushed. "I was just thinking…"

She broke off, and Chris made what he hoped was an encouraging sound.

"Martha said you would want to kiss me as soon as we were alone, and—" her blush deepened—"other things."

"Other things?" Chris was intrigued to know exactly what the knowledgeable maid may have disclosed.

"You know, Chris. Embraces and such." She leaned closer to him and hushed her voice, as if afraid that the driver might hear. "Touching me with your hands. In… places. She said men like it?" Clem sounded uncertain.

"This man likes it," Chris assured her. "Very much, when it is my hands and your body. And I hope you will like touching me, too. I did not want to start something in the carriage that would leave you rumpled and uncomfortable when you arrived at our house, for if I once start, beloved, I am not certain how much control I will have. I want you. Very much."

"Oh." Clem thought about that. "I'm not sure exactly what 'want' means, but…Will I like it, Chris?"

"You will like it very much," he assured her. He would make certain of that. "In fact, you can tell me what you like most about it, and I will do more of that, and if there happens to be anything you don't like, tell me, and I won't do it. But not here in the carriage. Not for your first time."

"Oh," she said, her face clearing by the moment, and her second, "Oh," sounded much more cheerful. "Not until this evening, then."

"Here we are," Chris commented, as they drew up at their own front steps. *This evening?* He could wait until this evening if she insisted, but he hoped she didn't.

By the time he had helped her from the carriage, the front door was open and the servants were lined up in the little entry hall, ready to greet their new employers.

Clem went down the line, greeting the cook-housekeeper, the parlor maid, the kitchen maid, the footman (who was going to provide any valet services that Chris needed), and the boot boy, and presenting them all to their new master. She had met them all when she interviewed them for their positions, and from what Chris could see, she had done well.

Martha was there, too. Chris greeted her. He'd be keeping an eye on this one. When Clem had said she planned to keep the maid, Chris had questioned her choice. "What if her loyalties are still with your father?" he asked.

"That could be true of anyone we employ," Clem said. "Since she and I made our bargain, she has been an excellent maid— loyal, as far as I know, and competent. She knows how I like things done. I'd like to keep her, Chris."

She was Clem's maid, so it was over to her. And Clem was

right, of course. Any of the servants could be reporting to Wright, to Billy O'Hara, even to Chris's grandfather. Time would tell, Chris supposed. He'd be careful not to leave anything that should be confidential where one of the servants could see it.

Meanwhile, he had a wife to kiss, and "embraces and stuff." She had seemed disappointed that he had not started in the carriage, and he hated disappointing his wife.

Clem was dismissing the staff. How did one ask a lady if they were open to the idea of moving the consummation from the evening program to the afternoon? Especially since Martha and the footman had not left with the rest.

"Clem, would you like Martha to help you into something more comfortable?" he asked.

"I am quite com… Oh. Now? You mean this afternoon?" Fortunately for Chris, she sounded more intrigued than scandalized.

"Yes, why not?" *Please, Clem. Please.*

Martha gave him an approving nod, and Clem smiled. "Yes. Martha, come along," she said. "Give me half an hour, Chris."

"Half an hour," he agreed, with an internal sigh. He used the time to order a tray of tea from the kitchen to be sent up immediately, and another with food and more tea in three hours.

Then he went up to the bed chamber they had agreed would be his dressing room—they planned to sleep in the same bed. He stripped out of his wedding finery, washed thoroughly, and put on a banyan—one that he'd bought only that week, since the robe he'd had for the past ten years was not fit for other people to see.

Ready, ready, more than ready he knocked on the door to their shared bed chamber and went inside.

CLEM HAD EXPECTED Martha to be full of last-minute advice, but all she had to say was, "I reckon Mr. Satterthwaite knows what he's about, Miss. Ma'am, I mean. Just trust him, I say. If he's the man I think he is, he'll make sure you enjoy it."

"I've heard it hurts," Clem disclosed. Several of the married women at the wedding breakfast had been keen to share their own opinions with the bride. They had left her no wiser, since none of them had been specific. Furthermore, their views on the matter, so presumably their experiences, varied widely. At one extreme was the matron who advised her to lie still and think about something pleasant. At the other was the young wife who blushed vividly while confiding that her husband was lusty and that she loved it.

Martha shrugged. "Maybe a little sort of a pinch-like pain the first time? You know he has to put his thing inside you, right? When you swive? Once you're used to it, it won't hurt at all."

His thing? What thing? And *inside* her? She supposed something had to go inside her, because after all, "swiving"—as Martha called it—was how a baby would get there, but Clem wasn't at all sure how swiving worked, or whether she wanted to find out. She supposed it was too late to worry now. She consoled herself that Chris's kisses felt wonderful, and that Martha, at least, and possibly her former maid, Amanda Brown, had enjoyed the experience.

And even the "lie still and think of something pleasant" matron did not appear to be damaged in any way.

A knock on the door was followed directly by Chris. Martha bobbed him a curtsey and left. Clem stared at him, hoping her trepidation didn't show. "The tea tray arrived. Would you like a cup?"

Chris seemed to be examining her. "Shall I pour you a port or a sherry, beloved? You seem anxious. A drink might help."

"Is it that bad?" Clem blurted. "Do I need to be drunk to bear it?"

In two swift steps he was sitting on the sofa at her side, his arms around her. "What have people been telling you, you poor darling? It isn't bad at all. In fact, I mean to make certain you find it wonderful. And, as I promised, if I do anything at all that you don't like, you need only say." He punctuated his sentences with kisses, and Clem could feel some of her worries melt away.

"What do you need to know to feel more confident?" Chris asked.

"What do you put inside me, and where does it go?" Clem demanded. "Is it your tongue, Chris? Because you have done that already, and I liked it. Am I with child now?"

Chris's eyes widened. "No, kissing isn't how we will make a baby," he said. His frown was thoughtful. "Have you never seen one of those naked statues? People sometimes have them in their gardens."

Clem shook her head.

"Or a dog or a stallion that is ready to mate?"

"Not that I know." It was annoying that she was so ignorant. As if the whole world knew a secret and she was the only one left out. "Can't you just tell me, Chris?"

"Give me your hand," Chris said, and when she did, he placed it on his groin. He had something long and hard—a rod or a cylinder—under his banyan.

"What is that," she asked. "Something in your pocket?"

"It is part of me," he said. "Put your hand around it, Clem. Feel it."

She gripped it, and Chris shuddered. She snatched her hand back. "Did I hurt you?"

He shook his head. "Not hurt, no. It's just—Darling, when a man wants to be with a woman the way I want to be with you, that part of him grows hard, ready to enter her. When you touch it, it feels…" He shook his head as if he was lost for words, and settled for, "Amazing."

"May I see?" Clem asked.

He showed her, untying the sash of his banyan and folding it back.

She frowned at the strange appendage. "I don't understand.

Where does it go?"

"There is a part of you that it is made to fit," he assured her. Let me show you. I'll just touch you with my hands, Clem, and won't do more unless you wish it."

"Kiss me some more first," she said, bargaining for time. She was not afraid of kissing. She was, however, afraid of this mysterious part of him that was, supposedly, made to fit somewhere on her body. She'd never seen the like.

Fortunately, Chris did better than just kissing her. He encouraged her to kiss him back until she forgot to be nervous. He taught her how to use her lips and her tongue and to share an intimacy with her mouth that she'd never imagined. Nor had she thought it possible that doing so would cause a heat to rise within her and kindle glorious feelings in parts of her body she'd mostly ignored until this very moment.

And then he was touching those parts, murmuring praise because she was unaccountable wet down there, and apparently that was a good thing. When he introduced first one finger and then another inside her, they slid easily in the moisture. "This is where we shall join, beloved," he told her, and she wondered if that part of him truly would fit.

But there was no room in her for fear, for her new husband filled her senses. With skilled fingers and mouth, with murmured words of love and praise, he introduced her to the pleasures of which her body was capable.

When at last he joined with her, placing that part of him at the entrance his fingers had so recently breeched, she was more than ready—and he was right. He and she were made to fit together. The pinch that Martha had predicted was so mild and over so quickly, she barely catalogued the moment before it was swept away by the rhythm they established between them.

It was the same rhythm he had been setting with his lips and fingers, but now it was all consuming, driven by the pumping of his hips and hers, and building her pleasure higher and higher until she screamed his name, desperate for…something.

"Let go, my love," he murmured. "That's it. Let your thoughts go and feel. *Be* what you feel."

Was it fireworks, or falling off a cliff, or a crescendo of music, or a combination of all of those? She did not have the words for the peak of sensation that left her floating, boneless, and satiated.

As she stilled, Chris pumped twice more, then stiffened above her. She opened the eyes she did not remember closing, and saw his eyes screwed shut, his mouth twisting with effort as she felt a warm gush deep within. Had she not just been through the same experience, she would have thought he was in pain. And indeed, the pleasure was so intense that the need for it to culminate was a kind of pain.

He slumped upon her, then after a moment apologized, and moved to roll the pair of them onto their sides, still joined.

"I like it," she protested. "I like your weight."

He smiled sleepily, and placed a sweet, friendly kiss on the nearest corner of her lips. "I hope you liked what we just did."

"You know I did," she said. "When can we do it again?"

Chapter Sixteen

T HEY RETURNED RELUCTANTLY from Harry's hunting lodge at the end of the week. Chris had never known such a week. He had never spent so much time with another human being, let alone with a lover.

They had talked, they had read together, they had walked in the country lanes, they had played card games and chess, they had tried to identify plants and wildlife—the country offered varieties of both that were never seen in London. And they had spent hours in bed, Chris teaching Clem the ways of passion, and discovering new pleasures himself as he did so.

For Chris, swiving had always been recreational. He had always thought it important to consider the pleasure of his bed partner, and he did, but the goal—the reward, as it were—was his own release.

Bedding his wife—his love, his partner for a lifetime—was very different. The goal was no longer pleasure, though pleasure there was, more than he had ever known for him, and he could not doubt hers, either.

Pleasure was important. Chris had fended off advances from several married women in his former neighborhood, all of whom justified their straying with disparaging remarks about their marital experiences. He was certain that the very least he owed his wife was his full attention to her needs in passion. But physical intimacy with her was more than mutual pleasuring. It was respect. It was love. It was union.

As the minister had said in the church, they had become one. A married couple. For as long as they lived, she would be his only lover, and he hers. What happened between them in bed was both a celebration and a reflection of what they were becoming together.

After the idyll of the last week, it was down to earth with a bump, when they walked in the door of their townhouse and were presented with the mail that had arrived for them while they were away.

Chris glanced at his three, ascertaining that they were from his mother's brother Lord Crosby, Wright, and his grandfather.

He opened his grandfather's letter first. It was a demand for compensation, since by marrying Clem, Chris had apparently lost his grandfather an extortionate amount of money.

Chris wouldn't even bother replying. With any luck, the other party in the marriage agreement Chris hadn't signed would run Grandfather out of town.

Lord Crosby's letter was simply a reminder to Chris to make an appointment so that they could arrange the transfer of authority for Chris's holdings from Lord Crosby, as trustee, to Chris. Holdings? That sounded as if there was more than the estate.

He expected the letter from Wright to be another irritation—annoying if not as infuriating as the one from his grandfather. But it was simple and matter-of-fact.

"Christopher.

> *You may have tomorrow to settle into your new townhouse.*
> *I will expect you at ten o'clock on the following day, ready*
to start work.

Wright."

"Here," he said to Clem, handing her all three letters. "Grandfather is up to his usual tricks and can be ignored, Lord Crosby wants me to make an appointment to talk about giving me my inheritance, and your father expects me at work the day after tomorrow."

"Mine are mostly invitations," said Clem. "Lady Halton and Lady Crosby have both arranged gatherings of the ladies of their families, and Aunt Fern wants to take me visiting."

She did not sound as if she thought that was a good thing. "You do not have to go if you don't want to," Chris pointed out.

Clem, though, thought she should put in the effort. "They are family, Chris. And they are trying to be kind."

"But you will have time to come with me to meet Lord Crosby?" Chris asked, and so it was with Clem at his side that he entered the Thurgood London townhouse the following day.

"How charming to see you, Mrs. Satterthwaite," said Lord Crosby. "I am sure my wife is at home, and some of my daughters. Shall I ask a footman to conduct you to see them?"

"I'd like Clem to stay for our meeting, my lord," said Chris. "She has an excellent business brain, and I value her input, especially on matters that affect us both."

Lord Crosby was taken aback, but too polite to say more than, "Oh, capital," sounding as if it was anything but. "Please take a seat, then, Mrs. Satterthwaite. I shall send for tea."

"Please," Clem said, "Call me Clem, or Clementine, if you prefer."

While they waited for tea, Lord Crosby asked a couple of polite questions. How was their new townhouse? Had she received an invitation from his wife, who had said she would write?

"Good, good," he said, vaguely, when Clem had replied that the house would be very comfortable once they had it arranged to her liking, and yes, she had replied to the invitation and was looking forward to the gathering.

Since neither of them seemed to be able to maintain a conversation, Chris decided he had better take a hand. Some paintings of birds on the wall gave him an idea.

"We spent the week at my cousin Harry's hunting lodge, my lord, as you may know. Neither Clem nor I have spent much time in the country—indeed, London has been home to both of us for much of our lives. Can you tell me, what is the bird that makes this sound?" He whistled one of the bird calls that had intrigued and mystified him and Clem during their walks.

It was the right question. Lord Crosby talked about birds until the tea tray arrived, while Clem poured the tea, and for at least ten minutes after that, with only the occasional question from Chris or Clem to keep him going.

He explained the habitats, the eating habits, and the differences between the great tit, the Eurasian blue tit, the coal tit, the long-tailed tit, and the yellow-breasted tit. He imitated each of their calls, and then did the same for a great array of finches.

He had begun on the thrushes when, at last, he pulled himself up. "My dear Lady Crosby would say I have forgotten myself, young people. I do love my birds, but I fear I have blathered on and on."

"I was fascinated," said Clem. "Chris and I argued for days about which bird produced the sound we heard so often during our stay, but we could never catch one singing where we could see it to identify it. I would not have guessed it was a thrush. They seem such modest birds."

"They are… But there. I must not allow myself to continue, Clementine. If you are truly interested, my dear, you and Christopher must visit us at Barthornton in the summer, and I shall take you out and show you as many birds as I can."

Clem's face lit up. Chris guessed that a visit to Barthornton—was it a village or the name of a house?—was now part of their summer plans.

"I would like that," she said.

"But I invited you here, Christopher, to tell you about your inheritance from my aunt, your mother's mother. Michael mentioned the estate, I know. She was the last of her family, and the lands were not entailed, so though the title reverted to the crown, your grandmother inherited the estate just a few weeks after your mother died. It has been doing very well, and I have been investing the surplus income in your name for sixteen years. You are a wealthy young man."

Chris tried not to let his jaw hit the floor. An inheritance, maybe. But wealth? He hadn't expected it.

Had Billy? Is this why he'd assisted Chris all these years, and especially now?

Lord Crosby picked up some papers from the table beside him, shuffled them, and handed the top sheet to Clem. "There, my dear. Show that to your husband," he said, sounding a little pleased and perhaps even amused.

"That" was a list of investments and their current value, with a total that made Clem blink and Chris's heart skip a beat.

"Maidenstone Court," the earl said next, handing over another sheet. It gave a description of the property—the house, the park, the woods, the home farm, the tenant farms, the acreage of each, the cottages, and shops in the village that the owner of the Court—that is to say, Chris—also owned.

"My goodness," said Clem. She turned to Chris, her eyes wide as if asking if he'd been aware.

"I had no idea," he said on an exhale. And then, "Where is Maidenstone Court?" The name of the village—Maidencraig Frampton—meant nothing to him.

"Three hours north-west of London," said Lord Crosby. "The home farm is currently rented out. The Court and its dower house have been rented, but the tenants did not renew their lease this year. I'd heard your grandfather had returned, and I hoped you were with him, so I did not look for new tenants."

They talked some more, since Chris and Clem both had further questions, and then Lord Crosby insisted on sending for Lady Crosby so she could welcome the newlyweds back to London. It was quite two hours after they arrived before they found themselves back out on the street again, Clem carrying a book of beautifully rendered bird paintings by an artist and ornithologist named Bewick that Lord Crosby had insisted on loaning to her.

"Clem," said Chris, "we are rich." He wanted to hear the words said out loud. He was not at all certain he believed them, but if Clem agreed, perhaps they would be true.

"We are," Clem said. "If Father becomes a nuisance, we can tell him we do not need him. And even better, Chris. Just think. We were hoping to spend the house money Father promised on a house for our orphan school, and now we have a house. Only three hours away from London. And it is all ours!"

THE TRIP TO see Maidenstone Court had to wait until Chris had put in the three days that he had promised to Father. Three days a week. "Do you have to go?" Clem asked. "We do not need the salary any more, and if Father cuts us off, we can manage without him."

"I gave my word," Chris said, and that was that. Clem valued Chris's integrity. Truly she did. But she could not help but feel that Father did not deserve it.

When she said that to Chris, he smiled and said, "I expect he shall cut us off after he finds out about our inheritance, and if not then, after I tell him about our plans for the school. Meanwhile, I shall keep my word. I'm sorry if that does not please you."

Clem sighed. "It pleases me that you are so reliable, Chris. I am just peeved that we have to wait to see the house. I do hope it is suitable for a school!"

"It must be," Chris said. "The most recent tenant was a school for girls. It is in the folder of records Lord Crosby gave me."

That made Clem even more anxious to view the property. However, she busied herself with ordering further furnishings for the townhouse and meeting with the Satterthwaite and Thurgood ladies.

At last, the day came for their excursion to Maidencraig Frampton and their estate. Chris had hired a chaise with a post rider to take them to the manor of Maidenstone Court and back to London, so there was neither room nor need for Martha or any of the other servants to come with them.

Three hours proved to be a generous estimate, even with the brief stop halfway to change the horses. They passed through Maidencraig Frampton and stopped at the bailiff's house, just before the iron gates to the carriage drive that led to the Court.

Chris had written letting the man know the probable time of their visit, and he must have been watching for them, for he opened his front door to greet them as they walked up the path between lush beds of flowers. He was a short, wiry man in a comfortable coat and moleskins, and with a loosely-tied kerchief at his neck.

Next to him, Chris, who had dressed more casually than usual, looked the picture of sartorial elegance.

"Mr. and Mrs. Satterthwaite, I presume," the man said. "I'm Wilson."

He stepped out of the way and waved them into a delightful little entry hall.

"Mr. Wilson, I'm Chris Satterthwaite and this lovely woman is, indeed, my wife." Chris and Wilson shook hands, and Wilson bowed to Clem with a smile that seemed comfortable on his face, as if he smiled often.

"I am very pleased you have come into your own, Mr. Satterthwaite," he said. "I have done my best, but a property only truly thrives when it is loved by its owner."

My! That was something of a scold, and they were only just in the door.

"My wife and I discovered four days ago that we own Maidenstone Court and the surrounding land," Chris explained. "I had a commitment in Town, but we are very excited to see the house, and anything else you have time to show us. As I said in my letter, it will be a short visit today, just so that we can form an impression and begin to make some decisions."

Wilson frowned. "If you are considering sale…" He shook his head as if reminding himself it was none of his affair or opinion and then declared, "It is a good property. You should find a buyer."

"At this stage, our hope is that it will be suitable as our main home, but we have not yet seen it."

Wilson quirked a one-sided smile that acknowledged Chris's gentle nudge. "Right. I'd better show you around then. Mrs. Satterthwaite, would you like a cup of tea first? I can tell you that there will be one for you up at the house. I told Mrs. Patterson, the housekeeper, to have sandwiches and the like ready for you. I know you must have left London early."

"Then let us wait until we arrive at the house, Mr. Wilson," Clem said. "Is it far? Could we send the chaise on and walk?"

With a brief pause to peer at her feet, which were clad in sensible country shoes, Wilson acknowledged that it was five minutes or perhaps a bit more by the path through the woods, so he fetched his cap from a peg in the front hall and showed them out. Chris went for a word with the post rider, and as the chaise drove off, Wilson led them around the side of the house on a flagstone path.

It was, in fact, a darling cottage, with white-plastered walls, small casement windows, and a thatched roof. The garden rioted with color and produce on all sides. Wilson opened a gate into the Court's park, but Clem could see around the corner of the house into an equally lush back garden, with a row of utility sheds along the side of a neatly shingled courtyard, and vegetable gardens all around.

If Wilson cared for the estate as well as he cared for his cottage, the place had been in good hands.

Walking at a brisk pace, they covered the distance in no more than five minutes. For most of the distance, the Court was hidden by trees. Clem's first glimpse was of the rooftops and chimneys over the top of a series of garden hedges and walls, and it was only toward the end of the walk that they came through a gate to see the house before them.

It slept in the sunlight—a long house in yellow and orange brick, three stories tall, with mullioned windows, crow-stepped gables, and tall chimneys that lifted high above the tiled roof.

"This is the east aspect," Wilson said. "The carriage drive leads in a big semi-circle to the main entrance on the west, but we'll go in through the garden doors." He stopped under the shade of a tree and took off his cap, which he turned around and around in his hands. Clem thought he was giving them time to take in the splendor of the house, but Chris must have noticed something she didn't.

"Is there a problem, Wilson?"

Wilson grimaced. "You know it has been a school, sir. Right?" When I went through after they moved out—not all of their changes were authorized, sir, and there's damage. Fixable, but I don't want Mrs. Satterthwaite to expect… the house is not what it should be, sir, and that's a fact."

"Got that, Mrs. Satterthwaite?" Chris said. "You can have all the fun of decorating, my love. Lead on, Wilson."

The place was shabby, but Clem could see how wonderful it must have been—and would be again, with some repairs and a great deal of plaster, paint, polish, and other redecoration. Furnishing, too, though when she said that aloud, Wilson mentioned that much of the good furniture had been banished to the stable loft when the school moved in.

"They left all their furniture," Wilson said, his voice dripping with disgust. "Cheap beds and cabinets in the bedchambers, and kitchen tables in the dining room."

Chris and Clem exchanged delighted glances and proceeded to explore the house from attics to cellars.

It was, perforce, a quick tour. They would have to come back. But they had seen enough to know the plan was not just feasible but already half-accomplished!

CLEM WAS EXCITED about the school. She had never thought a life of leisure and self-indulgence would be a life worth living, but had also not thought beyond a husband and family, preferably somewhere in the country. Her happiest memories were of her early childhood, when her mother was still alive and they lived on the outskirts of a village within an easy ride of Father's office in Sheffield. Ma had taught at the local dame school, and Clem had loved going to school with her, and having other children with whom to learn and play.

To work in harness with Chris creating opportunities for young boys like those she'd seen sweeping street corners or going up chimneys? She could not imagine anything more satisfying.

She and Chris spent hours at a time discussing the project and making plans. Wilson had been told about the school, though somewhat gingerly, given his disgust at the condition the previous tenant had left the place in.

After asking a lot of questions and making many suggestions, he had unearthed a floor plan that was somewhat out of date. It was good enough to form a basis for the new plan Clem was drawing to figure out classrooms, recreation areas, staff accommodation and bedrooms for the boys.

They had given up on the idea of the dower house, as it was small and cramped, and needed a major renovation, but they were setting aside one wing of the house for themselves. With a new kitchen built on to one side of the basement floor, it would provide completely separate accommodations from the main house.

Wilson had found them some builders who were doing the repairs and alterations, and Clem thoroughly enjoyed making up panels for each room with samples of fabric, paint, and wallpaper. She had more time than Chris, since he was working long hours on the three days a week he worked for her father.

Both the earls, Crosby and Halton, had been scandalized that Chris proposed to keep working for a living, even though he now had land and—as it turned out—investments to give him an adequate income for a modest lifestyle.

"But Chris," Lady Halton had said, somewhat plaintively. "Gentlemen do not work, dear."

"It seems to me, my lady, that his lordship my cousin works extremely hard—at his Parliamentary duties and running his estates," Chris had pointed out.

"True, by Gum," said the earl, much struck by the argument.

"I am learning the enterprises that will be my father-in-law's legacy to my son," Chris explained. "It is only proper that I be able to protect and guide my child."

"Well, yes," the countess conceded, "but Chris, dear, do you have to let the man pay you?"

The earl changed sides again. "That's true, too. Chris, a gentleman works for his estate or for his family's future, but he is not paid for it. Just tell Wright you refuse his salary, and all shall be well."

Chris shook his head. "No, my lord. I am earning the salary, and I will take it. After all, what difference will it make to Society? They are not to know whether I am receiving a salary or not. I am certainly not going to tell them."

The countess brightened. "That is true," she said. "I can let one or two people know, as a confidence, that you are being trained by your father-in-law so you can act as proxy for your son when he inherits. No one needs to know that you are taking a salary." She rubbed her hands together, and her smile lit up the room. "Oh, Chris, what fun it will be when your son is on the Marriage Market. Excellent bloodlines on his father's side and all that lovely money."

Chris thought of pointing out that Clem might have only daughters, but the countess was lost in a blissful dream. Perhaps she would have forgotten before the as-yet-unborn, and possibly-not-yet-conceived, son was twenty-one. And if not, Chris had time to come up with some defenses for the poor lad.

That was just one conversation of many about how Chris should adjust to meet the expectations of a bunch of people he didn't know and didn't care to know. People who thought he should be like the lazy self-indulgent dilettantes he had watched from the owner's balcony in Fortune's Fool. *Not a chance.*

To do them credit, though, the Satterthwaites, the Thurgoods, and Wright had closed rank over Grandfather's ridiculous claims. When his accomplice took a case of breach of promise before the courts, all three gave witness that Chris had been courting Clem the entire time Grandfather claimed he'd been making promises to the other lady's father, and between them, they were able to account for Chris's time and cast doubt on the lies from the other side. The case was dismissed. Grandfather disappeared. Whether he was still in England or not, Chris neither knew nor cared.

Chapter Seventeen

WHEN CLEM'S AND Chris's portion of the manor was ready, they moved in, and after that, divided their time between their London townhouse and Maidenstone Court.

When he was in London, Chris spent most of his days at Wright's offices, but he also found time to attempt to persuade his relatives and Billy to support the school.

The Earl of Crosby was cautiously in favor. "It is an appropriate activity for a gentleman," he said. "And the house has not been lived in by family for a long time. However, you will want to be careful that it does not become a Charybdis, sucking down your income, Christopher."

"We hope to make it self-sustaining, sir, with a combination of sponsored students, charity students, and paying students."

Billy O'Hara pointed out the flaw in that plan. "You'll not be able to sell the aristocracy on the idea of educating their sons with street rats. Nor the middle sort, either, probably." His frown was a thoughtful one, so Chris waited to see where his thoughts took him.

"I'll pay your fees for six lads," he declared.

Wright was not so supportive. "You'll not be spending my hard-earned brass on a swarm of gallows bait, boy," he declared. "They are scum, and they will always be scum, and that's that."

"No," Chris said. Meeting Wright's anger with anger never worked, but the man did not know how to counter calm determination. "I shall be spending some of the income from my estate, and money from patrons, on giving boys with promise a chance for a future. Boys like me, sir.

"You're wasting your time," his father-in-law insisted.

Lord Halton was of the same mind. "Your pupils will murder you in your beds," he warned, which was something of a startling prognostication.

Chris had no fear of that happening. His first pupils were going to be the children that Billy had already civilized. He would certainly need to be careful with others. He knew, none better, about the savage anger that burned in the breast of the neglected and abused child. They might seem—they were—too cowed to show it. But as soon as they felt safe, the anger would burst out, often in ways dangerous to the child and those around him.

Prospective pupils would need to be carefully vetted, and so would the teachers and other staff. They would not only need to offer a high standard of education, but also understand and have sympathy for the pupils, whatever their background.

He wanted people who genuinely believed in the mission of the school. People who believed his boys were nothing but "gallows bait" would not be allowed near them.

The first step was to choose the two people whose personalities—so everyone advised him—would set the tone for the school: the head teacher, who would set the curriculum, lead the teaching staff, and teach some subjects, and the matron, who would care for the boys' physical and emotional needs. None of those he interviewed proved to be suitable. In the end, it was, to his surprise, Lord Halton who found his head teacher.

Andrew Partridge was perfect. He had been a tutor to the three sons of an earl, a friend of Halton's. Before that, he had taught at a prestigious boys' school. He declared himself intrigued by Chris's vision for the school, and was not at all put off to discover that his first six pupils were ex-street children who were being sponsored by a gambling den operator.

His references were sterling, if one ignored the school's testimonial, in which there was clear disapproval of Patridge's preference for non-physical forms of discipline. There was also a veiled remark about a lack of respect for the school's tradition.

"What about the school's tradition did you find objectional?" Chris asked the man.

Partridge showed no hesitation in answering. "I should explain that, when each boy started, they were given a senior pupil as a mentor. A good idea, and I did not have an issue with the junior undertaking chores for the older boy. If the older boy was of good character, the system worked well. If the older boy was a tyrant, a dictator, or a bully, the junior boy had no recourse. As a teacher, I was not meant to interfere. Any brutality was excused in the name of 'toughening up' the younger lad."

He sighed. "The headmaster and I agreed that I was not a fit for the school, and we came to a parting of the ways. My next employer's middle son told his father that I had stood up for him, and he removed all three boys from the school and hired me as their tutor."

"How would you discipline a bully?" Chris wondered.

"Not by being a bigger bully," Partridge retorted. "Chores often work. Mucking out the stables. Peeling vegetables. Rewards for good behavior can be effective—the opportunity to ride, or a special dessert for dinner. The most effective thing, I believe, is to create an atmosphere where the boys themselves will disapprove of bullying. Boys, even bullies, desire the respect of their fellows."

Chris nodded. He had not analyzed how Billy got cooperation from his street rats, but he recognized the techniques Partridge outlined. Billy also used extravagant threats, none of which he carried out. Though Chris had known a few instances over the years of a boy who'd not been able to adapt, and who had suffered the one punishment that was irreversible.

"We need to make the school a safe and appealing place to be, then the ultimate threat—expulsion—should never be needed."

That prompted an appreciative grin from Partridge. "I like the way you think, Mr. Satterthwaite. However, if a boy is a threat to the other boys and refuses to change…" He shook his head, sadly.

"I'd like to offer you the job, Partridge," Chris said. "Let me tell you about the salary and benefits."

The salary was generous and benefits included bed and board—a small private flat that had been carved out of one end of the manor for the head teacher of the previous school, all meals, use of the stables for the head teacher's horse and any vehicle he owned, and cleaning services from the school's servants.

"The housekeeper is willing to stay on, but will serve under the direction of the matron," Chris explained. "We have yet to find a suitable matron, but when we do, she and the housekeeper will meet with my wife and decide whether they are a good fit."

"As to that," Partridge said, "I may have a suitable matron for you. That is, if she agrees."

It transpired that Partridge's sister was a childless widow, who had been a teacher herself, before she was married, and who had recently been matron at an orphanage. "The supervisor of the orphanage had been taking funds intended for the children and spending them on his own entertainment. When she objected, the orphanage's trustees dismissed her," Partridge claimed. "She is an affectionate woman. Firm, but fair. She would be perfect for turning your street children into gentlemen."

If the explanation of her dismissal was true, she was just what Chris was looking for. "Ask her," Chris said. "If she agrees, my wife and I will see her for an interview."

Mrs. Westbridge, Partridge's sister, was perfect, and Clem and Chris hired her on the spot. "I should like to accept the position, but I have a request, Mr. and Mrs. Satterthwaite," she said, when they reached that point of the interview.

She wanted Clem and Chris to admit two children from the orphanage into the school. "I wish you could take them all, madam and sir, but I realize that is unrealistic," she said. She sighed. "There are so many children, and then why one orphanage rather than another?"

"We cannot save everyone," Chris said, "but we can make a difference for a few, and perhaps they will grow up to help others. Tell us about these children, and why they would benefit from the education we plan to give our pupils."

They were boys—two brothers. According to Mrs. Westbridge, they were both very bright. "Their mother taught them to read and figure. The orphanage, for all its faults, at least offered basic schooling in the three 'R's. Martin and Gregory were already ahead of the class when they came to us. If I had told the supervisor, he would have put them straight to work, so I taught them myself. Please. The supervisor will let you have them, if you offer him the payment he always demands. I shall work for no more than my keep to pay for their tuition."

It was a real treat to exchange glances with Clem, know what she was thinking. They were of one mind, as usual. "That won't be necessary, Mrs. Westbridge. I'll arrange for their release from the orphanage, and they can be our first charity students. The other six all have a sponsor for their tuition."

The supervisor proved to be as venal as Mrs. Westbridge had said, and Chris had no problem securing the two boys. The supervisor did not even ask what Chris wanted them for. Indeed, he didn't believe the truth when he heard it, which was after he and Chris signed an agreement, while they waited for the boys to be retrieved from the oakum-picking workshop and delivered to the supervisor's office.

"The boys have been selected to attend a school for bright orphans," Chris volunteered.

With a nod and a wink, the supervisor indicated he didn't believe a word of it, but would keep his mouth shut out of respect for Chris's money.

The boys arrived hand in hand, both pale and rigid with fear.

"You are Martin and Gregory White?" Chris asked.

The older of the two boys nodded.

Chris indicated the small bundle each boy carried. "Are those all of your possessions?"

Another nod.

"Speak up, boy," said the supervisor, importantly. "This gentleman is taking you to a school. It is a school, is it not, Mr. Satterthwaite?"

Chris repressed a sigh. The supervisor's disbelief was clear. Hearing his tone would frighten the boys even more. Once he had the pair in the carriage, both perched on the edge of the seat opposite him, ready to bolt, he played his trump card.

"Mrs. Westbridge sent me. She is the one who suggested you for the school. Her brother, Mr. Partridge, is our head teacher, and she is our new matron. We have a three-hour drive, boys, but we are heading to my house first, where you will meet Mrs. Satterthwaite, my wife, and have something to eat."

The school was not quite ready to be lived in, but Clem and Chris were able to provide house room to Partridge, his sister, and her two *protégés*.

Finding other staff members was now a joint task. Mrs. Westbridge, the housekeeper Mrs. Patterson, and Clem interviewed for the positions of cook and maids. Partridge needed an assistant teacher, though Chris would take some classes. The school would also require a couple of footmen and a handyman.

Chris would give the school free use of his stables, where his stableman and grooms were already in place. Also the gardeners, who would look after his and Clem's private garden as well as the wider school grounds.

As they found more pupils, they would need more teachers and more servants, but time enough to cross that bridge when they reached it.

At last, all was in readiness. Partridge and Mrs. Westbridge moved into the school side of the manor, with the two boys from the orphanage. The servants and the new teacher all arrived and settled in.

Billy's boys arrived by coach. At first, they found the countryside oppressive and scary. Fairly quickly, however, most began to appreciate the space and the fresh air, even if they did jump at unexpected noises. The oldest—that same Tom who had been the oldest boy at Fortune's Fool—was one who remained cautious and jumpy, though he did his best to hide it, since he was something of a leader among the boys and took the responsibility seriously.

Tom—Mr. Fuller, he was called at the school, where all of the boys were addressed as if they were young gentlemen—was prepared to put up with a lot of smells and sounds he didn't know for the sake of classes. He had grown past the mathematics taught at Billy's and had never been introduced to the principles of scientific enquiry. Partridge tutored him in individual sessions on advanced mathematics and science, and he took to the subjects like a duck to water.

"We have our first pupil-teacher," Partridge told Chris one day. "I've given young Mr. Fuller the junior arithmetic class. He is very good, Mr. Satterthwaite. Very patient and thorough."

"Mr. Fuller is delightful with the little boys," said Mrs. Westbridge. "He is the one they go to if they have nightmares or broken toys, or if they cannot resolve their own disagreements. My brother says he should go to university, if he can win a scholarship, or if we can find funding. But I think he would make a superb teacher should he choose."

The boys all addressed Chris, who took them for English classes, as Mr. S.—an innovation suggested by Chris, since one boy had a speech impediment that made pronouncing Chris's full surname an exercise in frustration and embarrassment for the boy and stifled giggles from all within hearing, at least at first.

Since they all had chores, and some of those chores brought them to the kitchen garden that was fast becoming Clem's pride and joy, they soon began calling her, Mrs. S. Like Chris, they responded to Clem's warmth and kindness, and Chris was not at all surprised when Mrs. Westbridge, with a twinkle in her eye, told him one day that depriving a boy of garden duty was regarded as one of the most dire punishments in the school's arsenal.

As THE BOYS relaxed, some of them tested boundaries.

One broke the curfew, creeping out of bed after lights out to steal pears from the orchard. Caught on the way back into the bedchamber he shared with three other boys, he was sentenced to scrub vegetables in the kitchen for a week. For the pear offense, he was required to eat the pears he'd taken. They were not yet ripe, and he only managed one and a half of the hard, sour items before he was permitted to give up.

"The gardener tells me those are the late pears," Partridge said. "I will have had him bring me a basket of ripe pears from another tree, and all of you shall have one after our dinner tonight, except for Mr. Wilson here, who took his share without asking."

There was a private conversation between Partridge and young Mr. Wilson, too. Partridge didn't tell Clem the details, but Clem assumed it was a reinforcement of the prohibition on stealing.

A group who slid down the bannisters on trays they had purloined from the kitchen spent a long afternoon with a mix of beeswax and oil, a polishing cloth, and all the carved wooden panels in the halls and stairways.

Boys who fought were given chores to do, but Partridge also added boxing to the school's curriculum, for those who chose to participate and for any others caught fighting.

"He's a fair man, Mrs. S.," Tom Fuller told Clem one day when she found him in the kitchen garden, supervising a group of younger boys as they weeded the rows of winter cabbages. He waved a hand at the working boys. "This lot were caught holding a feast at midnight with food they'd sneaked from the table. Mr.

Partridge said they should realize how hard the gardener and the cook worked to feed us. They've already peeled a mountain of potatoes."

"A biff would be over quicker," said one of the workers.

"You'll remember this longer," Fuller retorted.

As well as punishments—kitchen tasks, chopping wood, polishing the floors, cleaning out the stables—there were rewards. Food treats, half an hour later in the evening to read, time with the kittens that the kitchen cat had proudly added to the school's complement of inhabitants, and—this was a favorite—riding lessons on the ponies that Chris had added to his stable.

The older boys were rewarded with trips to London, going up with Clem and Chris to spend a couple of days touring museums and seeing the sights. They were expected to write reports on what they had learned, but the trips were highly-coveted.

The school was expanding, and now had fifteen pupils. Two had come from dame schools—the charity schools that taught the basics of reading and writing to the children of the slums, but had no capacity to help those whose ability and thirst for knowledge exceeded what the charity school could offer.

One was another boy of Billy's, and three were paying pupils from families who had heard of the school from father. While surprised to hear he was recommending the place, Clem was pleased to have his support.

They added another teacher and an assistant matron to the staff, to make certain all of the boys had the attention they would accept.

The fifteenth boy was brought to them by Tom Fuller, a silent, frightened creature who clung to Fuller as to his only anchor in a storm. "Eight is my friend, sir," Fuller said, when the boy was discovered hiding in his room. "He needs us. Can he stay?"

Apparently, Fuller and Eight had met up on one of Fuller's

trips to London, and Eight had managed to follow his friend back to Maidenstone Court, clinging to the backs of carriages and, when no one was going in the right direction, walking.

Clem's heart said yes, Eight could stay. Mrs. Westbridge agreed, but the men were more cautious.

"I've seen enough in my life to know that this poor fellow has been through terrible times," Chris said to Clem, "but he is just the kind who will explode, and anyone could get hurt. You. Our baby…"

Clem put a hand protectively over her womb, which was even now cradling their child, but argued, "He needs us, Fuller said. Can we not give him a space and watch him closely, Chris? If we are careful, surely we can protect the other boys? And if we fail, we can send Eight to Billy, who might be able to help him. What kind of a name is Eight?"

"One given in a workhouse to a baby that is not expected to live," Chris explained. "It is a sensible solution. I'll talk to Partridge, and we'll both talk to Eight."

The boy would have to start at the beginning. Someone had taught him courteous manners and the elements of hygiene, but he had no schooling at all. Clem wondered where a boy like him might be expected to keep himself clean and be polite, and was horrified when Chris explained the use to which he must have been put.

Eight might have been as young as ten or as old as twelve. He, himself, had no idea, and nor did he have more than the one name. "You can choose another name if you wish," Clem suggested gently. Eight said that he would think about it. However, a few days later, he shyly suggested that he'd like to name himself after the Duke of Wellington.

A couple of the men who worked in the stables and gardens had served in the wars, and they had been keeping the boys entertained with stories about the great general and his armies.

"Wellington ain't a name," scoffed one of the other boys, amending his verb to "is not" after intercepting a stern look from

Clem. She didn't bother to explain she was objecting to his scoffing, not his grammar.

"Arthur, then," she told Eight. "That is his grace's Christian name. He is Arthur Wellesley, the Duke of Wellington."

"Arthur," the boy repeated. And he chose the name Stone as his surname as a nod to the school. The staff and pupils were delighted. The Duke of Wellington might have been less so, if he ever found out, but that was both unlikely and beside the point.

Chapter Eighteen

THE EXPLOSION OF anger, when it happened, was from an unlikely source.

Tom Fuller was caught beating up Martin White, the older of the two boys Mrs. Westbridge had rescued from the orphanage. While Partridge had dealt with fighting between the boys by organizing boxing lessons and imposing the Marquess of Queensbury's rules, this was not sanctioned and it was not fighting. White was down and begging for mercy, but Fuller was continuing to hit him.

"I'm heartbroken," Partridge told Chris and Clem. "I would never have taken him for a bully."

"We shall have to let him go," Chris said. "We cannot allow such brutality."

"What does Mr. Fuller have to say for himself?" Clem asked, but apparently, Fuller would not defend himself, nor speak on his own behalf in any way. White, too, was tight-lipped, though that might have been because speaking hurt. He was in the infirmary, with a broken arm, possibly cracked ribs, eyes that were swollen shut, a missing tooth, and multiple bruises.

"Besides," Partridge said, "nothing can excuse such a total lack of control."

Clem frowned thoughtfully. She like Andrew Partridge, very

much. But she had heard enough from Chris about the conditions that boys abandoned to the streets faced that she could imagine circumstances in which the anger and grief of years of abuse might break out. "Explode," as Chris put it.

"You predicted this," she said to Chris. "Not from Tom Fuller, perhaps. But he has wounds, even if he has learned to hide them. They all do, you said. All our street boys. I think we need to know what set him off, if we are to be just."

Chris couldn't argue with Clem's wisdom. So each of the adults spoke to two or three boys, dividing them up. The other boys claimed ignorance, even those who had witnessed what had begun as a fight. The one clue that someone let drop to Mrs. Westbridge was that Martin had been teasing Arthur. "Just pokes and words, like," said the informant. "And tricks, like. Tripping him. Pushing his cocoa over. Not stuff to get him half-killed."

"Perhaps not half-killed," Mrs. Westbridge told the other adults when they gathered to compare notes, "but certainly bad enough to see Mr. White on kitchen duty for months, if not expelled. But why did Mr. Fuller not come to one of us?"

It was a good question, but one to which they could not find an answer, until Clem thought of a possible way to break Arthur Stone's silence. She took him out with her to the garden, to the berry cage, where the autumn-flowering raspberries needed daily picking.

He had come out of his shell a little in the two months he'd been with them, but—now she came to think of it—she'd noticed a withdrawal in recent days, and now he was as white and as silent as he'd been when he arrived.

"These are the ripe raspberries," she explained. "To check, put your fingers gently around one that you think is ready, and tug without squeezing. If it falls off in your hand, it is ready."

The strained look around his eyes eased as he experimented, soon discovering the knack of it.

"Try one," she invited. "They're good!" And she had the satisfaction of seeing his eyes open with wonder and a small smile that vanished almost immediately.

"Good?" she asked.

His nod in reply was vigorous.

"You may eat one raspberry for every ten you put in the pail, Mr. Stone," she said.

For a while, they worked in silence, filling their pails. Arthur relaxed even more, and Clem wished she did not have to break the peace, which was doing the poor boy good. But they had to resolve this situation somehow, and Arthur was the key.

"Mr. Fuller will not tell us what made him so angry at Mr. White," she commented, keeping her tone conversational. "Unless we discover he had a good reason, we will have to send him away from the school, but he will not tell us, and neither will Mr. White."

Arthur said nothing, but he stiffened, and his hands stopped picking berries.

"I know that Mr. White was being mean to you. Bullying you. One of the other boys told Mrs. Westbridge. What I do not know is why you or Mr. Fuller did not tell one of the adults. Did you not know we do not allow bullying at Maidenstone Court?"

More silence.

Clem sighed. "You will miss Mr. Fuller when he is gone," she commented.

The boy sucked in a breath that was a series of gulps. "They said you'd throw me out if you knew," he said, his voice anguished. "Tom said it, and so did Martin. They said you wouldn't have the likes of me with the other boys." The next sentence was whispered. "Martin said you'd send me back to that place."

Clem cautiously touched Arthur's shoulder. He was usually wary of being touched, but this time he threw himself on her to weep against her chest. "Martin called me a Molly boy. He said he would tell you all if I didn't—" he whispered the next bit, describing an obscene act that Martin had demanded in vulgar terms that Clem, even now she was married, only partially understood.

"I don't want to do *that*," he wailed. "I don't want to do it ever again. When I told Tom, he said he was going to kill Martin. Mrs. S. Don't send me back to the place. Please, don't."

"Never." Clem made it a solemn oath. She had both hands wrapped around Arthur, holding him safe, patting his back. "Arthur, Martin was wrong. We will not send you away. Chris guessed weeks ago, when you first came. He knows what evil people can do to boys who have no family or friends to protect them. Even if he hadn't known, we would not blame you. None of what happened to you was your fault, Arthur, and we are never sending you back."

She repeated the message in different words over and over, patting Arthur's back, until the boy's noisy and relieved crying reduced to a few gulps.

"Come," Clem said then. "We shall go and speak to Mr. S. and then he shall talk to Mr. P.

"Will they hate me?" Arthur asked, in a very small voice. "Do the other boys need to know?"

Clem tousled his hair. "No and no," she said. "You shall see. All shall be well."

It was, too. Chris reassured Arthur, asked him to promise to let him or Clem know if he suffered any further bullying, and telling him that matters would be arranged with Partridge.

The head teacher was so distressed he had not noticed things getting out of hand that he offered his resignation, which Chris refused. "We all missed it. We shall all have to do better."

Mrs. Westbridge also had to be reassured. "I begged you to bring the White boys here. And Martin did this? How wicked! How terrible! How will you ever trust me again?"

Which left the two boys at the center of the disaster.

The adults agreed that they didn't want to lose either of them, but they needed to know that Martin knew what a terrible thing he had done and was truly sorry, and that Tom could be trusted to find healthier and safer ways to deal with his anger.

If this was the worst that could happen, it was not so bad.

Chris spoke to Martin White, and Partridge to Tom Fuller. They laid out the facts as they now knew them, then told each boy what he had done wrong.

Then, as they had agreed, they proposed that each boy decide who they had hurt by their actions and how to make recompense.

"Martin was a victim, too," Chris reported to Clem. "Until Mrs. Westbridge came to work at the workhouse, one of the night watchmen was an abuser. Mrs. Westbridge made sure he was fired, and warned Martin never to tell anyone what he had done. She was afraid that the self-righteous supervisor would blame Martin. As for the bullying, he saw it as toughening up. That was what the supervisor told the older boys—that they had to toughen up the younger ones, for it was a cruel world, and a person had to be hard to survive."

"You have explained the error of his ways, I hope," Clem said. She was still furious on Arthur's behalf.

"I've suggested to him that Arthur is one of the toughest people he'll ever know, surviving what he's been through, running away and finding Fuller, surviving Martin White. White agrees. I'll be interested in seeing what he comes up with by way of recompense."

Tom Fuller was the first to present his plan. "I am truly sorry I did not come to one of you as soon as I knew what Martin was saying and doing. I should have known you would not send Arthur away. I have hurt everyone here," he said. "Mr. and Mrs. S. first, because the school was their idea, and everyone thought it would not work."

He addressed Clem directly. "Mrs. S., I heard you say you wanted to put in a rose garden, and the gardeners haven't had time to dig the soil over, get out all the weeds, and add sand and stable manure. I would like to do that for you. If it is acceptable to you, Mr. S., can that be my payment to you, too?"

"Mr. Fuller, that is a huge amount of work," Clem said. Fuller was wiry and strong, but not very big.

"I can do it," he insisted. "I would like to do it." He grinned somewhat sheepishly. "And if I get blisters, perhaps they will remind me to make better choices."

"Mr. P. and Mrs. W., I thought maybe I could clean out your fireplaces for a week. In your bed chambers and in your parlors. You have both been very good to me, and I should have trusted you."

He frowned. "I have already spoken to Arthur and apologized for giving him bad advice. So there is just Martin. I... To tell you the truth, I am still pretty mad at him."

"What Mr. White did was wrong," Mrs. Westbridge said. "He must make his own recompense, and would have needed to do so, even if you have left us to apply justice. But you broke his arm, cracked a couple of ribs, and knocked out a tooth. You kept hitting him after he could no longer fight. You need to make that right, Mr. Fuller."

"I could help him with his geometry," Fuller suggested. "He is not very good at it, and he is falling behind, being in the infirmary. Would that do?"

"Ask Mr. White if that is acceptable to him," Clem suggested, hoping that, if the boys would only talk, they would find they had more in common than what divided them.

And so it proved. Fuller was nearly at the top of those to whom White wanted to make recompense, with only Arthur ahead of him. And he had come up with a surprising way of making things even. "I will tell Tom and Arthur what happened to me in the orphanage, and then they will know I am just the same as Arthur. If they ever want to hurt me, they can."

As far as recompense to the staff was concerned, he was still bedridden, but he said that would not stop him from peeling vegetables if someone would bring them to him. "And if you like, I can do the reading," he suggested. Mrs. Westbridge had formed the habit of reading a chapter from a story book every night, and the boys really looked forward to it. Since Martin had a dramatist's flair when reading, the suggestion was popular with everyone.

Peace was restored, or as much peace as could be expected when living next door to a school of fifteen boys.

Chapter Nineteen

ONCE THAT CRISIS was over, Chris suggested it might be time for them to let the families know about Clem's pregnancy.

The baby must have been conceived on the night of their wedding, or at least in the week that followed. Clem was growing rounder by the minute, and one of Chris's favorite times of the day was in the evening, when he sat at Clem's feet and put his cheek against her abdomen, his palm on the other side, to feel the child they had made moving against him.

They had kept her pregnancy to themselves for months, though Martha knew. Martha, who had been so difficult when Chris first met her, seemed to have undergone a transformation since Clem had challenged her. Clem's readiness to give her another chance had softened her and Clem's very real appreciation of Martha's skills and her fashion sense had gratified her. Moreover, the school had impressed her.

The respectful but sincere courtship of one of the grooms had wrought the final change, for when the groom inquired about the Satterthwaites' attitude to married servants, Clem had shared her answer with Martha. "As long as you do your job well, I am happy to employ you, Martha. Indeed, I cannot imagine anyone being better than you are with my hair."

Martha seemed as thrilled about Clem's pregnancy as Chris

and Clem were, and declared that she would wait to be married until after Clem's baby was born. "Pat won't mind waiting, Mrs. Satterthwaite," she said. "He knows how much I owe to you."

Clem agreed that she was growing too round for them to maintain the secret of her pregnancy, and they agreed to disclose the news to friends and family.

The two earls were thrilled for them. The school, from Mr. Partridge and Mrs. Westbridge all the way down to the youngest pupil, dedicated themselves to Clem's comfort. Billy O'Hara merely nodded. "Inevitable," he said. "Congratulations, Christopher."

Aunt Fern burst into tears because, she said, she was so happy.

Wright was indignant he had not been told as soon as Clem and Chris knew.

He became a constant visitor to their townhouse. He brought doctors to check on Clem's health, foods to ensure her good health, books for her read out loud so that the baby would be educated even in the womb, musicians to play for her.

He demanded that she remain in London for the duration of the pregnancy, so she could have what he called "proper attention." Clem refused. She also refused his choice of doctors, having made up her mind that a midwife would be better for her and the baby.

Wright had a tantrum, demanding she allow the team of doctors to examine her. But the only one who persisted in the face of Clem's objections recommended a starvation diet to counter her gain in weight, and proposed to bleed her because her color was too high. He left the house in a temper when Chris offered to have the footmen carry him off the premises, and Wright too, if the man didn't accept Clem's right to make her own decisions.

For once in his life, Wright found himself powerless to carry out his threats, since any of the repercussions he proposed would also threaten his much-wanted grandson. Wright refused to entertain the idea that the child might be a daughter. He was determined that Clem was carrying a son, and that the child would be the greatest prodigy the world had ever known. Clem said the baby would be her child—hers and Chris's—and that was wonderful enough.

The rest of Father's gifts, she accepted—the food, books, and musicians—and eventually he stopped seething over the loss of the doctors, especially since Clem continued in good health.

In defense of his bride's sanity, Chris settled them in the country at the beginning of December—they had been spending part of each week in London. Wright had been outraged when he first learned they planned to spend the winter at Chris's country estate. Chris and Clem had done as they pleased.

"After all," Chris told him, "you have refused to consider legacies for our other children, and so I need something of my own that Clem and I can use to give a future to our younger sons and dowries to our daughters."

Wright grumbled, but he came around, and managed to visit once a week, staying for two nights. On every visit, he brought several more items for the nursery, carrying them up to the third floor where a full nursery and schoolroom suite waited, fitted with all-new furniture and gleaming with new paint.

Chris and Clem did not bother to tell Wright that they did not plan for their child to use the nursery in the first months. They had turned the bedchamber adjoining their own into a room for both the baby and his or her nursemaid, for Clem was determined to feed the child herself and wanted him or her close.

Wright soon discovered for himself that coal mines and refineries in Yorkshire could be operated as easily from rural Berkshire as from London. When he stayed, he spent most of his time in the study he had made out of the sitting room attached to his assigned bedchamber, receiving reports from his various enterprises and writing responses.

"Your grandfather has reconciled himself to the country," Chris told the baby during one of his evening chats with Clem's abdomen. "On this last trip, he did not complain once about the noise from the farmyard, and he asked how the winter wheat fared with the recent storm. I told him that most of the young crop seems to be fine."

"Father says he will return in two weeks, and will then stay until the baby is born," Clem said, in late February, which was bad news, but not unexpected.

Chris was lying next to his wife, feeling his son or daughter shifting and kicking.

"I could swear this little fellow has at least three legs," he commented.

"Four, in fact," said Clem.

Chris lifted his head so that he could meet the eyes of his beloved. "I beg your pardon?"

"The midwife believes I am having twins. It is why I am so big. She is certain she can feel more than one baby."

"Good lord," said Chris, putting his face back on her abdomen. "You don't half do things properly, my love." He grinned at her. "Let's not tell your father. With any luck, he'll arrive when it is all over and our two children are with us. Two children! I can hardly believe it. You are a miracle, my love."

Chapter Twenty

AUNT FERN CAME to stay a week later. She announced that
Clem needed a woman relative with her through the ordeal
to come. Clem, who was trying not to think about the ordeal to
come, did her best to be grateful, and when her father turned up
two days later, she had cause to be.

"The two of them keep one another busy," she reported to
Chris, when he came back up to the house after a morning in the
fields helping with the plowing. "Which is just as well, for I shall
kill the next person who asks how I am."

"And how are you, my love?" Chris asked. She threw her fan
at him, and he ducked.

"Hot, uncomfortable, and bad-tempered," she replied. She
had retired to their bedchamber, which was on the west side of
the house, and was sitting in the chill breeze from the window,
but even the most comfortable chair Chris had been able to find
was not comfortable for long when one was approximately the
size of a whale, and provided with an internal heat source that
made one drip with perspiration even in February, when the day
was sunny.

"Shall I massage your feet?" he offered.

Bless the dear man. Sympathy was all very well, but a foot
massage was on another plane altogether. She didn't bother with

words but just held up one foot, and he sat down on her footstool and put both feet in his lap.

"No stockings," he noted. "Too hot?"

Clem sighed. "I shall have to put them on again before I go downstairs," she acknowledged.

"I don't see why. I won't tell if you don't."

True enough. Her legs would not show under her gown, anyway. She could wear her lightest slippers and no stockings. She might not be cool, but at least it might help to keep her from feeling so hot!

"The midwife says it is worse for those who carry through July and August," she commented. "I cannot imagine!" She leaned her head back against her chair and closed her eyes while Chris's clever fingers pressed and rubbed, until her poor aching feet relaxed and she wanted to purr like a cat.

She must have fallen asleep, for the angle of the sun had changed when she was woken by a sudden cramping in her abdomen that faded even as she became fully aware. She was alone in the room, with a pillow under her head and a light shawl covering her feet on the footstool.

The door to the room opened, and Chris entered with a tray. "You are awake," he observed.

"How long did I sleep?" she asked.

"About an hour. I went down to get you a tea tray, and to check on your father and aunt. They are plotting a trip to Reading tomorrow. Your father wants to see if the man who sold him those grapes you enjoyed has any more, and Aunt Fern thinks you might be short of what she calls 'essential nursery supplies'."

"I must have more baby clouts and frocks than any mother in the history of England," Clem said. "Help me sit up, darling. I would love a cup of tea."

Chris offered her his arm, helped her rearrange herself in her chair, poured her tea, and put butter and jam on one of the drop scones that the kitchen had sent up.

While she sipped her tea, she felt another cramp and froze for a moment.

"Is something wrong?" Chris asked. "What is it?"

He was watching her like a hawk. They all were, including Martha and even the least of the maids. If she mentioned the cramp, the whole house would be in turmoil. "Nothing," she said.

But an hour later she had to admit, if only to herself, that it wasn't nothing, and an hour after that, she asked Chris to send for the midwife, but not to say anything yet to Father and Aunt Fern. "Not until I know that I am definitely in labor," she said.

CHRIS SENT A footman, and went himself to let their two guests know neither he nor Clem would be at dinner. "Clem is a little tired, and I plan to sit with her," he said. True enough. But the midwife turned him out of the bedchamber that had been set up as a birthing room. She said he didn't need to be there while she examined Clem. Aunt Fern found him in the hall outside the birthing room door when she came up to get a shawl, and leapt to the correct conclusion.

"Clem is having her babies!" she said.

Chris cast an anxious glance toward the stairs. "Ssshhh," he said. "Clem does not want her father making a fuss."

Aunt Fern narrowed her eyes and glared at Chris. "Then go downstairs and keep Mr. Wright busy. This is not an occasion for men."

The midwife opened the door at that moment, and nodded at what Aunt Fern said. "Your wife is asking for you, Mr. Satterthwaite. You may speak with her briefly, and then leave her to us. The babies are impatient to be born, and the next few hours will be women's work."

If Clem had asked, Chris would have stayed. "Go and keep Father company, Chris," she said, instead. "Aunt Fern and Mrs. Greene will look after me and the babies."

But when Chris got back downstairs, Wright was gone. "He heard that the midwife had arrived, and he ordered his carriage," the footman reported.

What on earth is the man up to?

Chris could only wait. With no news from upstairs and no anxious grandfather to keep him company, he paced from the window in the study that gave him a glimpse of the stable yard, through the hall that held the stairs up which his wife was working to bring forth his children, to the window in the parlor where he could see the carriage drive.

He was interrupted once, by a message from the school asking for news of "Mrs. S. and the babies". He sent back to say there was none. There was no word from upstairs. Even the maids, who passed him in the hall carrying buckets of hot water and clean cloths, could tell him nothing except that the mistress appeared "well enough, considering."

At last, Wright's carriage came through the gates and proceeded along the drive. Chris rushed back to the study, where he watched Wright descend, followed by the London doctor whom Chris had ejected from their townhouse months ago.

That cunning old man! He must have had the man waiting at the local inn.

Chris met them both as they came into the house from the stable-yard door. "Wright, Doctor. Come through to the parlor, and I shall pour you both a drink."

Wright puffed out his chest and jutted his chin. "The doctor needs to see his patient."

"The doctor does not have a patient in this house," Chris said. "But he has been good enough to come all this way, so I am offering him a drink."

"My grandson..." Wright began.

"My wife and my children are above stairs, in the care of a highly-regarded midwife, who was recommended to us for her excellent record of live infants and mothers," Chris replied.

"I have every right to protect..."

"This is my house, sir, and these are my wife and children. I respect your concerns for them, but I will not have Clem bothered while she is giving birth."

The doctor was looking from one of them to the other like a man at a tennis match.

"Brandy, Doctor?" Chris asked, and led the way to the parlor.

"You are taking a serious risk, young man," the doctor said, as he accepted his brandy. "In general, midwives are ignorant old women, practicing old wives' tales that put women at risk. When there are problems, they do not know what to do."

As opposed to doctors, some of whom were ignorant old men, Chris thought. "The midwife says that Mrs. Satterthwaite is healthy and strong, and that at least one of the babies is well positioned for the birth," he said. "My wife is having twins, Doctor."

The doctor shook his head, dolefully. "Twin births are complicated," he said. "Midwives are not trained to handle the difficulties that can arise."

"Can arise," Chris pointed out. "The village doctor is standing by, and Mrs. Greene has promised to call him in if she is concerned about the progress of the confinement."

Wright, who had been brooding, broke in at that point. "We won't need the village doctor. My *accoucheur* is right here."

It was a fair point. "That seems reasonable. If he is needed, and if Clem agrees to his attendance." One thing would be a sticking point for Clem. "She will not want to be bled."

The doctor sniffed. "I have found bleeding to be most efficacious in preventing the fevers that kill many mothers."

Chris wondered how the man had counted the numbers who lived or died, and to what records he compared them. He forbore to argue. "We were about to have dinner when Clem decided that she needed the midwife," he said. "Would you gentlemen care to eat?"

Presumably, the kitchen would be able to produce something fit to serve. He left the two men to their brandy and went to make the arrangements for meals to be taken up on trays to

Clem's attendants and served in the dining room for him and the two men.

After that, he climbed the stairs and knocked on the door of the birthing room. Martha the maid opened the door, but only enough to look at him through the crack.

"Everything is going well," she said.

"May I speak with my wife and Mrs. Greene?" Chris asked, feeling both mildly outraged to be kept outside of a door in his own house and out of his depth in this essential feminine ritual.

"A moment please," said Aunt Fern's voice, and Martha shut the door in his face.

It was longer. Perhaps three or four minutes. But then the door opened again, this time wide enough for Chris to step inside. His eyes went straight to the bed, then searched the room. Clem was walking to and fro by the window, arm in arm with Aunt Fern. She wore a robe, at the neck of which he could see the strings of a chemise, and her feet were bare. Her hair had been redressed into long plaits and these had been wound about her head, though some strands had escaped to droop around her face.

Chris's feet carried him across the room in a couple of strides and he found himself looking into his wife's eyes while clasping her free hand. "Is all well?" he asked. She looked well. But shouldn't she be in bed? He glanced toward it and decided to say nothing. If Aunt Fern and Mrs. Greene thought she would be better standing, who was he to argue?

"Darling," he said, "your father has brought that doctor of his, the *accoucheur*, Mr. Corgumbe."

"I do not wish to see him," Clem said, firmly, before Chris could say anything else.

"I told him he had no patient here," Chris explained, "but would you object to him waiting here? Just in case? Since he is present?"

"We shall not need him," said Mrs. Green, "but since he is here already, Mrs. Satterthwaite, let us hold him in reserve, shall we?"

Clem huffed out a breath. "Very well, Chris. Let him stay, but I do not wish to see him."

"Understood," Chris told her.

Clem turned her face toward Aunt Fern. "Another one," she said, her voice high, as her hand in Chris's groped to grasp his arm instead.

"Breathe, my dear child." Aunt Fern said, transferring Clem's other hand to Chris's other arm. "Hold on to your husband and breathe."

Chris rested his hands on where her waist had been and would be again. Her abdomen was rock hard, he discovered. "Lean on me," he invited. "I have you, Clem."

"You are doing well, dearest," Aunt Fern said, probably to Clem, though his godmother might have meant him. He ignored the pinch as Clem's fingers dug into his arms. So, this was labor! He would bear it for her, if he could—the pain that drew lines across her face, and sent her gaze inward, her breath short.

He did not know how long he stood there before her grip eased and she relaxed against him. He kissed her forehead, feeling helpless. Was that the way it was meant to go? Yes, apparently, for both Mrs. Greene and Aunt Fern were praising Clem and assuring her that everything was going exactly as it should.

He had no idea what that meant. "How much more of that…?" he began to ask, but Mrs. Greene spoke over him. "All is going exactly as it should, and Mrs. Satterthwaite is managing very well," she said, firmly.

"Leave us to our work, Christopher," said Aunt Fern. "We shall look after Clem."

He would have ignored them all if Clem had not joined the chorus. "Go and keep Father from breaking the door down," she said. "Tell him that I am too busy giving birth to his grandchild to put up with his nonsense."

Chris left the room, and if he didn't pass that provocative message to Wright word for word, he at least made it clear that all was going well, and that Clem wanted no interference from the men in the house. "Not even me," he said plaintively.

"*Eee*, lad," said Wright, looking contemplative, "it be hard on men, this waiting." The Yorkshire accent he had lost resurfaced during this emotional moment. "I remember me when Clem was born." He recovered his poise and his pronunciation, and proposed, "Have another drink, boy, and you and I shall wait it out together."

The doctor waited with them for the next two hours, but then declared that if he was needed, he could be woken. He went off to the bed that had been prepared for him.

Chris and Wright continued to wait, saying little. Wright kept drinking. Chris tried to read, but he could not concentrate. His heart was a floor above him, and it was all he could do not to migrate up the stairs and, if necessary, park himself on the floor outside the birthing room.

Thank goodness he'd had the presence of mind to command information and messages from the maids who were coming in and out of the room to bring the occupants whatever they needed.

The most recent report was that Mrs. Greene was pleased with the progress and confident that all was as it should be, and that Mrs. Satterthwaite was nearly ready for the birthing stool.

What that meant, Chris wasn't certain, but it sounded encouraging. It sounded like progress.

Wright had drunk most of a bottle of brandy and was asleep in his chair. The grandfather clock in the hall, which Chris and Clem had inherited with the house, chimed the half hour. Half an hour past what? Chris took a candle out into the hall and checked. Half-past one.

It must have been ten minutes later when he heard feet hurrying down the stairs. He rushed to the door to see one of the maids disappearing through the servants' door. He waited. It was only a few minutes, but it seemed endless before the door swung open again and two maids came back through the door, one on each side of a bucket handle.

"What is happening?" he asked.

"Midwife wants more hot water, Master," said one of the maids.

"Mrs. Satterthwaite is pushing," said the other. "You'll be a da any minute, sir." They hurried up the stairs as fast as they could go without setting the bucket swinging.

Pushing? What did pushing have to do with it? But a father any minute. If that was true…

His excitement rising, he looked back inside the room to make certain that Wright was sleeping deeply, then followed the maids upstairs, where he stopped with the door still between him and his wife.

The maids came out, one of them carrying the empty bucket. "We're to heat the kettle and set out the tea makings," one of them said. "For after, like."

After? After the babies were born, did she mean?

He waited, trying to breathe normally. By the count of his breaths, he had been here for five minutes, though it felt much longer, when from within the room he heard the sound he had unconsciously been waiting for. A bleating cry. His baby! His wonderful wife had birthed his baby.

Chapter Twenty-One

T HE DOOR OPENED a sliver, just enough for the maid Martha to slip outside. She started when she saw him. "Mr. Satterthwaite, sir." She beamed. "You have a little girl, sir. She is a darling. Mrs. Satterthwaite is resting, but Mrs. Greene says the other one will be soon. She has sent me to fetch Mrs. Satterthwaite's tea tray, and to tell you the news."

"Thank you, Martha. Mr. Wright is sleeping. I won't wake him until both children are born."

Martha nodded and gave him a wry grin that was in itself a commentary on Wright. "As you say, sir." And she hurried off downstairs.

She wasn't gone long. Chris had heard nothing further from the birthing room and when she came up the stairs with a heavy tray, he was quick to open the door. He could not see the birthing chair even with the door opened wide, but he heard Mrs. Greene's voice. "Is that Mr. Satterthwaite? Lady Fernvale, give him the baby."

A moment later, Aunt Fern appeared in the doorway, and though Chris stepped back, she insisted on transferring the shawl-wrapped bundle from her arms into his, showing him how to support his daughter's head with his elbow.

"I doubt this will take long. Just walk up and down with her,

Christopher." She stepped back into the room and shut the door, and Chris did what he was told, staring down into the face of his new little sweetheart. She blinked up at him and yawned. Chris was enraptured.

He lost track of time, space, everything, coming back to himself only when another cry came from the birthing room, this one not a gentle little bleat but a loud and indignant protest. "Your brother or sister has joined us in the world, baby mine," he told the little mite in his arms. "If your mother is well, then I am the luckiest man alive."

His daughter had fallen asleep. The surge of protective love was familiar, yet different. Often in recent months he had woken up next to Clem and watched her sleeping, a warmth and a softening in his chest as the woman he loved slumbered peacefully under his loving gaze.

This time, the urge and need to protect was stronger, more focused. His daughter. The child that he and Clem had made. So tiny, so helpless, so perfect.

The door opened again, and Aunt Fern stepped out into the hall carrying a bundle similar to his own cherished burden. "Christopher, meet your son," she said.

⟫⟫⟪⟪

FATHER WAS CLEM'S first visitor, for she did not count Chris or Aunt Fern, who had returned to her, bringing her the babies as soon as Mrs. Greene sent Martha to fetch them.

That had been during the night. She had delivered the after-birth, then Martha had helped her into a clean chemise and the robe she had discarded some time ago. Then Mrs. Greene and Martha had assisted her to the bed so that she could recline against the pillows, and Martha went to bring her loved ones to her.

With Mrs. Greene's help, she had put each child to suck, and then Chris had carried her to her own bed, and Aunt Fern and Martha had followed with the children. She had fallen asleep with Chris beside her, holding her hand, and the two babies in a single cradle beside the bed. Clem was not yet ready to give them up to the care of their nursemaids.

They had been a part of her for so long, and now they were born she could not bear to let them go away from her. She needed to be able to touch them, see them, listen to them. The three of them—the four of them, with Chris—belonged together.

This morning, Father had apparently been awake early, demanding to see her son. Nothing about his daughter or granddaughter. Clem decided he could wait.

She fed the babies, and gave them to their nursemaids to wash and change. She had a cup of hot chocolate, and with a good appetite ate the breakfast that Martha had brought up to her. She had her own wash and change. Then she sent Chris down to tell Father that he might visit.

"Which one is he?" Those were Father's first words.

Clem nodded to the nursemaid with the little boy, and the girl stepped forward.

"He is small," Father complained.

"He is big for a baby born two weeks early, Mrs. Greene says," Clem corrected.

Father glared at her with his "I insist on being obeyed" look. "I want Mr. Corgumbe to look at him. To make certain."

"He has all his fingers and toes, Mr. Wright," Chris said. "And he appears healthy in every respect. As does his sister. Small, but the way they are feeding already, that will soon be resolved."

"I want Mr. Corgumbe to look at him," Father insisted.

Clem looked at Chris, who said, "What do you wish to do, my love?"

Father snorted and muttered something about apron strings. Chris grinned at him. "My wife, my children, my estate."

"If not for me," said Father, "you'd still be a glorified clerk keeping books for a criminal."

"If I'd not met my wife, you mean," Chris said. "Yes, probably. I am not going to fight with you, Wright. Not in my wife's chamber, anyway. Not in front of her and my children. Clem put her life at risk yesterday and needs to rest. If your only intent here is to insult me, then let us leave her and the children in peace. You can do so more comfortably downstairs, over breakfast."

Father let out a snarl of frustration, and turned to Clem. "Daughter, please would you allow my doctor to examine my grandson."

Well, and after all, what could it matter? "Mr. Corgumbe can view the child—both children if he wishes—in this room, with Chris and me present," she said. "Go and have breakfast, Father, and I shall send for you and Mr. Corgumbe when William needs to have his clout changed. By the way, our daughter is to be named Christobel."

"William?" Father growled. "Why William?"

"This way to breakfast," Chris said, firmly, and escorted Father out of the room.

Mr. Corgumbe was not as difficult as Clem had expected, probably because Chris had pressed him to accept the excessive sum of fifty pounds as a token of their appreciation for him coming all this way, and standing by ready to intervene if needed.

Since Father must have already paid him, the vast sum would be a very nice bonus. He had also been joined at breakfast by Lady Fernvale and Mrs. Greene and, according to Chris, he and Mrs. Greene had exchanged various gruesome stories that had scared Chris, retrospectively, quite out of his mind and put the pair of them vastly in charity with one another.

He was in a good mood when he examined little William, saying repeatedly, "Very nice, yes, very good," as he moved William's legs to test the baby's hip joints, listened to his chest, and performed other actions that had William protesting loudly.

When William's nursemaid took him into the connected room to dress him again, Mr. Corgumbe said, "You have a wonderfully healthy little boy, Mr. Satterthwaite. While I am here, would you like me to examine the little girl?"

Father growled, "I am not paying for any little girl," but in a low mutter that everyone else in the room decided to ignore. Chris raised his eyebrows in question and Clem nodded. Why not?

"Yes, thank you," said Chris, and he asked the nursemaid to undress Christabel, who had inherited her father's easy nature, for she merely hiccupped a little and tolerated the examination. Soon, she, too, was being whisked away to the adjoining room. Chris had had beds set up for the nursemaids so that they were within easy call, cupboards, and shelves to hold the children's clothes and anything else they might require, and a surface at an easy height for washing and changing the babies.

Not the cradles, which would remain in this room, at least for the present. Clem wanted the children under her eye.

"Another fine child," said Mr. Corgumbe, approvingly. "My congratulations, Mr. and Mrs. Satterthwaite. Mr. Wright, I shall take my leave, sir, and return to London. I called for my carriage before coming above stairs, and it should be waiting for me. Mrs. Greene, a pleasure to meet you. Lady Fernvale, your servant, ma'am."

And he went on his way.

If only Father would do likewise. "I have work to do," he said. Then stopped in the doorway and added, "Well done, Clementine."

That was a surprise. She could not think of an occasion on which she had pleased him, and she had long ago given up trying.

"For once," said her husband, "I agree with the old goat. Well done, Clem my love, and thank you for our two beautiful babies."

⤜⟫⟫⟩✳⟨⟨⟨⤛

THE FOLLOWING DAY saw two deputations from the school. Mrs. Westbridge came first, bringing two beautifully knitted shawls and a variety of other baby garments made by the female staff, plus a rattle that Mr. Partridge and the assistant teacher had selected at the village shops.

After class hours, Tom Fuller led a little delegation bringing congratulations and presents from the boys. They had, Tom explained, been stuck on what to get, for everyone wanted to contribute, and only a few of them had any money.

When they applied to the vicar's wife—"For we did not want any of the adults at the school to know what we were doing"— she had suggested they each knit a square. She had taught them to knit, had loaned them the needles, and had begged spare wool from everyone in the village.

The resulting blanket was a glorious mix of colors and textures. Five rows of three squares each, "And the vicar's wife sewed it together for us, Mrs. S. Is it… Do you like it?"

With tears in her eyes, Clem assured the boys that she loved it.

Later that week, Wright returned to London, promising to see them again in two weeks. By his next visit, Mrs. Greene had gone, since the two babies were gaining weight and Clem was in good health.

Lady Fernvale waited until Father's two-day visit was at an end, and also returned to London. "I shall be back for the christenings," she promised.

That would be in a little over three weeks. Meanwhile, Chris hadn't been into London for over a month, and Wright had been rather pointed about certain necessary meetings. "If you need to go, go," Clem said. "We will miss you, but we understand."

"I could do the trip there and back in one day," Chris suggested, but Clem disagreed.

"That would mean six hours on the road, Chris. Stay overnight. After all, we have the townhouse. Go, do your meetings, and come home to us."

But when Chris wrote a list of all the people he should meet and the places he should visit, they agreed that he'd be better to stay two nights. "Otherwise, you will need to go again in just a couple of weeks," Clem pointed out. "Which will mean another six hours traveling."

What she said made sense. Reluctant though he was to leave her and the twins, Chris had a job to do. It wasn't going to go away, either. "When will the children be old enough to travel?" he asked. "Your father is talking about sending me to Yorkshire, but I am not going on a month-long trip without you and the babies."

Clem had no idea. "I expect, as long as we did short days and stayed in comfortable accommodations, we could travel once I have been churched," she said. "I could ask Mrs. Greene. She might have an idea. And Aunt Fern."

They left it at that, and a week later, after some intensive letter writing to arrange all his meetings and visits, Chris left for London.

In addition to his duties at Wright's, Chris had a commission on behalf of his family that had him calling on his relatives, and Ramping Billy.

"You want me to *what?*" said Billy, shock showing in his expression for a fraction of a second before he reimposed his usual bland facade. Even so, his disbelief colored his voice as he said, "Me? Does Mrs. Satterthwaite know about this?"

"Clem and I agree, Billy. We would like you to be William's godfather. If not for you, she and I would not be married. I would not have survived on the streets if I hadn't met you, for a start."

Billy slowly shook his head, as if he could not believe his ears. "A godfather? Me? Christopher, I'm the last person you should ask. I haven't been in a church since I escaped the orphanage. Besides, I'm probably Irish. If anything, I should be a Catholic."

It wasn't a "no". Chris knew a plea to be persuaded when he heard one. "If you were in an orphanage, I imagine you were baptized in the Church of England," he said.

A quirk of an eyebrow was Billy's only answer.

Good enough. "That's all the vicar will want to know," Chris said. "Clem and I want our son to have you on his side. We don't trust Wright, and if anything happens to us, we need someone powerful to keep Wright in check. You look after your people. Will you please be one of William's godparents?"

He sat through a long silence while Billy stared at the wall behind his head. Eventually, the man took a deep breath and let it out. "You called him William to twist my arm," he accused.

"We called him 'William' to honor the man who saved my life and educated me to be a gentleman," Chris countered. "His name is not going to change, whatever you decide."

"Who are you choosing as his other godparents?"

The church required each child to have three godparents—two women and a man for Christobel and two men and a woman for William.

"Lady Fernvale and Lord Crosby."

More silence.

"I'll do it," Billy said. "Now go away and let me get on with my work. Tell Tiny the date, time, and place. I'll be there. Oh, and Christopher?"

"Yes, sir?"

"Tell the vicar that my name is William Harrington." Billy picked up a sheaf of papers from his desk and began reading.

Chris backed out, wondering what that was all about. William Harrington? But he knew that asking questions would get him nowhere.

Lady Fernvale had already been asked to be godmother to both children, and during his next two calls, Chris acquired the agreement of Lady Crosby to be little Bel's second godmother and his father's cousin Lord Halton, another powerful man, to be godfather to Bel.

Chris also took the opportunity to have dinner at Harry's club with Harry and Michael on his first night in London, and at Harry's brother Lord Thurgood's place on the second night. They were both much pleasanter than the two noon meals he shared with Wright, throughout which Wright had boasted to the other invited employees about his prodigy of a grandson, and shared grandiose plans for the child's future.

After the second meal, on his third day from home, Chris made his final report to Wright of what he'd accomplished since he arrived in London.

"Good. That's acceptable," said Wright. "When do you plan to return?"

"I will talk to Clem, sir, but I think three days every month should be sufficient, with the rest by correspondence. The twins' christening is in less than three weeks, so I'll see you then."

"And Yorkshire? It is not urgent, but I need someone I trust to travel up there and check that I'm being told the truth."

"September, we thought, sir. I'll plan to be up there for several weeks, so I shall take Clem and the twins with me." The babies would be six months old by then, and Clem thought they would be able to manage the journey.

Wright's eyebrows shot up. He frowned, but he said nothing except, "September should work."

"I'll be on my way, then," said Chris. In three hours, more or less, he would be home with his family. It could not be soon enough.

Chapter Twenty-Two

CHRIS WAS HOME! Clem felt she could take her first deep breath in three days. Her father had been uncharacteristically pleasant when he was staying with them, after his defeat over the doctor. She had been afraid he would find some way to reassert himself that might harm her husband.

But Chris returned safely, swearing to Clem that the children had grown visibly in the few days he had been absent.

Father would be back again in a couple of weeks, for the children's christening, and so would the other godparents. Others of the Satterthwaites and Thurgoods too, coming to pay their respects once Clem was churched and therefore officially back in Society.

And Billy O'Hara, who would—Chris said—be traveling as William Harrington. Clem had received a polite note from Mr. Harrington thanking her for her offer of hospitality and saying he would be taking accommodation in the area, which was a relief. Clem was by no means certain that she was up to being Ramping Billy's hostess.

Not, at least, at the same time as she was providing hospitality to her father, the Earl and Countess of Crosby, the Earl and Countess of Halton, and Lady Fernvale. Not to mention various cousins.

Father arrived two days before the service, and immediately protested that he had not been asked to be Will's godfather. "But Wright," Chris said, "I thought you were convinced you would not live to see him reach adulthood. Of course, as his grandfather, we hope you will be here to see him grow up, but I am sure you agree with the importance of choosing younger people for the role of godparent."

Chris always seemed to know how to draw Father's fangs, and Lord and Lady Crosby arrived at that moment, so they had an excuse to leave him so they could greet the new guests.

Having them all in the house was as difficult as Clem had expected. Not that the other guests were a problem, but Father made everything more difficult than it needed to be, and Chris and Lady Fernvale were hard-pressed to keep him soothed and as content as was ever likely to happen.

It didn't help that Will had a snuffly nose and was angry about it. Clem found herself counting down hours and days. How many hours until Father would go to bed again. How many days until he left?

Thank goodness she was feeding her own children! It gave her an excellent excuse to leave the company at regular intervals and for up to half an hour at a time—longer, if they refused to feed at the same time.

How grateful she was to the other ladies of the company, who took her disappearances in their stride, and to Chris, who kept thinking of new ways to keep the gentlemen busy.

She was relieved when the Christening Day arrived. She would be churched first, followed by the baptism. Will's sniffle appeared to have disappeared overnight, and she fed them both just before it was time to leave for church, in the hopes that they'd sleep until it was time to pour water on them.

The churching service was called in the *Book of Common Prayer*, "The Service of Thanksgiving for Women After Childbirth, commonly called The Churching of Women." It, and the baptism to follow, were celebrated as part of the usual Sunday morning service, so the house party arrived at the church in several carriages and were met by a crowd of villagers, countryfolk, local gentry, and the crowd from the school, who had walked to church through the woods.

Clem had met many of the locals before she went into confinement, and the gentry wives had visited while she was lying-in, so their way through the crowd was slow, as she and Chris introduced their guests to the local notables and everyone admired what they could see of the twins, who were bundled up in shawls against the chill spring wind.

The churching was done first. Clem left the twins with their nursemaids and knelt to say the prayers and receive the blessing. Next came the ordinary prayers of the service. When it was time for the homily, the vicar spoke on the significance of infant baptism, and the important role of godparents in bringing children up to believe in God and to be good Christians.

Then it was time for the baptism. Clem, who was by now holding Bel while Chris had Will in his arms, passed her daughter to Lady Fernvale. Chris, as he left the pew with his darling burden, was met by a man who was a stranger to Clem—a gentleman by his dress, which was neat, but unobtrusive.

There was nothing about the man himself to draw the eye, either. He was of medium size and build, his hair mid-brown in color, his features even and pleasant, with no distinguishing characteristics.

Chris passed Will to the man, who held him with accustomed ease. Then he looked at Clem with familiar hazel eyes and bowed slightly. It was only then that she recognized him as Ramping Billy O'Hara!

Lady Fernvale nudged Clem and she continued on to the baptismal font, where she found herself standing next to one of the most feared denizens of the stews of London while he promised solemnly on Will's behalf to renounce the devil and all his works, and to keep obediently God's holy will and commandments.

Will slept through the prayers, readings, exhortations, and vows, but when he had the holy water poured on him, he woke yelling.

Mr. O'Hara did not flinch, but held him steadily until the vicar was finished and moved on to repeat that part of the ceremony for Bel. Clem was itching to rescue her son, or was it Mr. O'Hara? But he held the little man with one deft hand while tucking the shawl back into place with the other, then lifted Will against his shoulder and rocked the baby gently, patting him with one hand while murmuring a song in his ear.

It was too quiet for Clem to make out the words, but it worked. Will settled, hiccupped, and went back to sleep.

Aunt Fern was equally capable with Bel, but then Clem had expected that. Nor was she surprised that Aunt Fern refused Bel's nursemaid's offer to take the baby. Clem would have taken her, too, but Aunt Fern was absorbed in her newest godchild, and Clem let her be.

More surprising was that Mr. O'Hara did the same with Will, watching the vicar with those calm hazel eyes, while continuing to murmur to the sleeping baby for the remainder of the service.

She noted, however, that he was the only member of the christening party not to go up to communion.

After the service, Chris introduced "Mr. Harrington" to his distinguished relatives, to Father, to the vicar, to the neighbors, and all without anyone showing the least recognition. Father, at least, had met O'Hara before, and so—she was certain—had several of the other men.

"My friend, Mr. Harrington, a gentleman from London," Chris said, and "Harrington" nodded, smiled, and made polite conversation, all without disturbing Will, who slumbered peacefully on the man's shoulder.

BILLY CAME BACK to the house, where their kitchen and the school kitchen had combined forces to put on a celebratory feast. He stayed only long enough to give Clem the gifts he had brought for the children—silver mugs engraved with their names and the date of the christening—and a bone teething ring each, one carved with flowers and one with dogs and balls.

"Something as a keepsake, and something that might be useful," he said, almost apologetically, as Clem opened the boxes in which the gifts were presented. After that, he made his farewells.

Chris walked him with him to the stables, where his carriage was waiting. "Thank you for coming. And thank you for agreeing to stand up for Will."

"Has Wright mentioned the alterations he's doing on his house?" Billy asked.

"No, he hasn't," Chris replied, his eyes widening, for Wright was not the sort to spend money unless he had to, and prone to boast about his plans when he did spend money. "What sort of alterations?"

"I don't know yet," Billy admitted. "He has builders in, and the painters are expected next week. He is redoing a room, or possibly more than one room, on the floor where he has his bedroom."

"He has said nothing," Chris said.

"Is that unusual for him?"

"It is."

"Hmmm." Billy nodded at his driver. "Straight back to London, Steve." He then held his hand out to shake Chris's. "Thank you for asking me, Christopher. Ask Wright about the alterations. I do not trust him."

Neither did Chris. And he trusted Wright still less when he managed to turn the conversation around to several months ago when he and Clem were preparing the country house for them to live in.

"We'd been advised not to live in the house while the main

part of the building was full of builders and painters. Even a room or two can disrupt the whole house, we were told. Have you found that, sir?"

Wright shook his head. "I haven't had builders working in a house I was occupying. Decorators once, long ago, when I first moved to London and purchased the current townhouse." He chuckled. "I ended up setting up a cot in my office."

"I remember that," Clem commented. "Our whole house smelled of paint for weeks, and my governess had to shout to be heard over the noise. We had terrible headaches." Which meant Wright had expected his daughter and servants to continue living in the mess and disruption.

No mention of the current work. Either Billy was wrong, or Wright was hiding things. Or, Chris supposed, Billy was lying to cause trouble between Wright and Chris.

"Michael," Chris asked, when he and his cousin had a moment to talk in relative privacy, "may I ask a favor? Would you call on my father-in-law and try to find out what building work he is having done?"

⇒⇒⇒⫸⫷⇐⇐⇐

BY EARLY AFTERNOON, the neighbors had all gone home, and some of the cousins had also departed. But Lord Crosby and Lord Halton remained. "Might I have a look at the school before I leave for London?" Lord Crosby asked, and Lord Halton nodded. "I would like that, too."

Chris sent a footman to ask Partridge if it would be convenient. Clem begged off, saying that she would be going upstairs to feed the children, but the remaining relatives and Wright all joined the tour.

It was the first time that Wright had shown an interest— Chris hoped he might be impressed, but if so, he did not show it. The earls both asked interested questions about the curriculum while their wives seemed impressed by the bedchambers and classrooms. All four commented on the excellent manners and neat appearance of the boys.

Harry, Michael, and some of the other cousins joined in a game of cricket that one of the teachers had organized on the back lawn, while the other gentlemen questioned Partridge about his educational methods and the ladies talked to Mrs. Westbridge about the challenges of housing, feeding, and raising fifteen boys.

On the whole, Chris was pleased. But the best part of the day was when they had all gone home, and he went up to his bedchamber to see what was keeping his wife. She had probably fallen asleep, and so he had told their guests.

Sure enough, there she was, in their bed. He would have loved to have crawled into bed beside her and woken her in the most delightful of ways. But Mrs. Greene had warned him not to press his attentions on her until she had finished healing, and besides, she needed her sleep.

His desire for her, which had only grown over time, would have to wait until she was ready. Until then, he was happy to spend his nights with the comfort of her beside him.

Then she stirred in the bed, opened her eyes, and smiled when she saw him. "How are our guests?" she asked, sleepily.

"All gone home," he said.

"Good," she said, sitting up in bed and letting the sheet fall away. She was wearing nothing at all. "Now come here, Chris. For I am well and I have missed you."

Chapter Twenty-Three

W HEN MICHAEL WROTE a few days later, he said that Wright had seen him in a downstairs reception room. Wright told Michael the distant hammering they could hear was from the house next door. "It wasn't true, though, Chris," Michael wrote. "I sat over a beer in the tavern on the corner of the mews, and saw the builders leaving by the back door. He has builders in, and he is not talking about why."

It was weird and disturbing. Still, Chris couldn't see how what Wright did with his townhouse could affect Chris, Clem and the twins three hours ride away in the country.

It was all a storm in a teacup, as Chris discovered during his next trip to London. He tried to invite himself to dinner, but Wright told him that there had been a leak in the roof, which had been mended, and now the painters were in. "The place smells, Satterthwaite," he said. "I'm staying at an inn, and would be glad to have dinner with you there, and hear more about my grandson."

Once Chris got home, he wrote to both Michael and Billy O'Hara to let them know that the builders were there to do repairs, and he told Clem. He'd kept it from her before, not wanting to worry her while she was still recovering.

She was furious.

"How dare you keep me in the dark, Chris? Especially when the topic is my father."

Her response annoyed Chris. "You have only recently given birth. You are feeding two children and sleeping poorly. Surely, I have a right to protect you?"

"Instead of which, you put me in danger, for if he was planning something that affects us, I needed to be warned. You are not here all the time."

"I did not want to worry you," he explained, but she wasn't having a bar of it.

"Yes, I would have worried, but if I cannot trust you to tell me your concerns, I shall worry the whole time. How would you feel if I said that Will had stopped bleeding, so there was nothing to worry about, if I had not even mentioned he had been hurt?"

Chris, who had been lounging until that moment, sat up straight. "Will has been bleeding?"

"No! But if he ever does, I shall tell you immediately, not when he's stopped bleeding, and I expect the same from you, Chris. Tell me problems from the start so we can work through them together, not from the end when they are solved."

He hated to admit it, but she had a point. She hadn't finished, though.

"As to Father and the roof leak, I do not believe it. What evidence do you have that the builders were there to fix the roof? Father's word, and we know he lies whenever it suits him, and without a scrap of conscience."

Which was unfortunately true. "I shall ask Michael to continue to keep an eye on him then," Chris said, with a sigh. Whatever the man was up to, they would undoubtedly find out, sooner or later.

It was sooner. A week later, Chris received a letter from Billy that asked him to come into London on a matter of importance. An urgent matter.

"What do you think?" he said to Clem. "Should I go? I wonder what he wants?"

"You still don't trust him," Clem noted, "but he has been nothing but kind to us."

"Because it suits him, for some reason," Chris insisted. "I'd feel better if I knew the reason. Though, to be fair, he does look after his people. He says it is good business, for it ensures loyalty."

"Which is why you are going, darling," Clem noted. "You do trust him, deep down. Why else would you have wanted him to be Will's godfather?"

She was right again. Chris called for his horse, and kissed his wife and his children. "I won't stay the night," he said. "Unless this crisis, whatever it is, needs me to do so. I'll send you a message, if that is the case. Otherwise, expect me before dark."

"I love you, Chris. Take care. Travel safely."

"I love you, Clem. Look after our babies, and I shall be home soon."

※

CLEM WATCHED HER husband ride away down the carriageway, and felt a sudden sense of panic. Ridiculous. She lived surrounded by people who owed their livelihoods to her and Chris, and who were—as far as she knew—happy to be working for them. What could possibly go wrong?

Nonetheless, she hurried inside and up to see the children, fast asleep in their cradles. All was, of course, well.

Despite that, the sense of dread would not leave her. When a couple of carriages rumbled up the drive an hour after Chris's departure, she hurried to the window. Her mind told her she was being silly. Her heart was certain that the threatened danger was there, outside her windows.

Carriages, yes. One of them, her father's. And outriders— burly men with stern faces. She ignored the common sense that told her to wait to see whether her father meant trouble, picked up her skirts, and ran upstairs, telling the footman as she passed,

"Delay opening the door. Keep them waiting."

She hurried through her bedchamber and into the nursery. "Hide the babies," she ordered. "My father is here, and I am afraid he intends no good."

The nursemaids stared at her.

Martha had followed her into the room and now she said, "Hurry. Ann, you take Master William. I'll bring Miss Christabel. Flora, take the pram out the back door by the stables and run as fast as you can into the woods, then walk along the other side of the lake. If they catch up with you, say that our lady was worried about the wheels on the rough ground, and you were testing the pram."

As she spoke, she was stuffing clouts and other baby supplies into a bag.

Distantly, Clem could hear a cascade of knocks on the front door.

"Hurry," she repeated, wondering if she was doing the right thing in trusting Martha.

Once again, her common sense and her instincts conflicted. On the one hand, Martha had betrayed her before—though not, to her knowledge, recently. On the other hand, Clem would swear that Martha loved the babies. And there was the matter of her engagement to the footman…

"I am trusting you with my heart," she told the maid.

"I would never betray you or Mr. Satterthwaite, or the twins," Martha declared, and Clem believed her.

Downstairs a second cascade of knocks followed the first, louder and more peremptory.

"Go," Clem said. They went by the servants' door, which would take them downstairs to the basement. Clem didn't ask where they were going. She had no practice lying. If she knew and lied about it, her father would see it on her face, and she had no idea what he might do.

She returned downstairs, and nodded to the footman. "Answer the door as soon as I am in the parlor," she said. "Then send my father to me."

Father entered the front door ranting about the footman's tardiness and threatening him with dismissal. She hoped her servant knew it was an empty threat even if he hadn't been following his mistress's orders.

More footsteps sounded behind Father's.

She didn't hear what the footman said, but she heard Father's reply. "In the parlor? Good. She can stay there. You two, guard the parlor door. You two, follow me."

Clem darted out of the connecting door to the dining room and from there peered into the hall. A glance told her that the footman was attempting to forbid Father the stairs, but two of the men with him were forcing him out of the way.

Hurrying down the service passage that connected dining room to kitchen, she told the servants there to arm themselves with brooms or anything else they could reach and to follow her.

"I believe Mr. Wright has come to take away my son," she said. She could not think of any other reason for this assault.

She sent the boot boy, to the stables for reinforcements, and then she raced up the servants' stairs, her servants behind her. They took the door into the main passage through the bedchamber section, fearing that Father would be before her, but the boot falls from the floor above told her that the intruders had continued upstairs to what would normally be the nursery floor.

Thank goodness! That gave them a bit more time. All they would find was the perfectly appointed nursery Father had been shown on his visits, ready for when the babies no longer needed to be fed during the night.

Good. The more time Martha and Ann had to get away, the better.

"Search this floor and then the rest of the house!" Father roared. "I want my grandson!"

"Mary, Gareth, with me," Clem said, her mind racing. "The rest of you, back to your work. Don't try to prevent the search. If anyone asks you where the babies are, say you don't know."

"We don't know," said the cook, either in obedience or because that was the truth.

Before the tramp of feet reached the staircase again, Gareth had taken both cradles down to the storeroom in the basement, and Mary and Clem had hidden the bedding and anything else that looked as if it might belong to a baby under the bed, which had been pushed into a corner, but was now back in the center of the wall, with a dust sheet thrown over it.

At a cursory glance, the room was now unused.

She and Mary left the room by the servants' door just as Father and the men with him began searching that floor. Clem had one more thought. "Mary, send a groom to go after Mr. Satterthwaite. Tell him that Father has come to try to take Master William away from us."

That done, Clem settled herself in the parlor, and took out some needlework. Her heart was pounding. Her mind went over and over every step she had taken. What next? The babies would need feeding again within the next two hours. Could she put Father and his men off before then?

Where had Martha taken the children? Would she give them up to Father? The questions were all unanswerable. She could only wait, sitting there calmly with her mind racing frantically while her father rampaged through her house.

No! This is a mistake! This is not the way she would behave if she was innocent of hiding her children from her awful father. She put the needlework aside, and opened the parlor door. When she tried to step out, one of the men on guard put an arm out to stop her.

"Sorry, ma'am. We can't let you leave this room."

"How dare you," she said. "This is my house. Who are you, and what is all this noise?"

"I don't know who they are, Mrs. Satterthwaite," said her footman, who was standing in the hall, glaring at the intruders. "They arrived with your father. He and three other men are upstairs."

Clem raised her voice. "Father! Come down here and explain yourself! You cannot come in here and rampage through my house without so much as a by-your-leave. I shall have the law onto you. See if I don't!"

The two guards exchanged glances. One looked worried, the other smug.

Father's roar preceded him down the stairs. "Clementine Wright! Where is my grandson!"

He came into view, stepping heavily, his face red with anger. With him came a man she had seen before, when they were negotiating the marriage agreement. Father's lawyer. He must have been in one of the carriages. The other two burly riders were presumably still searching the bedchamber floor.

"I am Clementine Satterthwaite," Clem said, far more calmly than she felt. "And my son and daughter are with their nurse-maids. What is the meaning of this rude invasion, Father?"

"I'll have my rights," her father grumbled, brushing her aside to walk past her into the parlor. "Tell her, Harcourt."

"Yes, Mr. Harcourt. Tell me what my father is about," Clem said to the solicitor.

Mr. Harcourt would not meet her eyes as he replied. "Mr. Wright has a warrant to take custody of his grandson. He is invoking clause one hundred and thirty-seven A, subclause three of the marriage agreement, Mrs. Satterthwaite. Magistrate Brannock has found due cause to suspect you and Mr. Satterth-waite of... moral turpitude." He mumbled the end of the sentence, but Clem understood him well enough.

"Show me," she demanded, holding out her hand. She and Chris had discussed the moral turpitude clause, and even laughed over it. It was meant to be invoked if Father saw his grandson's welfare being threatened, and they saw no reason to fear it.

But there it was in the warrant that Mr. Harcourt showed her. Chris's history as an orphan in the streets and then an employee in a gambling den, their ownership of and proximity to a school that took in what the warrant called "children of the worst moral character," the fact they had chosen Billy O'Hara as godfather, even her decision to feed the children herself. Furthermore, Chris's horrible grandfather had denounced his grandson as a degenerate.

"And I suppose you own the magistrate," Clem said to Father.

"Enough of this nonsense," Father said. "Where is my grandson? I have a magistrate's warrant and four constables to make certain you hand him over. If you do not do so, I have the right to have you arrested, and I shall do so."

What would Chris do? He would lie, Clem decided, and if ever there was an occasion for it, it was now. Clem frowned. "But you must have seen him, Father. Did you not check the nursery?"

"He wasn't there," Father growled. "Neither was the female."

Clem leapt to her feet. "My babies!" She rushed to the door, past the now-relaxed constables who did not move in time to stop her, and up the stairs. A thunder of boots behind her must have been the constables, but Clem was pretending that someone had stolen her babies from the nursery without her knowledge, and the pretense led wings to her panicked feet.

She was the first to arrive at the door of the unused nursery. She gaped at the empty cots. Was lying this easy? All you had to do was lie to yourself, first, apparently.

Turning to the constable who had crowded in behind her, she said, "They are gone! Where are my babies? You've taken them!"

The very real anger that fueled her acting must have shown on her face, for the men actually took a step back, and one stammered as he replied. "No, ma'am. No one was here when we checked."

Clem took two more steps into the room, frowning. "Perhaps the maids have taken them out for some fresh air. But they did not tell me."

Father had arrived, breathing heavily from the four flights of stairs.

"Father," Clem said. "They are not here."

"I told you that, stupid girl," Father said. "Where is he? Tell me, Clementine. I have a warrant to take my grandson, and anyone who stands in my way can be arrested. Do you want to go to prison, Clementine?"

Clem was pretending to ignore him. She was hurrying around the room from place to place, channeling her very real panic into frantic movement, stroking the blankets on the cots, touching the toys on the shelves, setting the rocking horse into slow motion. "The nursemaids must have taken them out for air. Do you not think? They could not have been stolen. Who would take a baby from its own mother? What kind of monster would do such a thing?"

She turned back to the constable who had told her they'd searched the nursery. He stood with one of his colleagues, watching her, frowning as if uncomfortable. And so he should be, the dastard.

"Will you check, please? See if they are out in the garden? Or in the summerhouse? It is too cold for the open park. The nursemaids must have taken them somewhere, mustn't they? They must be safe?"

"Two of you search the rest of the house and two of you search the garden," Father ordered.

"We'll find him, ma'am, said the constable. "Don't you worry."

"Them," Clem corrected him. "My son William *and* my daughter Christabel. They will be needing a feeding soon. They cannot be far, surely?"

The tears were a nice touch, and not at all an act. Her fear and concern had them rising without thought or effort on her part, and spilling down her cheeks. "Find my babies," she begged.

The constables nodded, and hurried away.

She surely couldn't keep them busy until Chris arrived home, but at least she was giving Martha enough time to take them somewhere safe. But where? And how would Martha and Ann feed them?

Clem sobbed, real tears.

Father snorted, turned on his heel, and stomped out of the room.

Chapter Twenty-Four

W HEN CHRIS RODE into the yard of the inn where he usually changed horses, Billy O'Hara was there, walking to and fro, occasionally slapping a riding crop against his boots.

He strode over as Chris dismounted. "Christopher. Come on. We must get back to your place. I've sent my men on ahead."

He turned on his heel and strode off to the road beyond the inn gate. Chris followed him, frowning to himself. What was going on? He very rarely—no, never—saw Billy be anything but under control but there had been a note of possible panic in the man's voice. A groom in the inn's livery drove up beside Billy in a curricle that Chris had noticed as he passed. The man had been walking his horses slowly along the road, something that wasn't common but then again, wasn't unusual. He might have just been warming them up for work, or cooling them off after a hard haul.

But now, he realized, the man had been waiting for a sign from Billy.

"There you go, sir," the groom said to Billy, who was taking over the reins. Chris climbed up as the groom climbed down, and Billy set the horses into a fast walk, and then a canter almost before the groom was clear of the vehicle.

Chris fell the last couple of inches onto the seat. "What's

happening?" he asked.

"Your father-in-law," said Billy, succinctly. "He has persuaded a magistrate to find you unfit parents. He has taken constables to pick up your son."

"The moral turpitude clause," Chris said. *Damn.* The lawyers—his own and Billy's—had assured him that he need not worry about it. It was intended to protect Clem and the children if he turned out to be the rankest of villains.

Billy nodded. "That's the one."

"Is that why you sent for me?" Chris asked.

"So that was it. I did not send for you, Christopher," said Billy. "Just after I found out about the magistrate, I learned that Wright had sent one of the post riders I sometimes use to your estate. Then he left his own townhouse taking with him a wet nurse, four constables, and his solicitor."

"And based on that you guessed Wright had got me out of the way by pretending to be you, asking me to come to London on an urgent matter?"

"I had a hunch he'd have sent you away somehow," Billy said. "I was giving it another fifteen minutes, then going after my men. They have instructions to delay things so I had time to arrive. But best if you are with me. Here's what I know, what I've done, and what I think we need to do."

Billy shared his plans. They didn't talk much after that. Canter, trot. Canter, trot. Chris sat beside Billy, wishing they could gallop all the way, but the horses could become lame if they tried it. They were traveling as fast as they could—quite a bit faster than Chris had traveled the same distance this morning.

Billy had even thought to have his men arrange a new team half an hour from home, and it took the hostlers less than five minutes to unhitch the exhausted team, hitch up the fresh horses and get them on their way again.

Two and a half hours after he left home, he and Billy drove up the carriage drive, to discover a stand-off on the lawn.

The children, being held by their two nursemaids, were at the center of a ring of servants armed with brooms, spades, rolling pins, and other such implements. Among them stood men that Chris recognized as Billy's. Clem, with Billy's bodyguard and lieutenant Tiny at her side, was facing her father, and at his back were five men, two of them with pistols, two with batons, and one with an expression that said he wished he was anywhere else, and that he was trying hard to vanish.

Constables, Chris would guess, and the would-be vanisher was the solicitor who had led the team that produced the original marriage agreement.

The older schoolboys, led by Partridge, were approaching from the school side of the house, with determined faces and clenched fists.

Billy didn't bother with stopping the curricle, but turned the horses to canter across the grass, slowing them so they stopped between the protective circle and Wright and his men.

Wright looked up at the pair in the curricle and screeched, "I have a warrant! You have to give me the boy."

Chris descended from the curricle in a controlled tumble and hurried to Clem's side. She grasped his arm, leaning against him in her relief.

"The warrant has been rescinded," Billy answered him. He scanned the constables. "Which of you is in charge? You, Miller?"

One of the two men with pistols—Chris gave him credit for the fact he was not pointing it at anyone—moved his other hand as if his instinct was to raise it in response to Billy's question, but his intellect said he was no longer in school. "O'Hara? What are you doing here?"

"I have a letter for you from the magistrate who issued that warrant. Further information has come to his attention, and he has rescinded his approval."

Billy handed the letter to the constable. Wright tried to snatch it from his hands, but the constable held it up out of his reach and said to his men, "If Mr. Wright tries to prevent me from reading this, restrain him."

"I'll have your badge," Wright screeched, but the constable ignored him.

"The gentleman is correct," the constable announced after a moment. "The warrant is invalid. It can be torn up, and we, my lads, are for London."

"No-o-o!" Wright wailed. "This man O'Hara is a criminal, constable. Arrest him. Do your duty. He may have forged that letter. In fact, he *must* have forged that letter."

"My apologies, Mrs. Satterthwaite, and those of my men," said the constable, ignoring Wright. His glance at the assortment of servants protecting the children was almost fond. "If any of you belong in the stables, perhaps you can help us fetch our horses."

It was over, then, though Wright didn't accept it, and continued to rant, at the constables, his solicitor, the magistrate, his daughter, Chris, the school boys. Clem ignored him, and Chris followed her lead. Eventually, her father left, taking his solicitor with him. Also, the wet nurse he had brought, who had apparently been sitting in the carriage the whole time.

Clem thanked the schoolboys and went upstairs to feed the children, returning half an hour later to join Chris, Billy, and Tiny for a nuncheon in the dining room. Billy's other men were being fed in the servants' hall.

By then, Chris had gathered that Martha had taken the children to the school, hidden them in the attic, and asked the boys to run interference.

"It would have worked, too, if Will had not started crying while the constables were searching the school," Clem told them. "Martha and the nursemaids ran again, before the constables could find the entrance to the attics, and were making for our attics when the constables caught up with them. Fortunately, Billy's men were here by then."

"Martha delayed them long enough for Billy's men to arrive," Chris realized aloud. "She saved Will." He would never doubt her loyalty again.

Billy shook his head. "It isn't over. Wright has withdrawn for the moment, but he has not given up."

"Mr. O'Hara is right," Clem said, her voice soft but firm. "The secret of Father's success is that he never accepts defeat. He never gives up. He will find another magistrate, or think of some other way, but he will not stop trying." She was oddly calm, but Chris, knowing her so well, could see that she was holding herself together with the last of her strength. Chris understood. He had not been here for the crisis, but he still felt an urge to find a corner and howl. Or, better still, find Wright and beat him to a pulp.

"Then we have to find a way to stop him," Billy said, adding darkly, "One way or another."

"Mr. O'Hara," said Clem. "You cannot *kill* my father."

The corner of Billy's mouth quirked up and his eyes regarded Clem with unmistakable fondness. "The lady who taught me grammar would say…"

Clem was clearly in no mood to debate the difference in meaning between "can" and "may". "You *will* not kill my father," she said.

"We could disappear him," Tiny offered.

Billy nodded, and explained, "He would not be the first person Tiny and I have known who suddenly took an unexpected and involuntary boat trip to the antipodes."

Chris could see that Clem was considering it. "Let us keep that as an option, but I would prefer to stop the threat to Will while keeping Wright at the helm of his businesses. I still have a lot to learn before I can run them on Will's behalf. Although perhaps after today, your father will leave them elsewhere."

That fetched a snort of disbelief from his wife. "Father's mind is made up," she said. "He has decided to leave everything to Will. That's what he will do. He has decided that we are unfit to raise Will. How do we stop him? For he will not change his mind."

Unless they could prove him unfit to raise their boy. "We

need to counter each of the claims he made to prove us unfit," Chris said. "Then, if we can, we need to find something that disqualifies him."

"You mean," said his wife, "apart from being a selfish, mean, old blowhard."

"None of which are illegal," Billy said, standing. "And all of which are forgiven in the rich. Tiny, collect the men. We need to get back to town. Christopher, Mrs. Satterthwaite, I will be in touch. Look after those babies."

❧

FATHER'S NEXT MOVE arrived before evening that same day. "Sir," said the footman who did double-duty as butler, "You have a messenger from Mr. Wright who insists he must speak to you."

Clem, who had been feeling utterly relaxed after a lovely afternoon interlude with her husband, felt all her worries crash back in around her. Chris covered her hand with his own and gave her a reassuring smile. "Show him in, please," he said to the footman.

The messenger was one of Father's clerks, looking highly uncomfortable. He handed Chris a letter, and stood, shuffling his feet, while Chris read it. Chris passed the letter to Clem and waited while she read it.

In essence, along with threats and complaints, the letter said that Father was dismissing Chris, and wanted him to give the messenger all material Chris held that pertained to his business.

"It is late," Clem said. "Shall we give poor Mr. Samuels a bed for the night and send him off in the morning?"

"Why not?" Chris commented. "It is not his fault that your father is throwing a tantrum."

Chris spoke to the clerk while Clem went to the door to send for the housekeeper. "I will pack up the papers Mr. Wright wants, and you can return for them in the morning. Did he send you in a

212

carriage, Samuels?"

"On a horse, sir. It is outside."

Chris sighed. "My stable will look after the beast, and in the morning, we shall see about some transportation for the boxes of papers."

"If you go with my housekeeper, Mr. Samuels," Clem said, "she will see you settled." She went to Chris as soon as the door shut behind the housekeeper and the clerk. "He is cutting off his nose to spite his face," she said.

"He is giving me a holiday," Chris commented, "and enough time to find out what secrets he is hiding. I think I should send someone to Sheffield to dig around in your father's past, Clem. If he has been up to anything illegal in London, Billy should be able to uncover it, but I will go into town with Mr. Samuels and hire an investigator. Also, I expect him to keep trying the legal route, so I need to set a lawyer of our own up to knocking down every reason he gives a magistrate for stealing our child."

"I want to go with you," Clem said, "But I don't want Will anywhere near my father. Chris, I'm afraid."

Chris took her into his arms. "I promise you, Clem. I won't let the old fraud take our son. We have the earls on our side, and Aunt Fern, and Billy—who has an army at his back. A ragtag army, but an effective one. And if all else fails, we'll take ship for France or even Canada."

For the moment at least, the determination and conviction in his voice soothed her troubled soul.

CHRIS LEFT FOR London in the morning, and for the next few weeks, he came home for only one night a week. Between his visits, Clem lived for his daily letters, though in them, he reported mostly frustrations. Father was continuing to push for custody of Will, and Chris's lawyer—Richard Anderson—kept knocking down all the arguments he put up. Both Lord Crosby and Lord Halton had made it known that they supported Chris and Clem as Will's parents and so had Billy, so London's magistrates and constabulary were being very careful to toe the line of the law, whatever Father offered them.

As for evidence of wrongdoing, Chris's investigators had discovered plenty of shady dealings and outright meanness, but nothing illegal. Father didn't even have a mistress. He gambled within his means. He didn't use brothels, or at least not the ones that Billy owned. He did spend nights away from home, as Clem already knew, but he must spend them in his offices, for no one could be found who had seen him out whoring or drinking.

The word from Yorkshire was more of the same. Whispers that Father had cheated his first partner out of his share of their coal mine. Grumbles about short-changed wage packets and stand-over tactics in contract negotiations. Mutterings about corrupt practices. But no evidence that would stand up in court.

The people Chris hired to provide guards for the estate, the house, and the school prevented three attempts to breach the defenses, two covert and one a full-on assault, but the men who were captured would not say who was behind the attacks. Perhaps they did not know.

Then Wright had a break-through. He found himself a magistrate with a mighty chip on his shoulder about aristocrats and a black-and-white approach to morality. Chris was at home when his lawyer arrived from London to show him the papers that had just been delivered.

Chris read them, with Clem hovering to take each page as he finished.

"This says that Will is to be handed into the care of an independent person while charges against us are being investigated," Chris said. "What person, and what charges?"

Richard Anderson gave him two more sheets of paper. "The charges," he said.

Chris scanned them. "These are nonsense."

"Then we'll fight them," Clem said, relieved.

"Yes," Chris agreed, but Richard was shaking his head.

"But meanwhile, Mr. Wright's appointee will have your son," he said.

"No," said Clem. "That cannot be allowed to happen. I will run away with him first."

"That would be taken by the courts as an admission of guilt," Richard warned them.

"What do we have on Wright?" Chris asked. "Perhaps altogether it is enough."

The lawyer shook his head, and began to list everything they had found: *morally suspect, legally dubious, humanly appalling*. None of it able to be proved illegal.

Clem told Martha and Mrs. Westbridge what was going on, and Chris mentioned it to Partridge. All three insisted that they had told no-one, but by the following morning, word had spread through the house and the school, as Clem discovered that when her housekeeper stopped her on her way to the nursery to say, "The whole house is with you, Mrs. Satterthwaite. If you need us to hide you and the little ones, not a single person here will give you away. And nor will the school."

She was cheered by their support, but she still pushed her food around her plate, and Chris had no appetite, either. Richard had already eaten and set out for town to see what else he might do.

"I'm frightened," Clem said to Chris.

"We'll find a way," Chris promised. "And if we have no success in the next few days, we'll defy the court order and run."

At that moment, a footman came back into the room. "Mrs. Satterthwaite, ma'am. There are two boys here from the school. Mr. Fuller and Master Arthur Stone. They say they need to talk to you, ma'am. About Mr. Wright."

"Bring them in," Clem said, although what Tom Fuller and Arthur might know about her father was a mystery. They arrived, and stood just inside the door. Fuller was determined and Arthur was white and trembling.

"Is it true, ma'am, that your father has found a way to take your baby?" Fuller demanded.

Clem nodded, and Chris said, "We will stop him, Mr. Fuller. We shall find a way."

"See?" Fuller said to Arthur.

"Don't let him do it," Arthur commanded. "He must not be allowed."

Something important was being said.

"What has my father done?" Clem said, in the gentlest voice she could manage. Arthur burst into tears and fell to his knees, burying his face against her gown so that she could only hear his story in mumbled words.

She could hear enough, however.

⇒》》≪≪⇐

Chris, with Billy and his lawyer, met with Wright at the magistrate's chambers. The magistrate had refused to allow Clem into the room, but had reluctantly agreed that she could sit in the next room with Will, Bel, and their nursemaids.

Also, Tiny and several of the guards Chris had hired. Chris was confident that he had the knowledge to make Wright—and if not him, the magistrate—back down, but he was taking no chances.

"Hand over the boy," Wright growled.

"I have new evidence to present," said Chris. "Evidence that counters your claims against us, and evidence that you are not a fit guardian for my son. I am prepared to negotiate to put things back the way they were, Wright, with you having supervised access to your grandson. Or, I can present my evidence."

"I'll have the boy, and you shall have nothing," Wright insisted. "I'm taking Morton's son in to learn the company, and you are out on your ear. And I'll break you, boy, for defying me. You, and the earls who supported you."

"Very well," said Chris. "Here is what I have... What I am prepared to make public if you continue to demand my child. I have evidence that you cheated your first partner, Caleb Horner, and stole his share of the business."

Wright sneered. "Horner's family has tried to prove that in court before. They've failed."

"You also short debtors and creditors alike in your business. For example, of ten large sacks of coal weighed at your Limehouse depot, marked as being two hundredweight, all were short by at least twenty pounds. And barge owners can attest you regularly underpay them for what they deliver."

"All nonsense. I am a careful businessman. That is all."

"I have one more," Chris said.

Wright sneered. "You have nothing."

"Let me whisper it to you. One word, Wright. You don't want your solicitor or the magistrate to hear this, I assure you. But the whole world will hear if I walk out of here without the agreement I am seeking."

For the first time, Wright looked alarmed. "Perhaps I won't let you walk out of here," he said.

"Mr. Wright!" the magistrate admonished.

"I could have him arrested, could I not? For maligning my good name?" Wright asked.

The magistrate pressed his lips together.

Chris ignored the by-play, and continued to address Wright. "If I do not cancel my instructions to a man I will not name, the information I have will be delivered to Bow Street and to all the major newsletters. One word, Wright."

He stepped closer and leaned to whisper in the man's ear. As promised, it was one word, and then he stepped back to see the effect.

The older man rose to his feet. He had turned white. "Nonsense. It is a lie. Hearsay."

Chris was inexorable. "I have witnesses. Names. Dates. Places. One of your victims."

"No. It isn't possible." Wright was shaking his head, his eyes wild.

"Give the man a drink," Billy suggested to the magistrate. "He has had a shock."

Indeed, Wright looked as if he had suffered a blow with something heavy. A mallet, perhaps. His knees buckled and he fell back into his chair. He was still shaking his head. His face was white.

The magistrate nodded to Wright's solicitor, who hurried to the decanters on a sideboard across the room.

"It will have to stop, of course. As part of our new agreement."

Wright rallied. "You are not fit to raise my grandson!"

"You are, demonstrably, not fit to be anywhere near my son—or any other boy," Chris hissed. "As I will tell his Honor, here, if you insist. As I will prove in court, if that is what you wish."

The solicitor returned with a glass, which he gave to Wright, who took a gulp. The eyes he raised to Chris burned with hate. "You have won. Much joy may it bring you. You'll not work for me. You and Clem will not see another penny of my money. I'll appoint someone else to run the company and be the boy's trustee."

Chris inclined his head. "My solicitor will leave a copy of the new agreement with yours. I will expect it to be returned to my solicitor, signed by you, tomorrow at noon."

"Not so fast," said the magistrate. I need to hear that word before I will dismiss the case."

Wright argued, but the magistrate insisted, and in the end, the magistrate ordered the whole room cleared of all but him, Wright, and Chris. He then looked expectantly at Chris while Wright buried his face in his hands.

"For the sake of my wife and children, your honor," Chris said, "I must ask you to keep this information in confidence, and take no action unless Wright goes back on his word to stop."

The judge frowned, but his curiosity must have overcome his reluctance, for he said, "In confidence, then."

Chris nodded, and Wright shrank further into his chair. "The secret word is 'pederast'. I have evidence going back twenty years, and I dare say I could find more in Yorkshire. I will not let that man, unsupervised, anywhere near my son."

The judge screwed his mouth up in disgust. "I do not blame you, Mr. Satterthwaite. Case dismissed. Now get this piece of filth out of my office."

✦

Chapter Twenty-Five

C LEM PICKED AT her breakfast.

"Not hungry, darling?" Chris asked, looking concerned.

"How do I go on?" The words burst from Clem as if breaking through a dam. "How, Chris? He is my father, and he has been doing these terrible things. I never knew. How could I not have known? Such evil! I feel soiled, Chris. Guilty, too. I should have known somehow. I should have stopped him."

Chris scooted around the corner of the table to take her in his arms, and she wept noisily on his shoulder. "Of course, you could not have known. He was at great pains to keep it secret, my love. And you are neither guilty nor soiled. We are not our fathers, and thank goodness for that."

"That is very logical," Clem acknowledged. "But Chris, I don't feel logical."

"I know. I know. But we shall get through this."

Disgust still sat in her belly, cold and heavy, but she did feel a little better. Dread was there, too, though. "Chris, he will find a way to get back at us. More than cutting us off, I mean. He hates us now. We have beaten him, at least for the moment, so he will have to do something to hurt us. That is how he is."

Chris took a deep breath and let it out with a sigh. "He is an evil man, Clem. Worse than my grandfather, and that takes some doing. We shall stay alert, I promise you."

They were interrupted by a footman. "Sir, there is a constable at the door."

"Give me a couple of minutes and then show him in," Chris said. He dipped one of the napkins in a finger bowl and wiped Clem's eyes. "Do you want to stay and hear him?"

Of course she did. "It will be Father," she said. "I know it."

It was, but not in the way Clem expected. The constable was uneasy about her being present, and she soon found out why he would have preferred to have spoken with her husband on his own. "I regret to inform you, Mrs. Satterthwaite, that your father, Mr. Bertram Wright, has been found dead in his offices. Shot, ma'am, perhaps by an intruder."

Perhaps he expected her to fall into strong hysterics. Instead, she could only sit there, frozen, thinking, *Will is safe. Chris is safe. My family is safe.*

"Mrs. Satterthwaite has had a shock," Chris was saying to the constable.

"Sir," the constable said, obviously embarrassed, "I understand you have had a disagreement with your father-in-law. I need to ask you, sir, where were you last night?"

Trust Father to attack them even in dying!

But Chris was explaining to the constable that he had won the disagreement with Father. "Now if I had been shot last night, you might have looked at Wright for it. But—you can ask the magistrate—I won my case, so Wright was not a threat to me." He went on to assure the constable that he had been at home all evening and all night, and that the servants could attest to that. He handed the constable over to the footman. "Take him through to the servants' hall and tell everyone to answer any questions he might have," he said.

When the constable was gone, Clem told Chris, "I am glad that he is dead. Does that make me a terrible person? But I am. I know you told him he could have supervised visits to Will, but I never wanted him to see our little boy again, and now he won't."

"I feel the same way," Chris said. "But best if we keep that between ourselves, my love."

The constable must have been satisfied with what he heard from the servants, for he apologized for disturbing the household and took himself off.

Billy O'Hara was their next visitor. "Have you heard?" he wanted to know.

"Wright is dead," Chris said, and Billy nodded.

"Shot," he said.

"The constable who called thought Chris might have done it," Clem blurted, looking at Billy in suspicion.

"I think I convinced him I was here all night," Chris said.

Billy smiled at Clem. "I didn't do it either, Mrs. Satterthwaite. In case you were wondering. I think it was a good idea, though. Whoever did crash that monster did everyone a favor."

"Not if the magistrates arrest Chris for it," Clem retorted.

"As to that, I have a suggestion. Chris, talk to the magistrate in charge. Show him your evidence against Wright. If ever there was a reason for a man to kill himself, Wright's secret was it."

"Father would never have killed himself," Clem objected.

"The magistrate doesn't know that," replied Billy. Which was true enough, and, indeed, whether the magistrate believed that Father had committed suicide or not, after seeing Chris's evidence, he dismissed the case, writing on the death certificate, "accident with a gun," which Richard Anderson said was magistrate-speak for suicide.

Clem was glad that women were not encouraged to attend funerals in order to protect their "delicate sensibilities". Chris went, and said that the congregation was very sparse, with only Morton, Father's business rival, the lawyer, Harcourt, and a couple of people from Father's office. "Harcourt wanted to talk to us about the will," Chris told her. "He is downstairs. Would you like to hear what he has to say?"

Father had not had time to change his will, which meant everything went to his grandson, with Chris as his trustee.

"I suppose this means we still have to take that trip to Yorkshire, my love," Chris said.

"It will be quite nice to see Yorkshire again," Clem told him. "Anyway, as long as we are together, dearest beloved, it doesn't matter where we go."

Chris gave her a deep and satisfying kiss. "Together," he agreed. "Always."

Epilogue

A S BILLY'S CARRIAGE pulled into the driveway of Maidenstone Court, he leaned forward to peer out of the window at the house and park. He had visited often enough over the past eighteen months that the view was familiar.

On one of the fields to the right of the house, enough boys to be the entire student body of the school were playing cricket, while three men ran up and down the sides of the field shouting directions and encouragement.

Billy allowed himself a small smile. Cricket! With a real bat and real wickets. And no doubt played to established rules. Billy himself, and at least half the boys in the school, had learned a version of the game on waste ground between buildings, with rolled up rags or a rock as the ball and any available stick used to bat the object away from an old plank or other improvised wicket.

Supporting the school was one good thing he had done. There were a few, though they were paltry when weighed in the balance against the men he'd ruined (along with their families), the people he'd beaten, and all the other harm he'd caused.

He didn't apologize for it. The stews of London were a hard school, and only hard men survived. Men who could take the pain and abuse, could turn the anger it engendered into a drive to succeed. Billy was, above all, a survivor, and he'd not ask forgiveness for his hard choices.

But he had had the opportunity to save other boys from those same choices. Only a fraction of the tens, perhaps hundreds of thousands that poverty chewed up and spat out. But some.

And here came one of them, striding away from the cricket game and cutting across the front of the house to meet Billy's carriage at the front door. Another smile, this one involuntary. Christopher Satterthwaite was, in some ways, just another of those boys. In other ways, he was Billy's greatest weakness, though Billy worked hard to never let anyone know it—not even Christopher himself.

"Billy!" Christopher greeted him. "Here's a pleasant surprise. Come in, come in. Clem is due home any minute. She went to visit the vicar's wife. The twins are here, though. I'll send for them." While he was speaking, he had been leading the way up the stairs and into the house and now he spoke to the footman who was crossing the hall as he opened the door.

"Roger, let Cook know we have a guest, have tea served to Mrs. S.'s parlor, and ask Nurse to bring the twins down to see our visitor. And Roger, ask the kitchen to look after Mr. Harrington's driver and groom, please."

"How is Mrs. Satterthwaite?" Billy asked. Clementine was with child again, and due to give birth in three months.

"She is well. Full of energy. She is certain she is only carrying one child this time, for she is much more comfortable."

Billy found himself smiling again. It was becoming a habit, and was not at all in keeping with his public image. He consoled himself that he was William Harrington today, at least to the inhabitants of this household and the school next door. With a few exceptions. Chris himself, of course. Clementine. His spy in this household. His spy had reported Clementine's excellent health. Billy could only hope it continued. Childbirth was a dangerous proposition.

"And here they are," Christopher said, with the doting expression and voice he adopted whenever his children appeared. "How are my children this afternoon? Look who has come visiting! It is Uncle William. Will, make your bow to Uncle William. Bel, give Papa a kiss and make your curtsey to Uncle William."

Will, put to the ground by the nursemaid, put one hand behind his back, wrapped the other across his stomach, and bent in the middle. He then ran to his father, who had just lowered Christabel to the ground.

"Bel kiss Unca Will," decided that dainty lady, stomping determinedly toward him.

Billy knelt to present his cheek for her peck. Although he was Will's godfather, he did not play favorites, treating Will and Bel the same, but he could not deny that the sweet girl had him wrapped around her little finger.

She knew it, too, the little witch. She tipped her head on one side and smiled at him. "Unca Will present?"

"Are you here to join the conspiracy to spoil my daughter, Mr. Harrington?" said Clementine, appearing in the doorway. She came forward with a smile, her hand held out for him to shake, stopping when a child grabbed either leg, making it dangerous for her to move.

Billy, grinning openly now, strode closer so they could shake hands. "How are you, Mrs. Satterthwaite?"

"Keeping very well, thank you. Yes, Bel, I see that it is Uncle Will. No, Will, I shall not pick you up, but if you run and sit on the couch, I shall come and sit there too, and you and Bel may sit on either side of me for a cuddle."

Will took off for the couch. Bel looked up at her Mama, and then at her father, and followed more slowly.

Once Clementine was ensconced on the couch, with a child tucked into each side, Billy and Christopher all sat down. Billy was feeling in his pocket for the packet of candied cherries he'd purchased for the children when the maids brought the tea tray in. Trays, rather, for there was one with tea makings, and one with cakes and sandwiches. A footman followed with a tea urn, which he placed on a sideboard.

Safely out of reach of the children, Billy noted.

"I'll make the tea, shall I?" Christopher asked.

Will was already wriggling down to investigate the food.

"I have brought a little something that might keep them both amused for a short time," Billy offered, showing Clementine the packet. He took one out so that Clementine could see. Bel reached out a hand, saying, "Pease, pease. For Bel."

"Yes," Clementine agreed. "Two each, Mr. Harrington, if you would. Bel, you and Will sit on the hearth rug. Uncle Will can then give you your treat."

The waiting nursemaids—the children had one each, working under the supervision of the nanny—came forward to lead the children to the hearth rug, where they sat and politely held out both hands. Billy, as he put a cherry into each of the four small extended hands, could not help but compare these two treasured children of wealthy parents to the endless number of unloved mites he had known in his time on this earth.

He did not remember being eighteen months old. Someone must have looked after him then, at least enough to see he was fed occasionally and had a place to sleep away from the rats. It certainly wasn't a team of clean and neatly dressed nursemaids. He didn't think it was his mother—Billy must have had one, but he had no memory of her, and no one he did remember from his childhood knew who she was.

That a protégée of his—especially this one—could give his children such a life! It made him feel that his ruthless drive to the top of the dung heap had not been entirely without merit. Little Will and Bel had a beautiful home in the country, the best of care, loving parents, adoring servants, a whole school full of older brothers, relatives, and godparents to pamper them and bring them treats—it warmed Billy's cold heart.

They kept the conversation general while the children and their carers were in the room. How had the weather been in

London? How were the boys at the school? How many words did Bel speak now? And Will? Physically, Will was the most able and daring, but Bel was far more sociable and did most of the talking for both of them.

Once the children were carried away for their naps, Christopher leaned forward to say, "I hear you have sold Fortune's Fool, Billy. And others of your businesses."

It was not quite a question, but Billy answered it anyway. "I've sold them all—mostly to the people who were managing them for me." Given them away, in some cases. His main goal had been to release himself from his empire while still taking care of his people. He had more wealth than he could spend in a lifetime. He hadn't needed to screw every pound, shilling, and penny out of the sale.

Clementine and Christopher exchanged their look. It was one he had become familiar with over the past couple of years, and he envied it greatly. First and foremost, it conveyed love and understanding. But on top of that, it communicated in a mysterious way that was visible but unintelligible to the onlooker.

In this case, it seemed they had made a mutual decision to remain silent. Billy had used the trick himself. People loved to fill silence. Ah well, he had come here to tell them. "I am going away for a while. I will be back, and I won't be Billy O'Hara or William Harrington when I am next in England." He needed to give his enemies time to stop looking for him, to change his appearance enough to go unnoticed, to build a credible identity different enough from those he had used before so that he could remain undetected.

He didn't bother saying that, but he did find himself explaining some of his deeper motives. "People don't grow old doing what I do. I find that I would like to live long enough to see William and Christabel grow up. And I do not want my connection to you and to them to bring trouble to your door, so..." He shrugged. "I will send you a letter from time to time. I won't use my name, but you will know it is me." He took a card from his pocket and gave it to Christopher. "If you would care to write, to let me know how you and the children are, my solicitor Richard Anderson will always know how to reach me."

Clementine regarded him gravely. "I hope you find what you are looking for, Mr. Harrington, or O'Hara, or whoever you become. You have been a great blessing to our family. We look forward to welcoming you back whenever that may be."

She was too kind. But then, she had only seen the benevolent side of him. Christopher knew better. "What can we do for you, Billy? We owe you so much, as you yourself have pointed out on various occasions."

In jest, and to maintain his reputation. In truth, he could never do enough to make up to Christopher for his failure to keep watch over the abysmal Reggie. Billy had loved Christabel Satterthwaite since the day he first met her and her little boy, when he'd turned up at the rooming house where they lived at the time to collect a gambling debt that Reggie owed.

Christabel had invited him in and given him tea. Him! Ramping Billy O'Hara! And so what if it was just a few tea leaves in hot water, all the poor lady could afford? Billy had managed to persuade his employer to give the useless Reggie an extra week to pay, and had personally pawned Reggie's watch and marched Reggie to a job handling cargo on the wharves to make up the difference.

Of course, Reggie learned nothing. After several more incidents in which Christabel had lost her household furniture, and in one case all the china her friend Lady Fernvale had given her, Billy had offered to take Christabel and the boy and set them up in comfort somewhere. "Thank you, Billy," she had said, tears in her eyes. "I know Reggie is a dreadful gambler, and will not stop. But he is my husband, and I love him. I cannot come with you."

She was right, in a way. Reggie was a compulsive gambler, and that came first in his life. But he loved his wife and son in his own way, and he was a gentleman. Billy was a rogue and a villain, the sweepings of the gutter underneath it all, however he tried to improve himself. He'd never gambled away the money for the week's groceries, but he'd done far worst things in service of keeping his body and soul together.

One of his worst crimes was focusing on Fortune's Fool, the first gambling den he acquired, right at the time that Reggie got himself in too deep with the wrong people. Billy had heard that the idiot had been killed and slung into the Thames, and had intended to visit the widow, but it was opening week. He had thought it could wait. He hadn't known that Christabel was sick.

By the time Fortune's Fool had enjoyed its successful first week, Christabel was dead, the debt collectors had stripped the house, and Percival Satterthwaite had done a runner—with Christopher, Billy had assumed, until he found the boy picking his pocket almost a year later.

Christopher was the first of Billy's errand boys, and the most important, though he cared for them all, in so far as the cold shriveled-up organ he called a heart was capable of caring.

In the moments it took him to recall all this ancient history, Christopher and Clementine waited patiently for his reply, hand in hand. He smiled at Clem and she smiled back. *They trust me,* Billy realized. What was even more astounding was that they could!

"Your happiness, the happiness of your children, and the success of the school," Billy said. "That is what you owe me, Christopher and Clementine. Achieve that, and the debt is paid."

Another of those marital looks. Then Clementine said, "Thank you," and Christopher said, "I shall spend my life on it, Billy."

"I have another question for you," said Clementine. "What really happened the night my father died, and where is Tom Fuller? Arthur and Martin also disappeared that day, but when they came back the next day, Tom was not with them."

"What did they tell you?" Billy asked.

"Nothing. They apologized but said they had been instructed to be silent. Who gave that instruction, Billy? Was it Tom? Or you?"

He could deny all knowledge, but it would be a lie. Billy had arrived after the ruckus. The boys had sent a street boy with a message to Fortune's Fool, to ask Billy to come. Apparently, the three boys had confronted Wright, demanding that he go away and leave William and his parents alone, threatening to tell Arthur's story and—as it turned out—Tom's story, too, since he was also a survivor from the place where Arthur had been known only as Eight.

Wright had threatened them in return, pulling out a gun to shoot them with—but Tom had jumped him, and the indolent old man had been no match for Tom's wiry strength. After the gun went off, Wright lay dying.

Billy had set it up as much as possible to make it look like suicide. He'd sent Martin and Arthur back to the school. Tom was in deep shock, and in no state to keep the events of the night secret.

What would it help Clementine to know all of that? "I cannot tell you, Mrs. Satterthwaite," Billy replied.

She was not satisfied with the answer. "Can you tell me if Tom Fuller is alive? And well?"

Tom was waiting for Billy in Canada, which was to be Billy's first stop on his journey. According to the people Billy had sent Tom to, he was doing well at school and was in good spirits. Soon, Billy would see for himself. He could give Clementine that much. "He is, yes." He bent a little more. "It was an accident, but Tom blamed himself. He wanted to leave."

"But you looked after him, just as you looked after me," Christopher said.

Next thing, they'd have him fitted with a damned halo. "I helped him for my own reasons, yes," Billy replied. He'd guessed Tom's problem when he first found the boy, and done nothing. He could have saved Arthur and who knew how many others if he'd done then what he did after Wright's death—closed down the brothel and ruined as many of the clients as he could find.

It was one reason he was getting out of town. He had annoyed some very powerful people. He'd also left a few surprises for them behind him. When the rumors built up momentum, they'd have a lot more to worry about than a missing gambling den operator.

"Perhaps I could visit the school one more time before I leave?" he said. He had a letter from Tom to slip to Arthur or Martin.

"Of course," said Christopher. "I'll take you over. It is nearly time for the mid-day break."

"Come back to say goodbye before you leave," Clementine commanded, and Billy agreed. In many ways, she reminded him of Christopher's mother—the same kindness, the same innocent enjoyment of life, the same tolerance for others.

Christopher Satterthwaite was a very lucky man to have had two such women in his life. For that matter, so was Billy, to have known Christopher's mother and then, his wife. Living up to what those two ladies expected of him was mission enough for the rest of his lifetime.

THE END

AUTHOR'S NOTE

This story was inspired by the tale of Rumpelstiltskin. As with my other twist books, the roles are reversed and other elements reinterpreted for the Regency era. I have the poor hero, the wealthy father with his marriageable daughter, the sponsor who sings the hero's praises, and the father who demands that the hero spins straw into silk—that is, turns his daughter into a lady who attracts the attention of aristocratic suitors.

The secret word that defeated the monster had to be something that would destroy him, and my inspiration here came from the power of names in diverse cultures since before records began. As folk tales hint and researchers have discovered, to name something used to mean to explain and describe it.

In many cultures, people had a use name and a private name—one that was known only to close family and the closest of friends, for to name someone or something was to have power over it.

In my own religious heritage, Adam's God-given task was to name the animals—to know them deeply enough that he could describe them.

In some cultures even today, children are given a baby name, but not an adult name until they earn it—and a wondrous or traumatic event could lead even an adult to being renamed, for the old name no longer describes them.

Thus, to defeat our villain, our hero and heroine had to find a word that described the part of himself that he kept hidden. Only that would free them from his power.

The name of my manor and village

Chris has inherited the manor of Maidenstone Court, near the village of Maidencraig Frampton.

The word "maiden" in English location names might come from the word for a young, unmarried women, or from the old word "magden", which meant *fortification*. So the girl's stone or the stone fort. A lot of places in England with "Court" in the name were, in olden times, the homes of local lords who were appointed by the Crown to hear legal cases, and who did so in a room at their houses.

And the first word in Maidencraig Frampton means the same thing, since "craig" comes to us from a Celtic word meaning *rock*. Frampton, as it turns out, could mean one of several things. Ton is town, or (earlier still) fortified farm. Framp? It could be fair, or brisk, or valiant. I'm going with the fortified settlement by the rock.

Putting on the top hat

In the first draft of this book, I used the term "top hat". Then I looked it up and found I was too early for the term. Though the first top hat was made in the 1790s and they quickly became popular, they were not called top hats until Victorian times. In 1810, they went by several names, depending on the variety. Isn't research fun?

Yes, Billy will appear again.

Billy popped up as a secondary character in an earlier novella, and fascinated me. He is still a secondary character, but now that I know more about him, I am even more fascinated. All I need now is a heroine. I know she is there, somewhere in the deep recesses of my mind. Give me time, and Billy will have his story—though he might appear elsewhere meanwhile, when I want a morally ambiguous sort of a villain with a heart of gold.

ABOUT THE AUTHOR

Have you ever wanted something so much you were afraid to even try? That was Jude ten years ago.

For as long as she can remember, she's wanted to be a novelist. She even started dozens of stories, over the years.

But life kept getting in the way. A seriously ill child who required years of therapy; a rising mortgage that led to a full-time job; six children, her own chronic illness… the writing took a back seat.

As the years passed, the fear grew. If she didn't put her stories out there in the market, she wouldn't risk making a fool of herself. She could keep the dream alive if she never put it to the test.

Then her mother died. That great lady had waited her whole life to read a novel of Jude's, and now it would never happen.

So Jude faced her fear and changed it—told everyone she knew she was writing a novel. Now she'd make a fool of herself for certain if she didn't finish.

Her first book came out to excellent reviews in December 2014, and the rest is history. Many books, lots of positive reviews, and a few awards later, she feels foolish for not starting earlier.

Jude write historical fiction with a large helping of romance, a splash of Regency, and a twist of suspense. She then tries to figure out how to slot the story into a genre category. She's mad keen on history, enjoys what happens to people in the crucible of a passionate relationship, and loves to use a good mystery and some real danger as mechanisms to torture her characters.

Dip your toe into her world with one of her lunch-time reads collections or a novella, or dive into a novel. And let her know what you think.

Website and blog:
judeknightauthor.com

Subscribe to newsletter:
judeknightauthor.com/newsletter

Bookshop:
judeknight.selz.com

Facebook:
facebook.com/JudeKnightAuthor

Twitter:
twitter.com/JudeKnightBooks

Pinterest:
nz.pinterest.com/jknight1033

Bookbub:
bookbub.com/profile/jude-knight

Books + Main Bites:
bookandmainbites.com/JudeKnightAuthor

Amazon author page:
amazon.com/Jude-Knight/e/B00RG3SG7I

Goodreads:
goodreads.com/author/show/8603586.Jude_Knight

LinkedIn:
linkedin.com/in/jude-knight-465557166